STAMPING GROUND

STAMPING GROUND

Maurice Leitch

Secker & Warburg
London

First published in England 1975
Martin Secker & Warburg Limited
14 Carlisle Street, London W1V 6NN

Copyright © 1975 by Maurice Leitch

SBN: 436 24414 4

ACKNOWLEDGEMENTS

The author wishes to express appreciation for permission
to quote from the following:

'Innishkeen Road: July Evening' by Patrick Kavanagh.
Used by permission of Mrs Kavanagh and Martin, Brian &
O'Keeffe, London.

Me and My Shadow © Copyright 1927 Bourne Inc. U.S.A.
Reproduced by permission of Francis, Day & Hunter Ltd.

Oh, Lady, Be Good! from the Musical Production *Lady Be Good.*
Composer: George Gershwin
Author: Ira Gershwin
Copyright © 1924 by Harms Inc.
Chappell & Co. Ltd (Used by permission)

Jealousy
Composer: Jacob Gade
Used by permission Lawrence Wright Music Ltd © 1926

Walkin' My Baby Back Home
Composer: Fred E. Ahlert
Author: Roy Turk
Copyright © 1930 by Chappell & Co. Inc.
Chappell & Co. Ltd (Used by permission)

Who Were You With Last Night? and *By the Light of the Silvery Moon*
Reproduced by permission of B. Feldman & Co Ltd
of 138/140 Charing Cross Road, London WC2H 0LD.

Printed in Great Britain by
Cox & Wyman Limited
London, Fakenham and Reading

For Paul

A road, a mile of kingdom, I am king
Of banks and stones and every blooming thing.
                                    Patrick Kavanagh
                        'Innishkeen Road: July Evening'

It is recounted that in those wild, solitary and mountainous places,
where they held their forbidden meetings, men, women and children
would sometimes feed in droves upon the wild fruit of the blaeberry,
or bilberry, as it is commonly called, when nourishment of a more
natural kind was denied them. And thus their persecutors found a
new name to further mock them. But fanaticism was merely re-kindled
and excess matched with excess, for as we know savage customs always
beget a corresponding darkness of the soul.
                                    The Colville Papers, 1717

Noon

1

Under the hedge at the foot of the Five-Acre the grass was thick and dark, a growth spared both by the first scythe that had opened the field and the mowing-machine following later; allowed to flourish, wither and die, free from human agency except for an occasional wind-blown fall of fertilizer. He liked the idea of it like that, dense and aloof from the stubble covering the rest of the expanse, and his feet swished luxuriously through its coarse blades. This place where he was rang with hidden, trickling springs. He was tracking a stream now, one he had discovered earlier while the other two sprawled and smoked in the hay, and presently he found a pool no deeper than a bowl and drank from it. The water coated his face and, when he rose, ran down over his bare chest, prickling his skin where the sheared stalks of hay had stung. He lay back deep in the grass then and looked up at the sky and the patterns pricked on it by the hedge's screen.

In a little while it would be mid-day. Hetty would appear, moving carefully, from the direction of the farmhouse, stepping high across the springy shorn field towards them, shading her eyes against the sun with one hand while rattling a can in the other. They had conspired together to ignore her, feigning deafness, backs carefully turned, three earnest toilers in the hay. The girl would advance on them, start to yell, insults changing to threats – her temper was well known – she might easily flail out at the nearest once within range and then all three, they would burst out laughing and race on ahead of her to the farm kitchen. A childish game, but it somehow matched the coarse mood of indolence and well-being they all felt. His own muscles throbbed pleasurably, his face and hands glutted with blood, as he stretched now, long in the deep grass.

Somewhere out in the glare a grasshopper trilled steadily.

The sound seemed to him to have a perfection. If he closed his eyes, could lose the heat and the blinding light, forget his body and where he was, such a sound would always evoke for him a hayfield in high summer. He thought of those other insects that rasped with disturbing foreignness on the sound-tracks of films he had seen. Night scenes on porches where lovers rocked or where prowlers kept steady watch on the windows of the big Colonial house.

Insects. Winding purposefully, deep among the giant stalks . . .

He put his hand down into the roots and felt the damp rise but was too lazy to raise himself. More important, he wanted to hoard these precious few minutes to himself. In the high field there was no escape from the others' presence and these last days working on the farm had reminded him yet again that he was solitary by nature. Coming here for the holidays, he had been hauled back to that earlier round where gregariousness was zealously guarded.

Something small and light landed on his chest. A leaf of some sort, he decided, eyes closed, dried to a hard tight curl. He visualized its slow shrivel at the top of a hedge-plant as the sun rose; a puff of breeze to loosen it, then to fall finally, whirling dryly. Between thumb and forefinger he would gently grind it to snuff. All of his thoughts moved slowly. Slow thoughts. Slow action.

So a closing in then on the doomed piece of tinder, readied pincer of finger and thumb, to squeeze then rub to nothingness. He touched the unexpected. A second of panic registered the reality of a live thing on his chest, chill carapace, something soft and cushioning underneath and legs, tiny but fearful, moving. He swept his skin bare with one vast obliterating and scouring motion. The insect, whatever its species, ceased to exist and he was sitting up still rubbing the spot. And trembling. He had almost shrieked.

He tried putting it out of his mind. In a little while it would be mid-day. Hetty would appear, rattling her milk-can, calling to them as they raked up the wind-rows. The sun and air worked on and through the loosened rolls of hay drying and crisping . . . A hard pellet stung his left shoulder, but this time it had been aimed.

As he turned quickly he caught a glimpse – less than a glimpse

2

– of two heads, scalps, cropped like his – crew-cuts were the fashion now – dropping out of sight into the long grass.

He found a lump of earth spun clear by the tractor the size of a large potato, solid but drying rapidly, red-brown and crumbling to the touch and, with nice calculation, he felt, lobbed it up back over his head, hoping it would drop, perhaps even break into pieces above them in the air to rain down, sweet retribution, and sure enough, to his delight, that was what seemed to happen, for Harvey came up out of the grass spitting – was it grains of soil? – rubbing his short thatch, swearing fiercely at the unexpected shower from above. Mack's reaction, on the other hand, was subtler, as was to be expected. He lay where he was, groaning.

—Oh dear God, came his voice through the stalks. —My skull is fractured.

Harvey laughed out loud.

—The young intellectual has done for me.

Sepulchral, mock tones of the joker. But his was also a twisted genius for rubbing raw sore places.

And Harvey too was not immune – Harvey who was now perched on crossed legs, bolt upright, grinning strongly. Yes, there were certainly times when the master-joker licked him with the lash of his tongue as well. Harvey burned then. His eyes gave him away, his hands too, raw farmer's hands that clenched and unclenched, lost for a walnut to crack or a tennis ball to squeeze flat in contest. His grip burned with frustration. He was continually breaking tools around the farm, senselessly, it seemed. Even objects as implacable as the heavy iron root-grinder, bolted to the concrete of the yard, received his ferocious touch. Harvey had managed to wrench that rusted block clear of its base at one corner. He had seen him do it and marvelled, had also felt a fear too at the terrible damaging thoughtlessness of the act. Although they had known each other for years it seemed to him that there was an invisible but doomed radius around his friend. He found himself skirting it whenever they were together in the same way he would unconsciously circle some large farm animal that might easily crush him with its bulk, unknowingly.

Mack, when he felt compelled to wound, called Harvey The Clydesdale. His cruelties seemed always to spring directly

3

from a fierce, unblinking observation. Perhaps he was secretly drilling him too with his eye now at this very moment, parting the grass stems low at their roots to form a tunnel along which he could spy, feeling safe, out of sight . . . *But I shall baulk you, Master Mack. Mack The Master-Spy* . . .

—At your devil's work!

The thought, but the words especially and their strangeness, startled more than their sound. Harvey looked taken aback. Rooks catapulted up out of the heavy, unmoving trees at the head of the field. Triggering roar, *but why had he shouted that?*

And curious, he was still pondering the mystery even as he was bounding in play towards Mack, still out of sight in the grass, Mack taken by surprise as well. Right in the middle of his plunging, leaping progress – *why did I?* And then Mack had begun to turn over and over like a fat white cylinder away from him, the grass in his wake flattening as though coming out from under a roller. It seemed a miraculous achievement that swath appearing as it did and to emerge directly from the other's body.

Out of deference to this magic under his very feet he held back for fear of treading on its human source. He contented himself with a war-dance, slow and menacing on the spot, feet pounding the bent carpet: he remembered the way grass had looked near the river after flooding . . .

The feeling of wildness grew, his face hot, his hands coarse and clumsy – but in a luxurious way. He thought he knew why men swaggered after a day spent working in the open air; that strong swelling of blood and heavy-handed power. He felt like a bludgeon, barely in check, charged. Mack rolled right to the edge of the long grass, came to rest, half of him on the stabbing quills of stubble, the rest in cool soft green. His hands lay crossed on his belly. He had his eyes closed. A crusader on his tomb. There was no doubt about it, a cool and stylish bastard truly, but he himself had lost any resentment now. No, the day was too fine and rich for that, and he had a lust for some kind of horseplay rising inside that made him feel grateful now to the clown at his feet.

Mack's body was pale and flabby. It never changed colour, even under the strong sun of the entire hay-making season. It seemed merely another extension of his bland and careless stance in life. He went his own way. Nothing interfered with Mack – not even Nature.

He began to pile the hay on top of him. He did it methodically, with seriousness. At least outwardly. With a set face in keeping with slow burial ritual he heaped the hay in armfuls over Mack. It was like covering a willing victim on a beach, for the sun beat down on them, his nape and shoulders burning, and instead of gulls there were the rooks, a black chorus of rising and falling specks against the solid sky. He began to hum to himself as the heap rose, something slow and funereal.

Harvey joined in the task. That was strange, he noted, for him to enter the spirit of the thing, and without embarrassment, but he made no comment, barely glanced at his new helper as they passed each other in silence, moving from the cut rows to the rising mound and back again. Beneath, there was a living nucleus, a kernel in the shape of Mack. Who was thinking what, he wondered; what swift, new and desperate scheme was engaging his brain as he held out, Houdini under the hay? And of course he would hold out, had to, if he were to win, and Mack studied the art of winning, just winning anything, anywhere, against anyone with chilling dedication. To the last unthinkable resort, even? Yes, for that was how he would triumph, of course, he had no other way. The pile would grow, a cock, neat and well-shaped (he and Harvey were showing no haste) until one of them, or both, would falter, the terrible thought seizing hold, they would look at one another for a moment, listen, then together begin clawing downwards to see a stiff replica of their friend, which after a minute of punishing horror – for them – would open one eye and . . .

But no, no, not this time and not this way, Master Mack, down there hanging on to your breathing, ticking off the seconds until panic up above, in the air, will turn the trick for you. Oh no, not this time . . .

The hay rose. Already it had broadened, squat-based, to a thatched nose, a modest rick. They were moving deeper into the field each time. A bald, spreading semi-circle marked their forays. The hay was still damp on its underside, warm to the touch, itchy; the roots of the sward where the blades had entered, almost solid turf. The trick, when turning it to receive

5

the sun, was to back down the row, sliding the teeth of the rake under the heavy fibrous butt with a twist, up and over. In this way a slow fat spiralling of the hay took place. It felt good unravelling the flattened rows. The cut crop looked as though it had been pasted there. But now of course they were destroying that pleasure and pattern; they were raping the rows faster and faster, racing out to the perimeter of their previous raids, then back to the growing heap. And still no movement, no startling sideways shift of the entire structure. Would Mack – could he perhaps – engineer the miracle of a living, moving hay-rick, his finest creation yet?

Harvey threw down what was certainly the heaviest armful of all. It whistled past, as he stood by holding his burden, with a violence that seemed more extreme than usual, even for Harvey. The face was sweating, he noticed, locked grimly. They looked at one another for a moment then flew back to the contest with renewed ferocity. Some curious quickening in the blood had united them against this lifeless yet living construction. It challenged them, mocked them too, so they flailed it with their sheaves, grunting. He felt the urge to damage. The tips of his fingers were raw with scraping the hay up off the field, his chest and stomach stung with sweat, his face was coated with seeds and stalks, but it seemed unimportant beside this need to force some form of submission, he knew not what.

Higher and higher – they were reaching up now with great chest-hugging armfuls – and he was tiring. He could hear his own breath whistle as Harvey stumbled past. Harvey's face rushed at him, just once, once was enough, blurred, red and white, out of the haze of heat and running sweat, and the eyes were set. And he stopped where he was. He looked at what their frenzy had constructed, was leading them to, and the terrible thing was that he wanted to go on with it.

He reached into the hay then, sinking up to the arm-pits, and pushed with all his strength. The cap began to move; it formed perhaps a sixth of the rick and sat in one piece, heavy, snub. It started to slide, but so slowly, parting with the rest of the layered bulk. The entire rick would have to be dismantled in this way, moving downwards; the hay had a stubborn quality, it had to be unpicked at its own pace.

6

He thought, *sweet Jesus*, that murderous slow descent, course by course, to what awaited them.

—Harvey! he shouted.—Harvey *Gault!*

The surname came out as a final cry of anguish. It shocked the air, single harsh bark, and it had its effect, although coming to his lips unthinkingly, born purely of desperation, for Harvey began heaving and tearing now at the heap of hay alongside him. They were shoulder to shoulder – to think of someone pierced by the sound of his last name – but rip at the sullen mass, tear apart the heavy twists and scatter, two frightened, rooting terriers. They flung it about them in desperate fashion, destroying what they had built.

An outsider viewing from a distance would never be able to piece together the events leading to such a sight. An outbreak of madness in a hay field in midsummer perhaps, motiveless except for the noonday heat? His mind spawned ludicrous images. They burst in a spate that mocked the slowness of his hands. A legionnaire staggering in circles over an expanse of corrugated dunes, then buzzards on a cactus stand, a discarded water-bottle. Pedro Armendariz with a broken leg croaking—*Leave me the pistol, muchacho. Go on without me—*

The last layer. They could see an outline now, a bulge, Mack covered by a thin coating of hay. They looked at one another for a moment. Both had paused. Who would strip away the final strands? Whoever made the move would somehow be responsible for all this.

Through the coarse stalks, clover and bindweed mixed with the crop, a sight of something that shocked, Mack's skin, his pale back, because there surely was the shape of his head, and there too his hair darker than the hay. *He was face down.* Had he shifted position at the beginning when they were both away from the heap, arching himself slyly to take the weight better, or – and this was horror – had some fearful moment occurred as he was being buried, that no one would ever know about?

The hay came off – Harvey did it – and Mack was crouched as though waiting for a game to commence, piggy-back, but his head drooped limply and they could hear no sound of his breathing. He and Harvey hung there too on their feet waiting, afraid to make the next move. Mack, he felt, might disintegrate at a touch like a dry puff-ball, or fall over in slow motion the way he had once seen an old mare do when it was shot. Harvey leant down once more and, gently for him, prodded the flabby back and, oh sweet relief, Mack sighed and the wind seemed to rush out of him just as if he were that same old spent horse, only reprieved, and he began to crawl shakily on his hands and knees out of the ring of tossed hay over to where he could be alone and could gather himself. They watched in silence, him panting, with his head and shoulders turned away.

Harvey lifted some of the scattered hay, walked across and threw it over him with contempt, then picked up a rake and began plucking at the tangled heaps, and it was as though he must break the wooden shaft at any moment, a natural outcome. The hay he had heaped on Mack still clung, demeaning.

He thought, *you twisted bastard, Harvey.*

He called out and the red face turned, receiving the full force of the armful of hay he hurled at it.

Then:

—*Hey!* he shouted,—*hey!*

And made a little jump, girlish skip really, landing with legs apart, arms outstretched, like saying *boo* without saying it, trying to show this too was a game, desperately, for his bravery had left him at the sight of that face, frozen still with its shock, but beginning to thaw, then set again into what must surely become black rage, murder in the eye, murder in the grip. Could he turn and run before the wooden pegs came whistling down to mash him? But then, almost as though there might after all be such a thing as divine intervention, he heard his own voice echoed – *hey!* but with mockery – *hey!* thin high cry of a sissy, and Mack was recovered, on his feet mimicking, and throwing in turn an armful of hay that blinded him.

Next moment all three of them were pelting one another as viciously as they could and laughing as each treble – *hey!* rang out.

Round and round they twisted and ducked, at times stumbling over the rolls of hay that littered their battlefield; Harvey, brutal and intent on delivering the hardest cut of all; Mack feinting, playing the fool; and himself – ? Well, what about himself? Not really involved, heart not really in it, voice not really in it either as he delivered his quota of simpering cries that set the tears running down their cheeks. He hoped it would end soon, as suddenly as it had begun, but didn't want the other two to know, so he kept up his own barrage of the flying crop – but who knows, perhaps they felt the same way. Perhaps . . .

But it was Mack who called a halt finally. At first it seemed just another of his tricks, not quite so inventive certainly, but he must be tiring as well.

—*Listen!* he shouted, dropping his load.

Harvey scored bulls-eye but Mack spat out seeds and shook his head impatiently.

—No, listen, you buggers! *Listen!*

Then they all held still and the sound came to them, metal on metal, faint but recognizable, above the rooks and the faint wind and the diminished drone of a motor-car in the Valley. Hetty. They looked at Mack.

He said:

—To work, to work, and then craftily,—Let's grab her when she comes up.

Each of them lifted his rake then and began tossing out the scattered hay. Again, to that imaginary observer, it would appear as though they were simply trying to bring back some pattern to this corner of the big field, working with seriousness to uncover aisles between rows, so that later the horse and mechanical rake could have clearance, but he himself felt an excitement that the work his hands found was barely able to conceal. The others, he felt, shared it as well. Harvey was giggling at the things Mack was whispering to him, his face lowered like a child who doesn't want the teacher to see his expression, biting his lip, shaking his head as though trying to fling loose the images being implanted there.

Hetty was coming closer, her rhythmic beat on the bucket rim gaining in volume. They couldn't see her because the bulge of the falling field concealed her and the gate through which she'd come. And now the tempo of the high metallic ringing changed and they all laughed, knowing that it signalled her growing impatience.

—Ssssh! called Mack,—keep your heads down and when I give the call – jump her.

They jabbed and manhandled the heavy drifts of hay, as though oblivious of everything but the necessity of the work,

9

three well-drilled labourers. Harvey broke wind loudly and expertly and again the laughter was quelled by Mack. They took cues from him, modelling their expressions on his serious and lordly one. And still Hetty was approaching, and at the same time declaring both her progress and her irritability with the rattling can.

It held watered buttermilk to quench their thirst. She would transfer it to the other can, now empty, deep in the cool shade of the hedge, a thin acid liquid that rolled easily down the throat and held its effect long and lasting. Now he tasted that remembered tang in his mouth and thought it would be no hardship to substitute the simplicity of a drink at the fresh can-ful for this game they were preparing, whatever it was. Something about it nagged at him, some uneasiness buried deeply, warning.

Hetty began shouting as though she sensed they were near.

—*Hey!* she cried.

Harvey giggled.

—It's good for horses, and again the word set them off, but a quiet shaking, no more.

Hetty came into view.

She was different today, dressed differently, startlingly, in a frock of pale blue with short, bunched sleeves and a neckline that left a vee of flesh exposed to the sun; and she moved warily on her feet too as though she might have silk stockings on.

—Hey, you lot! Are you deaf or what? Do you not hear me calling on you? Your dinner's ready.

She'd stopped some distance away and was studying them. There was no sound now but the rasp of the hay and the dry rustle their feet made over the surface of the field. They moved with lowered heads as though in a kind of dumb show, some secret pattern of movement that only they knew traced out among the scattered hay.

—It'll be getting cold. It's out on the table.

Slow and wary, the words spaced.

All she has to do is turn on her heel and go, he thought, *leave them to their mysteries* – but she wouldn't. He knew it by the sound of her voice, by the way she was looking at them; he kept shooting the barest of glances at her, under his brows, sly darts that noted each change in her stance, each fresh expression. She looked taller today, the frock she wore above her knees, the shoulders squared in a style that seemed slightly out of fashion, too old for her. Her lips were reddened too and her hair frizzed out. Why was she dressed this way?

—All right, you clever shits. If you think I'm going to stand here all day like a dummy, you've another think coming. I've an afternoon's work ahead of me.

Harvey's face looked as though it were about to split open, like a ripe tomato, at any moment. He was hunched over his rake with his back turned away from her. He, at any rate, wouldn't be able to contain his laughter much longer.

Then Hetty said—Right. Okay (with finality)—I'm going to leave your bloody old can here and you can do whatever the hell you like with it.

She moved to put it down beside the bulk of the largest remaining pile of hay. They all saw her legs bare above the knees, the satin frock stretching tight on her buttocks as she bent over, and Mack said:

—Now! and they rushed her.

She screamed and began to run, not turning her head, the sound of their feet warning her, and she was running like that, head up, holding her skirts high for some reason when Mack caught up and sent her falling into the hay with a two-handed shove.

Then they were all on top trying to touch her, contain her beneath their weight, as she flailed and screamed, muffled now but still a frightening sound and he had to admit, arousing too. The cry seemed to be running into his own body as his hands moved from area to area on this other warm heaving one. He felt sly, quick and criminal, as he jockeyed for a feel of uncovered flesh. Boldness grew in him, roughness too; he knew hands couldn't be identified. The thought excited him more. He began to be angry with the others. They baulked him. He found a place on one of her thighs, the skin soft, perspiring, and he gripped tight, fighting for his hard-won territory. He burned for a part of her for his own and squeezed cruelly in consequence. He didn't know whether her cries were because of him or not. He didn't really care.

Her knickers were exposed now, soft navy-blue, elastic sewn into the legs and waist, the sort that the girls at school used to wear. They seemed shockingly innocent, at variance with all the

11

earlier images of lust. Something tore – it must have been her frock – and he felt his mood dive even more steeply. Then, through the tangle of limbs, bare backs, and areas of straining blue satin, her face, and she was looking straight at him, and outrage had all gone from the eyes now. The look reproached him, mute cry for help, but it was worse than that. He had never seen her like this before, so – stripped. He couldn't conceive she could ever be like this, Hetty, the Hetty Quinn he'd known all his life. *He knew her.*

She began to sob, no fight left in her, and all three of them seemed to stiffen.

Again he had that irrational image of someone observing the scene and trying in vain to translate this pile of bodies and their game on a hot summer's day. Their isolation in this vast field, on this Valley slope high above the village, people and transport, pierced him with sadness, with a regret for something he'd missed and would never have.

They left her there. She was weeping, her face buried in the hay, one leg still bare above the garter, one of her shoes lying a few feet away. He picked it up and carefully placed it beside the uncovered foot. Then he and Mack moved slowly away, a little space apart, not speaking, heading towards the farmhouse.

Harvey had picked up his rake and was attacking the remaining scatter of hay. He worked with sullen energy. He had remembered whose field, whose hay it was.

Oh her lovely dress, her lovely bluey dress and why had she put it on today of all days . . . Just to show off to old Minnie Maitland, hoping she would make her turn around before her in the parlour . . .

—Now child, now that I'm settled, let me look at you. Mmm . . . her mouth full of pins and the work-basket with the red and green tapestry lid nesting in her lap.

—Well, I don't for the life of me see why you young people have to have your skirts quite up around your waists these days, but I suppose if it's the fashion, then there's nothing else for it. They'll talk in the village, of course, but then they always did. I was the first to wear bicycling bloomers. Did you know that? Yes, I was, yes. So practical. But did anyone appreciate that? No. The Reverend Mawhinnie humiliated me before all the corner-boys who used to prop up the window-sill of Semple's public house. There's always a new generation to carry on that important work. Miss Maitland, he crowed out – oh, an opinionated old jackdaw – Miss Maitland, do my eyes deceive me that you seem to have overlooked an essential outer garment. Its absence may be due to the exceptional clemency of the weather, but I'm sure you wouldn't wish to give rise to any hint of impropriety on your part. Hoity-toity and oh, how that man lusted after the sound of his own voice. Nothing but a midden rooster, or a rook, for that matter, a rook, in human guise of course; but oh, so high, so mighty and so righteous. I can forgive men most of their other failings but never that. Men, oh, men, why do we have to endure their inanities?

I had one of them things till the wheel fell off it – as old Bob Spence would say. She suspected that Minnie herself was foggy about some of the big words she used but went ahead with them anyway, knowing that no one in the company would, or could, correct either usage or pronunciation. And it was their sound

13

that seemed faulty. She would pinch particular words as though she were popping out a pip or a plum-stone. Her mouth would pucker like . . . She giggled, thinking of something coarse, then looked up and down the empty road (she had left Gault's hayfield far behind now) and said out loud:

—Like a hen's arse.

As she walked along she would renew the mood and the image by repeating it to herself but gradually went slipping back in her mind to what had happened earlier. To remind was the steady throb where the hay had stung the soft part of her thighs, and that made her feel hot and then cold, remembering how much of herself she had exposed. She pulled her frock down as she walked as if that might help to cover the shame of it, but she remembered. She began to cry again softly but without that earlier feeling, as if there was something tearing deep in her throat, that had come over her in the field.

For a long time after they'd left her there she'd lain, not even bothering to cover herself, sobbing until there was a bruising pain in her ribs. It was strange and she didn't know how to explain it, but she wanted to keep herself naked to the waist for as long as possible, as though to show someone, *something*, how she had been treated, now that it had been done to her to display herself, *look what they have done, look, look!* And even though it was only the sky that stared down on her and the passing birds – rooks, a seagull drifting over far inland, an aeroplane very high up, silvery with the sun on it – they helped some of the pain to leave her.

She felt empty as though she hadn't eaten for a long time. Occasionally she would stumble on the rough back-road; her new shoes with their thick heels and the straps around her ankles making heavy work of the pot-holes and the crumbling tarmacadam. It was a forgotten little by-road rarely used, and the grass and hedge-briars had been allowed their way with it; the broken, mottled walking surface gradually vanishing as each season passed and each crop pressed further in. At the best of times she liked this stretch of quiet roadway, idling along, picking honeysuckle or a spray of fuchsia or deep, hidden violets to give to Minnie Maitland when she arrived at the house for her afternoon's cleaning.

The old lady would cry—Oh how lovely! What a beautiful

14

surprise, and how thoughtful of you, Hetty! no matter how many times she presented the fresh blooms.

There would follow a great rushing about for vases and bowls to contain the flowers. She would be sent to find the best Waterford and very often the work of dusting and sweeping out of rooms would be suspended while Minnie talked excitedly about pistils and stamens and pollination and showed her collections of pressed ferns and leaves and musty picture-books on 'flora and fauna'. She had never been able to discover the difference between the two, and so far had managed to keep the fact to herself by nodding wisely as though she was taking all in on those long afternoons in the room where the books were kept, row upon row of pale soft bindings, like chamois leather they were, behind the glass doors of the high bookcases.

The sun beat down on the greenhouses outside the windows, sheeting them in gold, and tea would be served in fine cups. The pattern on the service was pink and brown, scenes of woodland and stream, and moving through that magic landscape on the bone china, a pair of lovers, hand in hand, or searching for one another among the thickets with pale worried faces. She felt the faces were pale because the artist had made the eyes large and beautiful, standing out from the rest of them, and, silly though it was, she thought of them as Flora and Fauna. The sound of the words was lovely enough. She said them to herself when she wanted to feel calm. Sometimes it worked. And it fitted the two on the tea-service.

While Minnie went on about Nature, she would take her gaze from cup to plate to sugar-bowl to milk-jug trying to work out a progression in their story. She hoped it ended happily for them there among the fine feathery bushes and the quiet pools, but had a feeling it didn't. On the largest plate the girl was lying beside the river with her hair covering her face, and there was such despair in the way she was stretched out that she felt sure the boy had been drowned. There were times she was tempted to break that plate when she was washing up in the scullery but the sin would have been too great and the consequences unthinkable.

Perhaps however that wasn't the end of the story but the beginning. Perhaps the girl Flora was weeping there on the bank one day, and she was heart-broken because – yes, because

15

her parents had just died and she had nowhere to live and nowhere to go, and this boy had come along and had seen her through the bushes and had fallen in love with her and they had gone walking together hand in hand, and maybe some little time later she had stopped to pick flowers and he had hid himself from her. That would explain the worried face and the searching on the sugar-bowl – and then perhaps she would hide from him, just in play too, and he would think he had lost her and then the one who had been hiding would leap out and they would see each other and kiss . . .

In school the master had called her a dreamer: Dolly Day-Dream, the nickname he had put on her, and the rest of the class would laugh when he would creep up behind her and yell it in her ear. He should never have done that; it was bad for her nerves. Sometimes she would shake for a long time afterwards and couldn't concentrate on the book before her.

Old Harper and his old school far behind her, a thing of the past; good riddance to bad rubbish!

On her last day she had set out to do as much mischief as she could, to pay him and his school back. She had scribbled on every school-book that came her way, changing words to dirty meanings; she stole his heavy black ruler – the one he had used on her – and his Parker pen, and she had put them down the girls' privy into that dark bottomless pit. She let the tyres of his bicycle down too, but when she had done all the damage she could and was going through the gates for the last time, she still hadn't felt satisfied. It wasn't enough somehow for all the times he had nipped her with his chalky old finger and thumb on the arm or the neck or the ear and pulled her by the stretched skin out to the front of the class to mock her, and nothing would ever pay for that worst day of all. It was the day the inspector was to call, and, standing out with the others around the room at reading time before he arrived, she had wet herself when her turn had come, and he had made her stand there with a puddle at her feet and her legs smarting and the class giggling.

No one would ever do that to her again, no one; she would stick a knife into them first, and on that last day she felt that only killing Master Harper would relieve her. After school she waited for him up a tree that stretched a single big branch over the road, with a heavy stone to drop on his head, as he rode by underneath, home to his tea. She felt just like Tarzan or Robin Hood once the scheme had got stuck in her head. She had to carry it out, no matter how hard it was to climb up with that big stone, but she managed it nevertheless, and placed it in a fork where a light push would send it down on the top of his head. He always wore a green paddy hat with a little feather in its band.

But of course when the time came she couldn't go through with it. She thought of him looking up and seeing her, just as the stone was falling and not being killed outright, just lying there paralysed and still looking at her. So she had climbed down out of the tree and ran home, but the worst part of it was that she had to leave the stone where it was, because she couldn't budge it. For weeks afterwards she had nightmares about it falling down on someone innocent, and having it on her conscience. But even that turned into one of her day-dreams, the one where she was sentenced to life imprisonment and died of a broken heart and refusing to eat anything, and thousands of people coming to her funeral and making speeches and discovering she was innocent all along . . .

She sat down on a soft bank at the side of the road to have a rest, but really it was to let the story in her head take a firmer hold and have its course. She kept thinking of that stone in the tree. Whatever had happened to it? Because when the autumn came and all the leaves fell away, the stone had gone too; it had disappeared, and though she searched underneath and up and down the dry grassy ditches on either side of the road, and even over the hedge in Ramsay's potato-field, nothing, no sign of it. It must have gone somewhere. Perhaps it had fallen down on an innocent party after all, and been taken away by the police for evidence. Finger-prints? But she would have heard about it. A thing like that would keep the locality in talk for a year – so, *Hetty*, she told herself, *put it out of your mind, you'll never know what happened, the ins and the outs* . . .

A lady-bird was climbing on her outstretched hand, slowly making its way over the heights and hollows of her spread fingers. It was one of the few insects she liked, little spotty thing with its beautiful shiny shell and its gentle ways. It always seemed short-sighted to her, as if it had been travelling a long time and a long way. Would it ever reach its destination, she wondered? If she could find out where it was going she might take it up and wear it on her dress like a brooch and carry it and then set it down, saving it all that needless travel. Little lady-bird.

Then suddenly as it lay there at peace in the palm of her hand for her inspection, its back split in two halves and, with a tiny whirring noise, wings came out of the opening.

She screamed and threw it from her, terrified at its ugliness, then rubbed her hand on her frock until the fabric burned her. Another second and she felt sure it would have stung her or pressed out some form of poison on to her skin. She began to weep with this new shock, crouched there on the bank, her two hands binding her legs, head buried in her lap, ears and eyes closed on the day and the noise of the birds.

Oh ugly, ugly . . . cruel, cruel, cruel . . . Why was everything and everybody like that? Why had everything to be spoiled and marred just when things were nice?

Into her head, for no reason, it seemed, came:

> All things bright and beautiful
> All creatures great and small,
> All things wise and wonderful,
> The Lord God made them all.

It was her favourite hymn. But all things weren't bright and beautiful, or wise and wonderful either, so why did people invent lies like that?

It must have been the lady-bird that made her sing the words in her head – *all creatures great and small*. She had noticed that things did come into her head that way, hymns or songs usually, suddenly without warning. Someone would say a thing or she would notice or think of something and there would be bits of music and words floating in her head and it wouldn't be for some time afterwards that the association would strike her. Did it happen to other people? She had never asked anyone. It wasn't a question you could ask someone. Maybe she was simple-minded after all. Her father told her so often enough, and Master Harper used to say it as well. He would point at his head to make the class titter when she was at the blackboard trying to go round the sides of an isosceles triangle or touch the capes and bays on the map of Ireland with the pointer in her hand.

She wished she had dropped that stone on his head after all, smashing all his brains in and leaving him there with his bicycle on top of him with the wheel going round and round in the air. She could see that part of it clearly, the wheel turning gently, the shiny spokes and the sound it made slowing to a *click, click, click*. It was like something she had seen in a film and although she had forgotten everything else about the film she had remembered that one little bit . . .

But old Minnie Maitland didn't think she was simple. She had said she was *sensitive*.

—I was the same at your age. Sensitive. Aware of the finer things, because, never forget, dear Hetty, there is another world outside Tardree and the poor half-creatures who live there and think it is the only world. Ah! music, pictures, literature, fine concerts and brilliant company! They're all waiting for you – and you're so young, so young . . .

But although she enjoyed the conversation – it was one of her favourites, as they sipped tea from the pink and brown cups – she would change all the things Minnie wanted for her into her own dreams of what was really out there *in the great big world*. When she felt depressed, if they had been shouting at her at home or if her father wouldn't let her stay out to go to a dance, she saw herself getting on a bus – the green Transport one that stopped in the village twice a week – and travelling to the city, and there in the bus-station waiting for her would be someone who looked like Farley Granger in a white car with the hood down, and he would take her suitcase, and put it in the back-seat and then drive her to a shop and buy her a fur coat and high-heeled shoes, perfume and earrings and a little fluffy dog like the one Gloria Grahame had in that picture she had once seen. She fed it chocolates and Broderick Crawford hated it and kept trying to lock it out of the apartment . . .

No, Minnie was welcome to her *finer things*, as she called them; she preferred her own. She had no interest in the books that lined the walls and smelt of mould when you opened the tall glass doors, or the pictures on the landing of foreign seaside places or of *Oh, For The Wings Of A Dove* coming out of the big green horn on the old gramophone.

19

That was Minnie's favourite piece of music. Once she had heard it on the wireless at home but hadn't recognized it for some time because Minnie's record was so old and scratchy – nearly played done, the red label with the listening dog on it going round and round thousands of times over the years in that house. That was sad when she thought about it; Minnie sitting there getting older and older and the record going the same way.

—Don't be like me, she would say.—Don't stay in this frightful place of small minds and tiny ambitions. Spread your wings, little bird, and fly, fly!

She always had to excuse herself to go upstairs to the bathroom whenever she said that, could hardly keep it in until she was safe behind the locked door and then she would roll over the cold floor in hysterics, and every time she flapped her arms up and down in front of the big mirror she thought she'd die of laughing.

—*Fly, fly,* she whispered to herself in the glass,—*fly, little birdie*, and fell down with the giggles.

Once she had heard Minnie cough quietly outside the door when she was at her antics, and she had felt sure she had heard her, but, when she went downstairs, old Minnie had carried on as if nothing was amiss. That was a bad time. She had felt ashamed because Minnie had always treated her well, like one of her own. And it wasn't funny really because she knew the story of how Minnie was never able to leave the old house because of her father, old Hutton Maitland, not even when she was young and beautiful and it was tearing the heart out of her with all the things she was missing and would never ever have. There had been a man too who wanted to marry Minnie, but, funny enough, she never talked about him at all. It was only by adding little bits to other little bits she'd let slip that she knew about it.

Old Dadda, as Minnie called him, was dead now, but he'd done the damage; he'd seen to it that she would always be tied to Hollybush House and the musty books and the pictures and the records in the stiff brown albums. There were photographs of *him* in nearly every room just to remind that, even though he had gone, he was still boss.

In one of them he was in a funny sort of chair with a little wheel at the front to steer it by. The chair was made of basket-work and there was a rug over the old man's knees. His hands were under the rug, but you could just imagine them clenched as hard as iron balls underneath. He had a pointed beard, and he was looking straight at you, fierce as an old billy-goat. The beard suited him all right; a goatee, she'd heard it called.

The other men in the photograph had moustaches and carried tennis racquets. The only one she recognized was Barbour Brown, the retired schoolmaster – even with his moustache. He was standing with his hand on Minnie's shoulder and he looked young and smiling, very different from the old man she sometimes passed walking on the roads. He always looked at you in an odd way with his eyes very bright as if he wanted to take in every little detail in that one glance, because he might never see you again. She was often tempted to speak her mind and say in passing —*You'll know me the next time, Master Brown,* but she felt afraid of him and his bright gaze. She was certain he often stopped and was staring after her until she disappeared from sight.

It was strange to think of them – Minnie and him – both being the same age and playing tennis on the court at the back of the house. Nobody had played there for ages. The stinging nettles covered all traces of what she'd only seen in photographs from those long ago summers; Minnie holding up her skirt and racing like mad for the ball, her hair pinned up under a big floppy hat. She looked as though she was in great demand by all the men who wanted to play with her, all waiting their turn on the kitchen chairs that someone had brought out for them to sit on against the wall of the greenhouse.

How many of them, she wondered, had asked her to marry them? How many had wanted to take her for a walk in under the monkey-puzzle tree up at the head of the avenue? Had Minnie ever gone with them, she wondered, into that dark green shadowy place?

She had gone in there crouching once herself, searching for a hen's nest, and the quietness and airlessness of the place had made her feel funny. It was hot too, like being in the greenhouse, only dark, and she had thought things that made her blush whenever she remembered. Had some man's hands ever loosened Minnie's buttoned blouse or crept up under those wide skirts? Lying back on the soft moist mounds, she had imagined it happening to her and not wanting to do anything about it, only stretching there with her eyes closed and feeling her limbs loosening in the close heat . . .

Would it be like that when it happened to her, slow and pleasant and drowsy? She had no way of telling, only what her imagination prompted, because the ones she had asked about it, married women in the village, only laughed and joked with her and said—*You'll find out for yourself soon enough*. Only it mightn't be soon, it mightn't be ever – like Minnie. And maybe that wouldn't be such a bad thing either, for it seemed men were such tearing, panting creatures whenever they were roused, whenever it came to *IT*. *Did you get IT last night?* she'd heard their voices sniggering at Semple's corner in the darkness . . .

In the hayfield it had been the sound of their breathing that terrified her most. She could think of what happened a little more calmly now. What would they have done to her if she hadn't begun to cry? It changed them in a moment, getting up from her with the bumps still standing out in their dungarees. They all pushed their hands into their pockets, she noticed, turning away. She knew what it meant, and in the past it had always struck her as comical, about men and their peculiarities. That was another of Minnie's words. *Men's little peculiarities*, she often said. It sounded just an ordinary thing to say but now all innocence had been taken away from it.

Thinking of Minnie brought into her head the time. She had no watch, but it felt late and she knew she had been wandering in her thoughts sitting here on this bank. Her seat felt damp and she rose, smoothing out her dress, pulling it away from her skin. Her legs prickled.

To avoid more of that line of thought she began to sing to herself.

> *Cherry – Berry – Bin, I love you so,*
> *I love you so, I love you so . . .*

Those were the only words she could remember and she sang them over and over, hoping that the rest of the chorus would creep in on their heels, falling into place in the tune from out of nowhere, from somewhere in her head that she didn't know contained them like *All things bright and beautiful*.

She marched along the road conducting with her arms, then began to dance in time to *Cherry–Berry–Bin* (funny words those) whirling around over the empty road with her arms outstretched now, as though dancing with a partner. It was an old-tyme waltz, one, two, three; one, two, three; round and round until you staggered, released, dizzy at the end of it and had to sit down with the room spinning.

She'd just seen this lovely picture a few weeks ago called *The Grace Moore Story* and Kathryn Grayson had sung it in that. It was her favourite film to date and she kept seeing Kathryn Grayson's little rosebud mouth singing the words. How could anyone so beautiful be such a good singer too? Grace Moore was just an ordinary American girl who sacrificed everything so that she could be a great operatic star. She never married, although she loved a man all her life, so great was her ambition. But the beginning of the film was the best part when she'd just arrived in New York and couldn't get a job. She met these two other girls and they all shared an apartment and told each other their problems. They were always sitting around in their pyjamas on top of their beds talking and making plans and that was the sort of life she would love to have and the girls were the sort of friends she'd like to have too for the rest of her life, just three girls being all together with no men to spoil things. Men always spoiled everything. Even in the picture one of the girls left to go and get married and then the other girl fell in love with Kathryn Grayson's boy-friend. Everything spoiled as usual . . .

She was in full voice, in her fantasy, Kathryn Grayson in the opera house, dancing in time to her own singing, if that were possible, when she heard the sound of an approaching motor. Its engine had suddenly burst into life out of the silence and she turned and saw it was Charlie Lord the bread-man in the red and cream Inglis Bakery van. He must have been coasting silently downhill towards her all along. She felt sickened that he must have seen her and was having a good laugh at her expense. It was just like him to take pleasure in watching her while she made a fool of herself.

Hot in the face, she plunged through a hole in the hedge to hide until he passed, then regretted it immediately, for what if he stopped and came in after her, hoping to catch a sly look at her with her pants down? She moved further into the plantation. Was there to be no end to her humiliation? Why should she have to suffer the attention of every dirty-minded blackguard abroad this day?

She stopped and listened. Over her head the tops of the trees made a noise like the sea and there were wood-pigeons as well, perched and cooing out of sight. She listened. She couldn't tell whether the bread-van had stopped or the engine was running very quietly. Then she heard the sound of a hand-brake being applied, and she got down on her knees on the moss behind one of the thickest trees. Her cheek touched its rough, dry bark and she put her arms around it for comfort.

—*Oh God*, she prayed, *Make old Charlie Lord go away and leave me in peace* . . .

But, in her imagination, she saw him coming in after her with the long pole he used to pull down the loaves with and poking it around for her in among the bushes, the little cold cruel cleek at its tip feeling for her between the legs. She pressed her knees together on the damp moss and held the tree more tightly. Would she ever get to Minnie Maitland's this day? And how would she explain her lateness?

She heard herself saying—*Well, for a start, Harvey Gault, Mack McFarlane and Frank Glass grabbed hold of me in Gault's big hayfield and tried to pull the clothes off me, and then Charlie Lord the bread-man followed me into McGookin's plantin' and* . . .

Not that she would of course. Things like that were never to be mentioned before Minnie. *Bodily matters*, as she referred to them, were forbidden topics. Cats didn't have kittens, cows weren't served by the bull and poor Maggie Spence down in the gate-lodge didn't have an illegitimate baby every other year by the different drunk men who knocked on her door after dark when the pub closed. Och, Minnie could go to hell, her and her *sensitive* ways! But she was the only one she could talk to, even if they were never going to discuss that subject she worried about more than most others . . .

Again she listened to the distant sound of the motor. It still ticked over out of sight and she could imagine Charlie with his hands in the pockets of his long white duster coat standing beside it and weighing up the possibilities. Should he leave it unattended or not? She knew he hadn't followed her in yet because she would have heard his noise. Should he or not, should he or—? She enjoyed his dilemma, thinking of him there, torn between his lust and his fear that some of the young Gillespies might plunder his pastries, all his delicate little boxed apple and custard fancies, carried off to be devoured in some quiet place. She almost felt like laughing, thinking how good that would be if it were to happen, his face at finding the emptied cardboard boxes. She almost called out to him to tempt him away from the van, when she remembered . . . Her imagination getting the better of her again.

She felt afraid once more. Then the engine roared up and she heard the clutch going in, and soon the sound of the driven bread-van faded away, leaving her and the wood and its rising soft summery noises. It was peaceful beneath the trees again, a calm and safe place.

Standing up, she began to smooth down her dress, her poor dress. What had they done to it; what had they done to *her*, the men of the parish out abroad on this day with some summer madness in their heads? Lifting her clothing, she examined her blue knickers carefully for sign of a rip or stains. She began to cry, the tears wetting her cheeks. She stood there with her clothes hoisted in the middle of the wood weeping and not really knowing why she was doing either . . .

What a stroke of luck it was, a bonus surely for all the hours spent in ditches or propped on walls, his elbows chilling to numbness on the stone, as his old Zeiss glasses crept across the landscape or sharpened in on some lighted window. The binoculars shook; his finger and thumb fumbled its hold on the milled wheel before the image sprang clear, a single spyhole, strangely, never for him (his eyesight perhaps?) the linked circles as in that conventional shot of the Western film when they rake the horizon for the awaited stage-coach. He had been nervous certainly, trembling, no less, but then of course, why not, because wouldn't this delight disappear at any moment, vanish into the air or be obscured and he would be left (he knew the sensation well) shaking and feeling the perspiration cold as ice-water on his brow, and resolving once again – he groaned – *oh never again*, to be tempted and tempt this damnable, dreadful ache, the consequence of his habit . . .

Barbour Brown held the field-glasses steady, fiercely too. There would be faint bruises later as recompense for his ecstasy. The finely stretched skin of black leather covering the metal under his grip felt damp. His own sweat oiled the tubes, his sweat leaked out by his own overwhelming excitement at the image. It was inside his head now, imprinting itself on his memory steadily like one of his French photographs.

He was lying fully stretched on an upward-sloping bank by the side of the road, his head and shoulders framed in a gap in the hedge, the toes of his polished brown brogues denting the grass, mere inches from the gravel. An ache had already started to spread upwards from his elbows. The thought of damp entering his joints certainly disturbed, but nothing must interfere with his moment of passion, not even a passer-by seeing him at his occupation. Of course he must be a familiar figure by this time creeping about the hedgerows, safe in what the local

26

people considered his eccentricity. He smiled at that. Bird-watching, a study of Nature, the little furry and feathered creatures of the field and copse – his daylight obsession. Night-time too, if they could only see him prowling near their homes after dark, drawn like a moth to their uncurtained windows, the brown leather case still hanging from his neck by its straps. For, if they only knew, these innocents in the heart of the country, *they* were his study and not the field creatures, they and their habits, much more fascinating than any dumb thing feeding, mating or dying under a sky. He could watch a man ploughing until his own arms dropped, or the children in the school-yard, or two women gossiping over a garden hedge. No human activity was too trivial for him as long as he was hidden.

The glasses held steady now, burning its picture into his brain. Like an experienced photographer his aim was locked tight once he had focused on his subject. He had taught his hands and wrists to take on a life of their own, to become mechanical instruments manipulating coldly and precisely, separate from the rest of him which, more and more these days, felt old, tired and trembling. His mind seethed but the glass always remained icily objective in its reproduction. His dependable little old German friend. Curious how he had rediscovered it, found qualities there he had never suspected, after all those years of neglect in the attic, first bought when he was younger and couldn't really afford it – for a silly reason. He remembered he felt he had to have the glasses when he went to his first important point-to-point meeting with the Mait-lands. Like any raw hobbledehoy he wanted to be turned out exactly like the rest of his party, and then of course promptly regretted his shiny new purchase when he saw the others with their battered and superbly offhand machines . . .

Oh yes, a grandly unexpected bounty this now and no mistake. What the Master saw – only immensely superior to those flickering pier-head images inside their gaudy metal box; fleshed reality as opposed to all those white-faced antics full of silent *oohs* and *ahs* and widened eyes. Frozen for him. A living cameo.

He settled his body in its Harris tweed into the fine moss of the bank, forgetting the moisture it held, even on this hottest of days. His waistcoat buttons, his looping watch-chain and his bloodstone fob pressed deeper, finding easy passage into the softness. In his imagination he himself was sinking into that yielding holy-of-holies framed in his sights. He felt himself stirring beneath the tweed, beneath his second layer of buttons. Maidenhair under its covering, a tiny damp wisp escaping perhaps from beneath the stern elastic? His glasses, alas, weren't as probing as that. Imagination would have to penetrate the final mystery.

And then – a chilling development – a movement on the lens, barely perceptible but he knew, almost as though he could anticipate the signal from brain to limbs he was observing, that his spying was at an end; that tremor of indecision, enlarged by the retina across the distance, the warning. And he was powerless. Oh, if only by some miracle he could control it, as though on a microscope slide, a touch of forceps nudging it back into position. But no, he watched for the outcome now, saddened, his blood easing, slackening its pace and pressure. He began to feel the damp in his clothes, but still he remained, lying full-length, waiting. He always had to have the last drop, greedily, obsessively. Then the glass blurred as though a mist had clouded his sight, and he was left with only the tree trunks in McGookin's wood. Thin silver birch, two exotic specimens growing among the ash and the humble thorn. He could see, in the finest detail, their bark, curling, peeling strips that when pulled threaded a pale ring right around the stem.

His eyes closed wearily behind the warm sockets, shutting off the sight, and he kept them like that for a moment before rising from the impression he had made in the grass. It brought to his mind the hollows that courting couples left behind them these summer nights on the banks where they lay. When he was abroad prowling after dusk he often passed along a lovers' lane which they used. His blood would race as he walked that way, hearing the soft tones of the girls and the deeper murmur of the men. They hid their heads in the grass as he approached. Sometimes he would be almost upon them before they heard him – his soles were soft – and their lighted cigarettes at such times looked like fireflies ebbing and brightening in the darkness. He was drawn to the place and the arousing sound of their whisperings, for some reason he couldn't understand, because the experience always made him feel old and finished with life.

But it wasn't mere prurience that sent him out on his forays, *it wasn't* – he brushed his clothes down with sudden energy, stamping his feet to restore circulation – his interest was a serious one; he was interested in the human condition, the species itself. His journal was proof of that, and the notebook in his side pocket where he carefully wrote down his impressions, which later became the basis of his written work, rich raisins in the literary confection. Already he had filled five, each the thickness of a hymnal and with the same red-dyed edges to each page. A pressure on the cover deepened the shade from blotting-paper to blood. Inside were pale blue feints. He had taken, from the stock in the school store-cupboard before he retired, a dozen at least; but he still had an irrational fear that he would run out, and he knew that it would be impossible ever to replace that style and brand. To use any other, would in some way, he felt, mar the continuity, not only in the bindings of the row of filled notebooks on their shelf, but also in their content.

He patted the side of his jacket with affection. On the right it dropped like a poacher's pocket. There had been a time when he would change the burden from right to left so as not to ruin the fall of the cloth – it had once been a good suit – but he rarely considered things like that any more. As one grew older one had to prune ruthlessly at the more pointless obsessions of daily life. Each tiny worry added its own weight to existence.

Teaching had bred in him too much fastidiousness. His habits had become as rigid as iron out of the necessity to survive in the face of the freshly primed and daily onslaught of the children. At times he felt like a breakwater braced against that tide of youth. He had become even more rooted in his idiosyncrasies while at the same time knowing that they had become the basis for his several nicknames. It struck him as more and more obvious that the middle years of a man's life, his so-called prime, were wasted and spoiled by such indulgences. Early youth enjoyed ignorance of them and old age was a despairing race against time to erase them. And time was of the essence, as each day merged into the next and he was no nearer the completion of his task. Rather, it seemed to him sometimes, as though it receded further and further away as he discovered yet another side-track to lead him astray from the firm, unyielding advances he had once determined upon.

How in fact, *why* had he begun to keep his book of the Valley? He could recall with some haziness an ambition to compile a modest history of the area. Church records were consulted – copperplate the colour of dried blood; gravestone inscriptions copied – he used a kitchen knife to dig into the moss, rearing it up into a fine emerald strip before his blade. Curious but all he could remember from all of that grubbing were probably the most banal lines of all:

> *At the river's crystal brink*
> *Christ shall join each broken link.*

Poetry of the Christmas cracker, and as recent as nineteen twenty-four. An oddity of memory.

But then after a time he wearied of his dull researches; people merely were born, married, died. Records spelled out to him nothing more than names and places. The places remained always the same and the surnames repeated themselves with just as much boring regularity. He found himself unable to accept the smug circling continuum of such existence; out of the womb, aloft for a brief spell, then back into the soil again. Dust to dust, dung to dung . . .

Perhaps it was really only the thought of his own fate at the end of that same existential treadmill that made him look elsewhere. The Valley itself, its changing countenance with the weather and the seasons, its stones and soil above and below its face, the plants that grew there, the animals, birds and insect life – became his new study. He drew up lists – dimensions, colours, ingredients, materials, the feel of surfaces – bark, thatch, planed and unplaned lumber, whitewash in its many layers (one for each July when the flags and banners flew celebrating Loyalty – *This We Will Maintain*) as though by sheer accumulation alone he would somehow strike an answer out of the environment. He had spent all his life here in this one place and now he was an old man – it was best to face it – an aged male, unmarried, living alone, as grey as a rat (one of the crueller country expressions) and he would die here too, nothing surer, dust to dust, etc., and he had never found out *why*, never even asked the question until a short time ago.

His life had narrowed to the quest, the question. And at first he was certain the Valley itself would communicate to him in some way, almost as the biblical Rock opened to give up water at the right nervous touch. He had a clear image in his mind of a reply as direct as that taking place. It was the unchanging element after all. Oh, roads and railways had eaten at its contours, the river changed courses, and its inhabitants had quarried and cultivated and added their own marks over centuries to its profile, but it *withstood*, seeing all, knowing all. Surely it must have the secret if anything should. But then impatience set in as his lists of rocks and plants and buildings remained obdurate, yielding nothing . . .

At times he wondered if he was becoming senile, holding faith in such theories, the sort of crazy belief a child would convince itself of. Was he entering, or had he already crossed over into, his second childhood? The phrase itself sounded, looked delightful. A state to be embraced, with its implications of new innocence and a carefree return to an earlier golden age – but it was fraud. Reality was twitching limbs, incontinence and others' disgust. He thought of his niece and her husband. He took his meals with them, and could imagine their feelings, the looks they would pass between them; later – comments spoken directly in front of him; then, outright annoyance, then . . .

An old man in the village, a hell-raiser all his life, had been committed to a Home by his family. He had been impossible to restrain outside, but soon died in the Home in Belfast. Someone had said that there were bruises on the body in different places, and not all consistent with falls. The worst nightmare of all, an end like that, a dumb football to be bumped about.

But he could understand such brutalities. Hadn't he been a teacher all his life? The frustration born of being faced with blocks day in day out. Answer, answer, he would rage, *answer!*

And now he had gone back to the forked animal again for revelation – inanimate Nature had yielded nothing. The men, the women or the children of the townland might. He felt too a sense of quickening impatience, a need to change course once a way seemed blocked. So he had become this spy creeping about the hedgerows, holding his quarry at a distance. On the invisible thread of his glasses he could draw them to him at will, never happier when he knew that they were unaware and innocent of his regard.

It made him shy of meeting people face to face – even past acquaintances – of talking to them. Exchanging a common greeting about the state of the weather could constitute a major defeat in the course of a day's campaign of secrecy. He realized that already he must have formed a rich reputation for oddity, but hoped he had fitted into the current gallery of characters of the locality without too much uneasiness on the part of his neighbours. His habits might endanger him – as the habits of all eccentrics can – but it was a risk he had to run, and the risk certainly had its reality here in parts where persecution and intolerance in the past came as naturally to mind and then to hand as pike or pitchfork . . .

He was now walking along the road and the buzz of his brain had stilled. He had time to look about him, to feel the rhythm in his legs settling to a pleasant action. A smell of cut hay came in waves to his nostrils. Breathing it in deeply, he felt almost overcome by the richness of scents on the air. In winter his walks were devoid of such pleasures. The contrast between the seasons seemed perverse. That remembered one with the earth and all its life sealed so cruelly – it was like walking on an iron lid – and this now, too abundant. He felt heady with the bounty, a drunken bee. He was ageing rapidly, that was obvious; the blood too thin, and reacting violently against what it considered extremes of heat or cold, drought or damp. His clothes stifled him, yet it would have been unthinkable to carry his jacket across his arm, or even unbutton his waistcoat. Certain niceties of dress and behaviour must still be observed, despite what he told himself more and more these days about the tedium of presenting appearances.

In his wardrobe there hung a pale linen suit, the colour now of a sun-blind; narrow shoulders, long in the skirt of the jacket, tight across the chest and under the arm-pits, trousers, narrow and cuff-less. The buttons were mother-of-pearl, a rich lustre, and the stitching hand-done. 'James Dunwoody, Gentlemen's

Tailor, Garfield Street, Belfast', on the inside label. A beautiful suit, never losing its elegance, despite changing styles – yet he never wore it. It hung neglected on the rail, flat against the back of the large mahogany 'robe. He never wore it, not since the day he took on his uniform of sober, stiff tweed (a darker herring-bone for use on the Sabbath) marking him in the community's eye as Master Brown.

And now that he had retired from grey granite schoolhouse and residence – the two tethered by a niggardly little walk of the same stone in chippings – he still didn't dare to flaunt his independence in the shape of a fine work of tailoring; too fine, now as then, for the district's sensibilities. He had been stamped, inside as well as out, by that stern vocation . . .

The three boys he had watched earlier at work in the hay-field . . . They adapted as easily to the weather as young animals, their hides offered to the sun, seeking ease and light-ness; or perhaps it was their vanity in having a tanned skin. When he was that age it was considered a sign of bad breeding to brown like a gipsy. Paleness of complexion was a virtue among ladies – gentlemen as well – caste-mark of the leisured. Like most affectations it found its way in descent to the labour-ing classes who, if they couldn't protect their faces and arms from the sun's rays, at least could keep the rest of themselves covered . . .

The men and boys bathing at the weir on a summer's evening, two-toned as though they had been dipped in stain – half-submerged and turning to stare as he and his companion had strolled past, high above them on the bank walk . . . Eyes in dark faces watching . . . A mixture of anger and fear rising in him as he imagined the flood of coarseness to be loosed the moment they passed out of earshot . . . Barbour and Minnie and what they would do together . . . the hows and the where-fores and with what variations . . .

He smiled to himself. So long ago, so long ago . . . All of that had shrunk to the size of a speck, a shrivelled little pod squeezed dry by time of all its former intensity of flavour and odour. He sniffed the present. It made his head swim. Honeysuckle poured out of the hedge, then reappeared further on as though its pressure could not be staunched.

He made his way through an opening in the hedge, man-

33

made and recent. It led to the site of a newly built one-storey house of the type known as a bungalow. No one seemed to want to climb stairs any more. Existence spread itself out, room opening upon room, and building was a speedy process, biting into good farmland for its snug pebble-dashed and sowed lawn compounds; the ambition of every young couple to own such a place, sinking a well and a sewage pit, bringing in the electricity, watching the Japanese cherry-tree in splints grow and shed its pink leaves every year of their lives. The farmers aided the process. They parcelled out their land in tiny plots – a corner next to the road – unable to resist the high prices. Ownership was pursued as savagely by the young – commuting clerks, salesmen, teachers, for the most part–as by the older farming stock. They were mutilating his beloved countryside, careless about what they left behind. Like this raw wound of a place.

He picked his way over lifeless subsoil, red and churned by lorry wheels and boots. Grey planks lay in tangled heaps; there was an up-ended bucket, a cement mixer, a pile of concrete blocks – painful in texture – and the new house, windowless, doorless. Roof, walls, a chimney complete, and a flag, the Union Jack flying above all, traditional touch by the workmen pointing out that they had finished the basic structure and were waiting to be paid.

It was a time for flags. He saw another on top of a silo across the Valley. The spirit of 'the illustrious past' smouldered still; only in these peaceful times there was little smoke except in midsummer when the flags flew out and bunting roofed streets and the arches went up, red, white and blue, orange and purple, with their prancing two-dimensional King Billys in painted plywood. The Valley had flowered with a bright harvest of hate. *To Hell With The Pope* and *Remember 1690*. He had often been tempted to add his own *Why?* to walls, sparking off a thunderous chalked correspondence . . .

But these were things not for him. He was the silent spy creeping about the lanes and skirting the places where people gathered to celebrate, sing and listen to speeches. He observed but never took part. His existence was as set now as the mould of concrete that someone had carelessly left in the bottom of this bucket. His toe pushed it over. It fell like a weighted skittle, slow to budge, then in a rush. It had taken much abuse, its life-span no greater than the length of time it would take to finish this dwelling-house. Old-fashioned word, biblical even, to describe such a harsh modernity.

He leaned on the new wood of a window-frame and looked inside. Cold grey walls, smooth and slick, smudged here and there by the workers' paws; a piece of flex with raw ends dropped from the centre of the ceiling – desolate and inhuman. But soon the new owners would move in and wait patiently, surrounded by their furniture, for the plaster to dry out. Six months, a year, before painting and papering would begin. He thought of living inside these chill confines for such a time. It needed a hardness of purpose, a tenacity, that at times frightened him. Generation after generation waiting to put down roots, waiting and accepting discomfort and ugliness in their present, for the sake of the future . . .

Barbour Brown laughed aloud then in the hollowness of that smooth-walled shell, and prolonged his laughter after the joke had ceased to amuse, because of the sound. He boomed like a genie in a cave. Laughing at himself. Transparent old rogue sermonizing again, and this time caught out in his own narrowness, for wasn't it because he himself had only a present and no future worth talking about that he moralized thus? Ach, let them have their lives, these people! They wouldn't change his existence and he couldn't change theirs. He kicked the bucket – *kicked the bucket*, that new-fangled, slangy phrase – and laughed once more. An old goat too immersed in his own skin, picking among his own detritus, a walking rubbish-tip of scurf, nail-parings, nose-pickings, ear-wax and toe-dirt. The children in school used to rub their palms together until little dark grey twists appeared. It always entertained . . .

He moved round to the rear of the house. There it was even uglier than at the front. He would have thought that hardly possible. How could anything be ever coaxed to grow out of this tortured soil after the last labourer had left and moved on to the next outrage? But he would be well out of it before the whole place was a rash of new brick, crazy paving and McGredy's roses . . .

He lifted his eyes from the ugliness at his feet and looked up and out, around and about this broad deep Valley. The further side, ink-blue, chequered here and there by the pale rectangles

of hay and corn fields. The patchwork changed colour throughout the seasons as crops ripened and were harvested, fields
lying fallow, then planted once more. It never looked better.
Even the houses seemed tiny distant granules of light, perfect
in setting . . .

Then he heard voices. Someone was coming up the road.
What if it were the workmen, or, worse, the new man come to
inspect his property? He would be discovered, questioned; for
ownership was never as jealous as when it was freshly acquired.
And he knew he couldn't face an accusing stare, couldn't carry
off the rôle of respected elder figure, wise in the weight of his
years. Instead he felt disreputable, a hooligan in a Sunday suit.
His heart began to beat violently, his palms sweating. There
was nothing for it but to face it out. If he moved now away
from the cover of the house he would be seen making for the
fields and that would prove his guilt in the eyes of anyone
approaching. And there could be nothing worse than to be
halted in the middle of that no-man's-land by a shout, among
the dead grass and the brutal drainage ditches.

He held on to the corner of the building, pebble-dash pressing, and listened. A woman's voice, scolding. Then a child's in
answer, and another's. He relaxed, feeling safer. Her accent
was coarse. She would never live in a house like this.

—Ach, come on, will you? Keep up with us or oul' Johnny
Christmas will get you, so he will.

He remembered a family demon that had its hidey-hole
under the stairs in his own childhood. Green eyes in the dark,
he'd imagined, like a cat in a coalhouse. Beelzebub waiting for
him among the galoshes.

—Eric, will you come on to hell outa that! That plant is
poison. Throw it away.

She came into view and he pulled back out of sight, but,
unable to resist, peered round the corner again. The woman
trailed disconsolately past, a couple of her brood whining and
pulling on her skirts. He could see pots of jam in her basket,
home-made by the look of it, transparent covers taut and
gleaming like mirrors, held in place by elastic bands. A family
visit to an old relative perhaps, some crone who always laid
by more preserves than she could humanly get rid of by
herself? This horde would always be relied upon to devour

36

any surplus. By the looks of them. The legs of the woman dragged along; her hips shook with fat under her apron. She communicated a heavy lassitude that seemed to leave the air dead in her wake. The last two of her offspring followed as though asphyxiated, listlessly dragging switches of ash through the dust.

The sound of their passage dwindled, died, and Barbour Brown shook himself. New resolve quickened in him as though celebrating his release. He set off briskly over the bumpy mounds of caked earth, swishing through weeds that flourished in the gullies at the rear of the new house. He was headed for the fields beyond and a way he had never taken before. He felt bold. He would tack across farmland, free and careless, taking his own right-of-way, travelling true and straight to a small wood he could see in the distance, holding the blueness of it in his eye. The fields drowsed in the afternoon heat. Grasshoppers filled the silence with their concert, rising and falling, like an invisible haze.

The wood was coniferous, trunks heaped about with pine-needles, soft drifts unimaginably deep. Silence in there, green gloom. A pigeon racketing out of the foliage overhead. They had both laughed, feeling each other's hearts beat. Falling back on the feather-bed piles. How high were they above the earth? How soon would the slow falling rain of seeds raise them to the branches? Years wouldn't matter; they would wait, they whispered, lying back and looking up into the roof-beams of their own house. A couple of romantic fools. He would like to see the place again though. It would start off memories just to peer into those dark tunnels of love among the scotch fir . . .

A fine thread of smoke rose from the centre of the wood. Life still went on at Hollybush House. He'd heard she lived on her own now. He might even see her. From the safety and distance of the trees. Watch her . . .

Soon the talk would commence in earnest, now that eating had
slowed to a few desultory stabs of their forks at any scraps still
remaining on the thick white plates. The meal had been a
heavy one: dumplings in a broth, thick and afloat with swollen
peas and lentils, followed by boiled potatoes from the heaped
basin in the middle of the kitchen table. Each person seated
around the taut shiny surface, American cloth, chequered
red and white, would reach out in silence to the steaming pile
and snatch one and then peel it deftly. The trick was to find the
firmest, otherwise the potato would crumble in its jacket at a
touch and valuable eating time would be lost in scooping and
paring away the bluish skin. Marathon gorging at speed was
the order of the day in the Gaults' big kitchen at meal-times,
as though the habit had long ago been assimilated from the
farm animals and fowl, fed and watered daily from troughs,
pocked tin lids and the halves of old car tyres set out in the
fields or in corners of the cobbled yard.

As bellies filled and the amount of food still on the table
was silently calculated by each person for his own remaining
needs, relaxation set in – a kind of dulled stupefaction, out of
which grunts, monosyllables, words, finally whole sentences
would emerge. Tea, black and strong, was poured by Mrs Gault
over each shoulder into each mug right around the table, with
a deadly accuracy. Milk then, from the white enamelled jug
with its navy-blue lip and rim. On occasions, if working late in
the fields was called for, the evening milk would be frothy and
still warm from the cow. It repelled him then. He had never
thought until such moments of drinking almost directly the
flow from an animal's glands. But now in the middle of the
day the milk was flat and chill. It had been taken from the
cooling-house where water ran incessantly and where churns
and wooden bowls dried out slowly to their strongly scoured

finish. He had always enjoyed the contrasting touch of the grey-grained wood, generations old, with its brass banding . . .

But the talk, the talking was beginning. It needed only one simple, single incident like an upset cup or some other misfortune at table; perhaps a person burning his tongue or his finger, followed by a curse or a cry of dismay, to set it off. Then, as though linked by a slow-burning fuse, each cracker of country slyness and wit would follow, comment feeding on comment.

Up at the far end of the table, isolated as always, because of the reek of his work-clothes and whatever moist rags of wool covered his feet deep in their wellington boots, sat Cooley, the Gaults' serving-man. He belched, then blushed, raising a hand to his mouth. It seemed a curiously feminine gesture for one so coarsened by the existence he led.

Old man Gault said slowly—Better in nor out, is what I always say, and laughter broke eagerly around the table.

Cooley made a convenient butt. He muttered to himself in a low, rapid stream of confidences that only he could understand, as he went about his duties in the byres and pigsties. Some war experience had deranged him and he shuffled along on flat feet – he had fallen arches – pushing a mound of manure before his yard-brush, his private colloquies dying to a whisper when anyone approached. He could be heard laughing aloud at such times as well, short mirthless bursts, as though he were impatient to race on to the conclusion of a debate with himself that never came.

The Gault household sheltered, if that weren't too charitable a word, a succession of misfits and outcasts, none of whom ever stayed for long; slattern girls from Homes, tramps who would work for their meals and housing; men like Cooley wrapped in their own private madnesses. All slaved relentlessly, paced by the never-tiring master and mistress, until a fresh and stronger labouring human animal came to the open back door of the big dark kitchen. They arrived like some form of hopeless human debris washed up for a temporary stay.

Crouched down at the base of the kitchen range on a low milking-stool was another of these casualties from the world beyond; but, unlike the others, Lizzie had remained a year, perhaps two. Half-witted, not quite mongoloid, she had become pregnant soon after she'd first drifted into the place.

39

The baby was despatched swiftly to a suitable Institution, but for some unknown reason she was allowed to stay. She sat there pressed against the side of the Modern Mistress, despite its great heat, smiling as though sharing the joke, but abjectly like a dog with eyes always trained for the first signs of its master's displeasure and, sure enough, Mrs Gault, as, though divining her expression through the turned back of her own sternly rigid head and body, snapped out to the air in front of her—The biscuits, girl. *Now!*

Lizzie scrambled to her feet and disappeared into the pantry, returning with the square tin, a metallic block gleaming dully, stripped bare of any trace of its original festive wrapping, as though the sight of a bright colour or decorative image might cause frivolity to creep into that dark and sombre place.

The girl's nails were bitten to the quick. The sight of those tiny pink fingers prising at the lid on the table before him made him turn away and pull back in his chair. He thought of the child she had borne; its hands surely not much smaller, and of that one creature emerging from this other babyish body. What sort of brute could have fathered it, he wondered, taking her in some ditch or barn or pressed up against some wall or tree in the dark fields. And what could have brought him to it? Drink leading to blind lust, or a patient stalking until the occasion seemed right; muffling her, covering and forcing his way? Then, ignorant and animal pain. Or perhaps something unthinkable, which seemed to him somehow more disturbing – compliance and enjoyment? Could she ... had she ...? He felt himself shrink between his legs. It was a similar sensation to the one he felt when he saw blood or a bad wound, un-explained and sudden identifying with the source, a shiver going over and through the body, but momentary. . . .

The lid came off the big tin and Lizzie moved back into her half-world down by the base of the range where the farm dogs lay and panted on the tiles. Not for her the luxury of delving in among the red corrugated papers that separated layers of the assortment. But the other hands went out and then down, rustling. One made one's choice silently and without hesitation. Mrs Gault's eye drilled to the very soul. The ritual of the biscuits seemed her only concession to what she considered softness of living. He himself touched the yielding red centre of one that held its dab of strawberry jam – not a particular favourite. Taking it out and having first bite made him feel as though his indulgence in some private shaming vice was on public show, for all to see.

Cooley took one too and crumbs rained finely on the table before him. Munching and blushing, he tried to sweep them under his plate. He had hands that shook continually. Their backs were hairy, but each pore was clearly picked out with its individual residue of dirt, from all the countless hours spent dipping among mashes in buckets and troughs and into sacks of dry dusty grain. A section of that unwashed skin under a microscope . . . He could see it in his imagination, enlarged, a forest of thick growths each planted in its own dark filled crater, then all beginning suddenly to heave as the hidden waves, magnified as well, but invisible, in their power, made that terrain quake and come alive. Other forms of life, but more minute, would be revealed lurking as well perhaps . . . scuttling . . . His brow felt clammy. Passing his hand over his face he drank his tea in gulps. The image passed . . .

—Cooley has a sweet tooth, haven't you, Frank? Fond of sweet things – eh, Frank? Eh? Sweet things?

Old Gault bent on a final stirring. He liked to leave the table on a rise of laughter, cutting it short in his own good time.

Harvey, Mack and he himself loosened in their hard chairs, faintly grinning, lying back to savour the last moments. One learned quickly to hoard each second of respite from the farm work waiting and stretching out ahead through the long afternoon, the slowest and sorest pressing part of the day.

—Did you like that biscuit, Frank? Eh? Did you like it? A good one, eh, Frank? Eh, Frank?

Prodding Cooley into some reaction took a certain perverse skill. He was mute usually in the company of others using his face alone to convey a range of servile responses to what was being said.

Harvey laughed out loud. He felt unsure of himself before the old man; could never do the right thing – like now, a nervous mistiming. His father eyed him.

Henry Gault was a man in his sixties; his only son had come late in his life, in his wife's too – but it hadn't changed him. His existence was as undeviating as a furrow he would set himself to plough, scorning to use anything other than the big roan gelding kept stabled in the darkness of its stall, seemingly for no other purpose. He moved through each day along a similarly straight course from dawn to an early bed-time and he judged everything and everyone he came in contact with – wife, son, servant, beast, implement – by the same standards he set himself. Now when he looked at his own flesh and blood, Harvey was on an equal plane with the poor half-demented servant-man he had decided to poke at a little, the way he might touch one of his farm animals with the point of his stick, not maliciously, but coldly, devoid of any emotion except one of unfeeling curiosity. Henry Gault was a man who, in his relationships with other people, resembled nothing so much as someone turning over stones to see what lay beneath and never once betraying any response as to what might be found there.

—You like a wee biscuit now and again, don't you, Frank? A sweet tooth, eh, Frank? Eh, Frank?

Cooley bobbed his head and moved his hands clumsily about on the table in front of him. The action was pathetic pretence for he had swept his place clean so often during the meal that the surface glistened, sending off streaks of light.

—What's your favourite, Frank? What sort of biscuits do you like best? Eh, Frank?

Cooley had now reached a pitch of embarrassment and nervousness almost painful to witness – that is if the three watching hadn't felt so drugged by the heavy food and the need to loll, indifferent to anything other than the chance of minutes, even seconds, being sliced off their afternoon's labours. Like farm animals they were, recouping lost energies, holding in and on, cunning, watchful . . .

—Eh, Frank? Eh? You must have a wee favourite one, surely now. Tell us. Go on, Frank. Ach, come on, Frank, tell us now, – gentled the old man, most patient of inquisitors.

Yet Cooley writhed as though each soft almost caressing murmur was a whiplash. Cooley was a dog whose training had unnerved him; his master, perverse in his methods; punishment instead of reward, praise in place of chastisement. But he had to answer – no way out for him – for he was rarely spoken to directly, so rarely wrenched out of his private world. He stuttered something incomprehensible and his hands moved even more frantically over the stretched shiny cloth.

—What was that, Frank? Speak up, man. Has the cat got your tongue?

Another laugh and a poor foolish grin from the clown at the head of the table.

—Frank?

Words were on their way. A slow and painful rise to the lips, eyes betraying that anguished ascent.

—A wee favourite, Frank? Maybe a ginger-nut – (more laughter)—or a digestive, or one of them wee chocolatey ones now—?

A stuttering rush of words at last, as from a child desperate to answer in class.

—*Or-or-orange cream!*

There was silence. How many around the table, he wondered, were feeling the pity of it all. With drollery, old Gault spoke up.

—Begob, Frank, I never knowed you were so loyal as that now.

The laughter this time was rich and unrestrained, as all caught the joke after the first second of hanging fire.

—Aye, a right good loyal colour indeed, Frank.

And then a further sly mockery.

—I suppose the next thing you'll be telling us is that you'll be walking on the Twelfth the year. Is that the way of it, Frank?

This time even Mrs Gault herself smiled wryly at the fantasy of a shambling wreck like Catholic Cooley in the midst of all those hard-hatted, sternly marching Brethren, as alien in their ranks as a tramp would be in a crack regiment. Her finely honed features softened, but only momentarily – then she snorted, bustling out of the room.

—I declare to Heavens the poor softie has more sense than the lot of you put together. Stuff and nonsense!

Old Gault by this time had lit a pipe and was coaxing it to draw, puffing out smoke while his keen eyes never left their target. Cooley was fair game now. He would torment him until he grew tired and then, with a word or a sudden movement, put an end to it, dismissing all of them to their tasks, Cooley as well, whose mutterings that day out in the dark stables and barns

43

must surely reach crescendoes of frustration and rage little short of outright murderous hate. The graip, the fork and the cutting spade would thrust, sever and rend apart as never before. Mountains of toil would be toppled before milking time. And perhaps the old man had this, another and more subtle purpose, behind his gibes. Looking at him now, as set and as powerful in his oak chair as though carved from the same substance, it was easy to attribute almost any depth of cunning knowledge to him and his motives.

—And I suppose you'll be taking a girl with you to the Field as well and treating her . . . Aye, we must get a lassie for Frank.

From the pantry, overriding the din of pans and dishes being clashed about, came the voice of Mrs Gault. —No bad talk now! I want none of it in this house.

The old man continued to suck on his briar. He smiled. —What does young McFarlane think, eh? Who will we get for Frank to take out on the Twelfth Day? Well?

For some reason he showed a respect for Mack and his opinion. It seemed a strange quirk because he certainly could have no admiration for his hard-working qualities. Everyone knew of Mack's laziness and his careless disregard about hiding it. He recalled with shame his own pathetic attempt to wring some word of praise out of the old man for himself and his muscle before he knew him better. The example of Harvey should have cracked any illusion on that score. If he had never stirred a response, then no one could, for Harvey sweated mightily to no avail and always bitterly. Rancour heaped on rancour.

—Well, young McFarlane? Have you a candidate for Frank here? There must be many a lassie who would be glad to promenade with such a strong, well set-up cut of a man . . .

The cruelty was going deeper than he'd ever known it, yet he found himself wanting it to continue. They were all closing in on the quarry now and the hunted one twitched and twisted.

Mack said—What about Hetty then? his eyes sharpening above the rim of his lifted mug, watching the old man's, meeting the other's look boldly.

They were on equal footing, raised high above the rest, their superiority displayed openly, contemptuously. He hated them both for this alliance, but Mack particularly. To make use of

44

her name like that so soon after. It was like a broken trust, even though none of them had spoken a single word after the incident in the hayfield. Yet he must have known. Even Harvey, behind heavy, sun-scorched features – coarser always at meal-times – felt it. He knew he did. He tried to penetrate that reddened forehead. The jaws ground rhythmically, moving the scalp under its stiff crop of fair hair, but the eyes remained cast down.

Old Gault said slowly—No, I don't think Hetty's the one . . . already preparing to give the game a little twist.—No . . .

There was silence in the room except for his sucking draws on his pipe.—Frank would favour, I have the notion, someone a wee shade older, someone with a lot more in her head than gallivanting and dance-steps.

Again he felt himself burn. The words from the old man's lips and the harsh criticism somehow doubled the sense of shame he already felt. Yet he knew he would laugh himself at the next cut along with the rest. It was easy to join in the raw chorus, mirthless mirth, adding his voice to theirs. What a weight of derision darkened the air of this countryside and the minds of its people.

—No. Someone with maybe a wee bit of money. Somebody well-doing and at herself. A widow-woman . . .

It was Mack – but who else? – who supplied the name.

—What about Minnie? Minnie Maitland? he said, and old Gault grinned with delight.

A moment of silence held the room as though idea and image needed a space in which to fill the mind. Mrs Gault had come silently out of the pantry and stood stockstill in the doorway, a plate in her hand. All thought hovered and then the great yell of malice broke like a wave over the kichen. The farm dogs sprang up in fright, Lizzie cooed and bubbles blew on her lips, Cooley jittered and shook as though buffeted from within and without, and the rest, himself included, fell backward and forward, hammering on the table. The perversity of that match, oh but beautifully so, Cooley with the shy eccentric from the Big House, and both walking out together, a mating so grotesque that the mind, the mind of the Valley, would never tire of it. They were witnessing the birth of a new and great local running joke. Oh, the embellishments to be added, and what a storehouse of rich ridicule to brighten the dark nights in pub, on village corner, farm and cottage fireside. And Mack its author sat smiling, neither modestly nor smugly. As always he was the still hard centre of whatever excitement he had engineered.

—Minnie it is then! exulted the old man.—And young McFarlane is the matchmaker. Do you hear that, Frank? Minnie Maitland and all that big house and land. Not to mention the father's money. Eh, man? Have you nothing to say?

But Cooley was truly spent, ravaged. He looked like someone on a death-bed unable to lift a finger or croak out a last word to save himself. Mercifully, he was to be left alone however. An ancient enemy had drawn the hunt away from him.

The Gaults were held in silence now. Minnie. The one they all hated. Bound together by blood and family feeling for land and everything that grew or stood on it – even those very grey-blotched stones of the march-wall that divided their two properties and over which both families had wrangled for generations. But whereas they had pursued the feud with crude peasant rage, the family beyond in the shelter of their fine plantation of scotch fir had waged a more subtle warfare, using all the educated wiles of the law courts. That running battle between the families was an old story in the countryside. Mack certainly was aware of it. There seemed no limit to the risks he was prepared to take, but then as usual he had weighed his chances carefully. The three now were blind and deaf to anything because of a sudden rush of venom. Their minds had sharpened to a single point—one person, rather—and everything outside had become a distant blur and murmur.

They sat there, father and son, united as never before, and behind them, apex of that family triangle of spite, stood mother, wife, more bitter, if that were possible, because the object of their animosity was a woman like herself.

—He's welcome to that old Home Ruler, she grated.—Her and her important ways and her airs and graces. Miss Minnie and her wee sips of sherry wine . . .

—Aye, Frank, said the old man with glee.—At least you'll never be short of a dram at Hollybush House. They say there's a bottle under every cushion in the parlour, just in case she's caught out. You'll not suffer from the drouth, I can tell you. No. No fears on that score. Eh, young McFarlane?

Mack smiled prettily and winked as one equal to the other.

He was leaving them to do all the talking. And sitting back to warm himself at the blaze he had kindled. His achievement was an impressive one. To have tickled out all those deeply buried hates, and tapped well-springs of resentment so deftly without any one of the three suspecting the manipulation, was a brilliant feat.

It seemed dangerous also, for a single wrong remark, a careless look or reaction would have that trio stripping his bones. They would never forgive being led to perform for any-one. Display of feeling in front of outsiders meant weakness to the Gaults. It might be retailed in gossip and used to damage the tribal fabric of their secret ways. Areas of their existence in and around the big stone-walled farmhouse set in its courtyard and topping its mount were never opened up to anyone. Just as he himself had never seen the inside of any of the other rooms, save the one in which they now sat, so there were closed places of the spirit as well, deep and dark, he liked to think, at those times when his imaginings took on a more Gothic twist. Even Harvey, who surely could be counted as a close acquaintance, for the three of them were rarely apart, would not talk about his family or the daily privacies of life within those thick and ancient granite walls.

Harvey's forearms, freckled and immense, lay unmoving on the chill top of the table. He had finished eating and his emptied cup was pushed away from him almost to the centre of the board as though he needed space, no distraction from the thoughts rising in his head. He looked grimmer than usual, hedged about by a brooding power all his own. Suddenly he spoke.

—She's no right to that low field, I say! She shouldn't be let away with it. The best grass in this townland and she doesn't graze it. She does it deliberate, so she does. I know what *I'd* do . . .

—What *you* would do is neither here nor there.

The old man's voice was quiet but authoritative.

He tapped his pipe in his cupped hand. The action was the one they had been waiting for; they had been dismissed.

Mack rose and stretched himself almost impudently. His

own chair grated backwards over the tiled floor. Harvey sat where he was, sullenly, with his head lowered, bunching his fists, watching the power coming and going in his heavy hands and wrists. There was too much strength there for his own good.

Old man Gault spoke directly to Mack and himself, ignoring Harvey.—Will the crop be fit to go into cocks in the morning? Mack said—Sure. It's nearly dry as it is.

Reply was a grunt, and the old man began to pick his teeth with a spent match. They started to move out of the kitchen then, stiffly, because sitting had caused their muscles to tighten up. Harvey remained where he was.

They waited for him outside in the courtyard where the sun never seemed to reach the perpetually damp flagstones underfoot; a cold clammy place, surrounded on all sides by lofty two-storeyed outhouses. All the doors around them lay open. From one came the sound of Cooley at work in the darkness. He was growling to himself as he wrestled with something heavy and intractable.

They stood there shivering a little and listening to the rise and fall of the two voices in the kitchen. The words were blurred to unintelligibility but Harvey's stronger tones now clearly dominated. Mack glanced over and winked knowingly.

Then the voices ceased and Harvey emerged, red in the face, and rolling up his sleeves a further inch. It seemed a needless gesture, for his arms were already almost bare to the shoulders. He gloried in his biceps and their superior size and action. It was something he and Mack occasionally laughed at behind his back. Mack called him Joe Palooka and both felt a comfortable sophistication, delighting in his frustration when he suggested contests of strength and they professed unanimous disinterest, presenting their bored faces to him and his immature he-manship.

They moved out under the archway and on to the back lane and the sun struck down suddenly and bewilderingly. The heat was a drug; they felt sleepy and full of food, and the work awaiting them seemed an impossible commitment.

Mack said—Have a fag, Harvey, and produced his packet of ten Gold Flake.

Lazily they took a light and breathed in tobacco smoke, then

48

ambled on between the heavy thorn hedges. He brought up the rear filling his own lungs with the scent of white blossom – he didn't smoke – and so, reluctantly, the trio made their way back to the Five-Acre. Like old men they creaked wearily up and over a stile and sank into deep grass in the field beyond with grunts and groans, wobbling on their legs. The blood pounded behind their temples.

—Christ! exploded Mack.—I'm bate . . .

The others laughed at him and fell back into the grass. It seemed the finest luxury in the world to rest on that soft and growing bed.

Cigarettes were again lit and smoked and they sat up and stared into the distance. Across the fields and in the middle of its protective clump of trees was the house and its occupant they had discussed earlier. Harvey puffed thoughtfully and narrowed his eyes to study the landmark, bluish pine trees sheltering a glimpse of soft red brick.

He said—They say she keeps a box of money in the house.

The others turned and looked at him.

Overhead a lark palpitated anxiously. They must be almost on top of her nest.

She was whirling around in front of the cheval-glass in Minnie's bedroom with a feather duster in her hand, pulling faces and letting her imagination play in and out of that latest Barbara Stanwyck picture, when she heard Minnie calling from downstairs.

—Coo-ee . . . drifted up the thin cry and she giggled.

—Coo-ee, Minn-ee, she whispered to the tall tilted mirror, and then skipped off to see what she wanted this time.

The staircase became a grand curving one, wide white marble, and the shock of feathers on its bamboo stalk turned into a fan as she flounced down to the ballroom below packed with admirers. She was wearing one of Minnie's old gowns – Minnie was stitching her own dress in the parlour – and the fur at her throat smelt of lavender sachets, cologne and past parties. Minnie had shown her the dance card with its tiny gilt pencil she had carried the last time she had worn it. Every waltz and polka had been taken and Minnie's eye was moist as she remembered.

She had been having a sly little drop, of course; always easy to tell because the parlour reeked of peppermints. Every time she smelt them on anyone else's breath now, even in church where a lot of people sucked sweets, she couldn't help supposing they were trying to cover up that other stronger scent.

Minnie drank sherry – the dry variety, never the sweet – and she had her supplies, a dozen bottles at a time, sent to her from a wine merchant's in London. They arrived unlabelled except for her address, but everyone in the village knew of the contents.

They would say to her slyly at intervals—Is Minnie still having her medicine sent over from across the water? with the great big innocent eyes of them, or again—Isn't it awful the weight poor old Joe Taggart the postman has to carry up to the

Big House on his bicycle! But she would act the prize dummy, pretending ignorance.

Her own father – or stepfather, as she had taken to naming him privately to herself, because it was true, and it also made it easier to harden herself against him when he abused her – carried on as though Minnie was never sober.

—Nice habits to be picked up in that establishment, nice habits certainly. Show me a woman who drinks and I'll show you one who isn't too particular about the rest of her doings.

That last part made her blush. In her thoughts, far back and shadowy, bcause it didn't bear too much going over, there was something bad and ugly involving *him* and her mother and doing *it* with each other and to hear him hinting at any coarse thing made her dry up all inside. Angry too in this particular instance, because she knew Minnie was as pure as the driven snow . . .

She looked up now over her rimless glasses, gold, and with a fine safety chain looping around her neck, when she entered the parlour. The blue dress was spread across her knees in folds. Minnie's hands lay on top, dainty and ladylike. She had only one ring, a brownish stone set in gold on her left hand, big middle finger. One move sideways and it would be on the engagement finger. Had that once been broken off?

The smell of lozenges was really killing.

—Hetty, lamb, why don't I take this hem down a fraction? It would be simplicity itself to manage and I do think it would be a little more becoming, despite the current fashion . . . Well? Shall I?

Oh damn, she thought to herself. I hate it when she comes out with things like that. Now I have to think of something to say that won't offend her . . . but what? I can't say that I might want to change the dress – it's too late for that now – and I can't say it's a present, no one knows at home I've even bought it yet. Anyway to think of *his* face if he ever saw it – not that it is too short anyway. All this fuss about a couple of bloody inches. Would they have you going round like something out of the Ark?

—Never mind, said Minnie, quickly glancing at her.—Youth should be allowed its head, as well as its folly.

51

She felt like kissing that little old face, so grateful was she for deliverance. Delicately she took the dress offered to her and said:

—Oh, how did you manage to do it so well? It's *lovely!*

Minnie blushed with pleasure and her jaws ground even more rapidly. She had better teeth than she herself had, as fine and as white as pearls, strong as well; nothing too troublesome for them to tackle when she sat down before a plate.

—Well, even if I do say it myself – and self-praise is no recommendation – I always was a better than average needle-woman. Of course young ladies of today don't have the same priorities in their upbringing . . .

(There were times when Minnie talked like a book.)

—I can remember having splitting headaches when I was your age. Three hundred stitches that the eye could hardly distinguish, was our daily discipline. Three hundred of them as exact as . . . as regular as . . . as . . .

Poor old thing, she had run out of words, out of steam too, by the looks of her. The sherry was taking its toll, little doubt of that. How many bottles, I wonder, does she go through in a week; and what does she do with the empties?

She smelt her breath, hot and sweet, as she bent closer. The needle was tucked into the material carefully like a signature, and she pulled it out and was replacing it in the soft green satin of the inner lid of the work-basket. It was unpleasant; an old woman's breath. Old people's breath, old dogs' too – Bruce the family's spaniel panting the last of his life away, his eyes following you in dread as he heaved in his basket under the kitchen table. His breath if you came too close. Decay was a terrible thing. Teeth and the things deep down in your stomach. She tried not to think about it; too horrible. *You shouldn't let such things bother you,* she told herself. Then in a panic – *maybe my own breath is bad!* and couldn't wait until she could put her hand before her mouth to breathe on it . . .

—Why don't I make you a nice cup of tea, dear Miss Maitland. You'd like that, wouldn't you now?

Poor old thing, it was what she needed to steady her up a bit. A nice strong cup of Earl Grey poured with care through the silver strainer and allowed to draw a little, then two lumps of fine white sugar from the china bowl with her two young

52

lovers on it going around endlessly searching and never ever meeting . . .

Just as she had got to the door, all intent on making the tea, Minnie spoke up.

—Hetty. Hetty, she said. Twice.

Her voice sounded different and when she turned to look at her she saw she was no longer slack in her chair but was bright-eyed and alert, perked up with her warm cheeks as red as two cherries. There was a look in her eye as well . . .

—Over here, that's a dear girl.

Crooked forefinger, beckoning.

—Over here.

She turned obediently and waited, thinking, *I've never seen her like this before.* Naughty, yes definitely naughty.

—I think . . . a pause, then, —Yes, I think we might partake of something a little more – shall we say, festive, than the customary China blend of the cup that cheers? Yesss we shall . . .

Oho, she thought to herself, *this is a revelation.*

—If I'm not mistaken, Hetty, my poppet, there should still be a bottle of Dadda's fine old amontillado in that corner cupboard . . . Yes, that one. And here is the key. Fetch it, there's a precious, and also two glasses. A little sip of sherry surely hurt no one . . .

Face to the glossy wood – her reflection showed clearly in the rounded door – she thought *you bad old article you, Minnie Mouse. Fancy such guile.* And sure enough, inside on a top shelf among the glasses was a tall bottle – the first one she'd ever seen in the house, she reflected. After all these months what could have got into her? But now it was her turn to play a little game.

—Oh Miss Minnie, she cried out in mock alarm, turning to present her shocked face.—Oh Miss Minnie, someone's been at it!

The bottle in her grasp indeed showed a good third lowered. *Let's see her get out of this one,* she thought to herself, not mal-iciously, but hoping instead that she would and could be plaus-ible, for this had all the makings of a fine old game of cat and mouse. Come on, pussy, come on . . .

Minnie said, as bold as brass—I expect the loss is due to evaporation. It must be a very old sherry. Dadda passed on in 'forty-two, you know . . .

Dadda may have passed on in 'forty-two, darling Minnie, but Dadda was temperance mad. Sure, didn't he try to have Semple's pub closed one time and didn't he used to run meetings in a marquee on the green every summer. Even I remember that, because I went to them. I even took the pledge that time when I was nine. Still, he was a right old bastard and I don't blame you at all, darling sweet Minnie ...

They touched filled glasses – a little *chink* – always the test of true Waterford, as Minnie had taught her, and the golden liquor ran down her throat and began to burn gently.

It was really very pleasant and not at all what she'd imagined it to be. The men she'd seen drinking on hot days outside pubs – she'd never been inside one – frequently made a face after swallowing their whiskey. Of course it might well be just another of those masculine rituals that they were careful to observe. She'd noticed that men behaved like little boys in this respect, always afraid to be different. But she also thought the taste of the stuff must still be vile. But this wasn't, no, it was quite nice; it was more than nice, it was ... She felt herself loosening in her skin, spreading on the chair, warm and sleepy. It would be so pleasant to take her new shoes off; better still, kick them off, not too strenuously of course, all her actions slow and relaxed, and gradually slide down further and further in her chair ...

Minnie said—Let's have some music, and she struggled up. It was difficult, hard to believe after such a tiny glass, but her legs did feel jelly-like, with a tremble in them. Jelly on a plate ... sister Kate; she felt like giggling but held it in as she crossed to the gramophone.

Going through the motions of getting the thing to play, a simple three-part operation – hold the turntable with one hand, wind with the other, then put the record on the soft brown pad, finally lower the needle – had its problems. Her hands slipped – on the swithering wheel, off the wooden handle; it was hard to centre the hole on the spindle and the needle kept sliding over the edge of the record; but eventually that familiar voice, thin and scratchy as if it was coming from hundreds of miles away, instead of out of the great green horn in the parlour, sang:

> *Oh for the wings,*
> *For the wings*
> *Of a dove ...*

Clara Butt. She must have been very fat, a great big lump of a woman, with a name like that. Wobbling all over like a jelly ... This time she laughed straight out, couldn't keep it in any longer, and fell down in the chair, disgracing herself. Oh it was awful, awful, but could she control herself? No, not for all the tea in China, not for all the sherry-wine in ... But Minnie was laughing too, a further revelation, her eyes shrunk to bright points no bigger than pinheads and from the wrinkles surrounding them squeezed tears, large rolling drops of mirth.

—Ah, she gasped, searching for her handkerchief,—the gaiety of youth, the gaiety of youth.

She dabbed at her cheeks with the tiny ball of embroidered linen.

—Oh dear Hetty, how lucky you are. To have everything before you. At your feet; before your very feet ...

She felt daft now, a bit ungainly and kept her gaze down, directed at those famous feet. Minnie made her sound like a footballer. Again the giggles broke and again Minnie followed her, shaking like a schoolgirl, but then she began to feel sober again. It was odd but there were times when it almost seemed as though she and Minnie were changing places and ages. A determined mood came over her. Time for play; playtime had come round, time for a game of house – mother and child, or schoolteacher and pupil, and guess who would be taking all the baby parts ...?

—Now Miss Maitland, she said, and she sounded just like a scolding elder,—Miss Maitland, you need a cup of tea, so you do. It won't take a minute to put the kettle on. It's what you need, you really do ...

Minnie looked at her and then at the bottle and then at her again. Her eyes said, *just one more please, a little one,* and so she relented and filled both glasses for the second time and sighed, sinking back in the buttoned chair again ...

So nice it was in the parlour with the old gramophone going full tilt and the birds outside in the fruit trees full of song. She felt the sherry creeping through her veins like a warm rising tide. It drove all idea of decision or action ahead of it. Her thighs seemed to be loosening and spreading over the warm velvet of the little chair until they would cover it completely, a second skin of upholstery.

Minnie sat facing her, thin bony white fingers tight around the stem of her glass. She didn't put it down but kept raising it to her lips for tiny bird-like sips. Every time the glass tilted her ring flashed, catching the sunlight. Dazzle, dazzle in her eye like a cutting stroke. If it hadn't been for that, dear knows how long she would have sat on, getting more and more like a graven image every minute, the two of them facing each other in a stupor in the hot stuffy room and Clara Butt's song sounding more hilarious every minute.

> *Oh for the wings,*
> *For the wings*
> *Of a dove*

The wings of a bomber would be closer to the mark.

All these operatic singers were the size of elephants. She'd seen pictures of them, all big bare white arms and bosoms. Jelly on a plate. She lurched to her feet laughing, then felt frightened at the swimming sensation in her head. What if this feeling was to last and couldn't be shaken off? How could she ever go home and face *them*?

She went out of the room, steering herself carefully past the furniture. There seemed to be an awful lot of it all of a sudden. Was this what being drunk meant – felt like? But she couldn't be drunk, couldn't be. Tipsy, perhaps, yes, tipsy; the very word Minnie might use, that is, if she ever could bring those ladylike lips to discuss such a thing. Cruel thoughts, cruelties directed towards the old woman nodding and sipping away at her consolation in its cut glass, swarmed suddenly in her head. She felt vindictive, had this odd urge to force some form of confession out of her. *Admit it, admit it,* she heard her own voice crying out, in anticipation. Her turn to play Master Harper's tune, hectoring and punishing. She could hardly wait to get back to the parlour and her naughty pupil.

But first, naughty Minnie must have her cup of tea, whether she wanted it or not. She found she was gritting her teeth. She must have the look of a hard taskmaster by now, cold eyes, stern mouth. But first the tea . . .

Slow progression of tea to pot, kettle to pot, then leave to sit. From the press she took two cups and two saucers and placed them on a wooden inlaid tray, then removed them and covered the tray first with a linen cloth. Back went the cups and the saucers, then sugar-bowl and tongs, two spoons and the tea-pot in its pink cosy. She couldn't be bothered fetching out the best service today; this would do just as well and, anyway, Minnie was in no state to notice or care about such niceties. She didn't give a damn herself either for that matter, come to think of it . . .

With the tray held out before her and her lip curling in what she imagined must be total aristocratic fashion, she entered the parlour.

Minnie had disappeared; her chair was empty. For a moment she held there in the doorway, clasping the brass handles of the tray and feeling disdain. Hiding was she, the bad thing, hoping to give her a start was she, when she jumped out with a cry from her hidey-hole, make her upset the tea-things, give her palpitations, would she, *did she, indeed?*

The tray was settled on the low gate-leg table carefully without fuss.

Now where was she? What a silly creature Minnie was, to be sure, indulging in such tricks. Second childhood was certainly a phrase that held a lot of truth. She sent her eyes around the room on a sly tour of inspection, on the look-out for a movement or a betraying glimpse of the old thing's skirts. Nothing, nothing – and silence, except for the rasping of the needle which had come to the end of plump Madame Butterfly Butt's recital. Lifting the arm from the spinning black disc, she thought to herself, *this will flush her out if anything will,* for she had a sudden insight, sensing how unbearable and final the throttling of the sound would be to the old ninny, wherever she was. But still nothing moved in the room at her back.

She stood listening to her heart. It began to beat faster as a terrible thought came to her, a terrible fear and possibility. What if something had happened to her? The whole house seemed to have grown so still all of a sudden. If a house could catch its breath, then . . . Not a creak of any living thing, nor of anything else for that matter, rafter, floorboard or stair-tread. She felt sick at the things she could see in her head. Minnie stretched lifeless, her face blue – a seizure of some kind, in one of the rooms, or in some inaccessible place where she couldn't move her, so heavy a weight for such a sparrow. *Dead* weight; oh terrible! And she'd be held responsible. Worst of all, how to explain the state they were in, the smell on their breath, both of them. She looked at the bottle, the glasses, thought stupidly to hide them, moved one way, then another, in a panic, a sob breaking. *Oh dear God, don't let anything have happened to her* . . . Minnie's virtues, dear kindly old Minnie, were now racing, a spate of them, through her head, the earlier mood gone like snow off a ditch.

—Minnie, she heard herself utter no louder than a whisper, praying to the furniture.

Behind her she heard a chuckle, a giggle. She turned, and Minnie stood in the doorway, her arms laden with furs and finery from the big wardrobe upstairs in her room.

—Treasure trove! she cried, her eyes big with mystery, a child's eyes full of her game.

—Treasure trove! and she let her load fall to the floor, spilling the garments carelessly. A long wriggly thing like a scarf, only made of something white and feathery, touched her feet. She felt like giving it the biggest kick. Oh . . . she ground her teeth with rage . . . oh.

Minnie said—Try on the boa. Please. For me. Feel it touch your neck. Oh feel it!—and began to waltz around the room with the thing pressed to her cheek, it flying in the air out from her like the tail of a kite.

In some ways the antics of the old lady were more unsettling than the fears she'd had earlier. The look in her eyes, her voice crooning, the way she dabbled her hands in the air as she revolved, all reminded her of that picture she'd seen. Was it *Gone With The Wind*, where the heroine goes demented in the big house all alone, in and out of the empty rooms, her head quite turned? Her own head was turned, that was closer to the truth of it. All this nonsense must stop.

—Now, Miss Maitland, she began, her voice cutting.

—Oh, don't be cross, said Minnie.—It does one good to push the boat out occasionally. Don't you think?

Her look was as mischievous as ever; she hadn't taken a hair, not a hair out of her . . .

—But, Miss Minnie, what about my cleaning? I've still the return-room upstairs to do, and then there's the—

Minnie waved her hand grandly in real Lady Muck fashion.

—Today is a special occasion. Dreary household duties are

forthwith suspended. I feel young, *young*, and that is a rare experience. Dear sweet Hetty (she had taken her by both hands now and was gazing pleadingly into her face), have patience with an old woman's folly.

Her cheeks were flushed and her eyes were bright as two glass beads. She *did* look younger, no doubt about it, but again the dread took hold of her, for what if all this excitement proved too much for her? A little pulse fluttered in the hollow of her throat at a terrible rate, her old heart too, must be thumping away like billy-ho inside its rickety rib cage. Oh why did people have to grow old and feeble? She felt herself relenting, weakening, as her hands were gripped in that tight, hot embrace. Minnie's ring, flashing, bit into her fingers, cold as ice . . .

—Well if you say so, Miss Maitland . . .

Oh so humble, nice as pie, butter wouldn't melt in her mouth, but she knew, didn't she, who was boss? The feeling was a nice one, she had to admit. She would play the game of naughty nursery to the hilt, so she would, of course she would . . .

Outside the sun beat on their side of the house; it passed through the windows and lay in a bright oblong on the carpet. At their dressing-up they would move into the glare then out again, as though it were a stage.

The clothes were very old but lovely to touch, satins and silks and crêpe, materials you would never see in the shops now. They felt cool and were perfumed, and soon the pair of them were on their knees delving up to the elbows into the tangled heap. Minnie at first was the only one to cry out and hold up some garment to the light – she had genuinely forgotten that she ever owned such a collection – but then she herself began to be carried away as well. Her blood raced at some of the vanities her hands found buried deep. These were the very dresses and blouses, skirts, hats and scarves that the dark-faced women in the photographs wore, posed long ago in gardens or in boats or against old ruins on holiday. She longed to find out if she would look the same wearing them. People in old photographs always seemed so different, not quite human, a different race. Was it the clothes?

Gradually a small pile grew at her side; her own choice – a wide-brimmed cream hat with a feather, a long pleated tan skirt, a sailor's blouse, a jacket with pinched waist and sleeves like narrow tubes that fanned out at the wrists; the jacket was of black silk with jet buttons.

She glanced sideways at Minnie; they hadn't got to the trying-on stage yet. She felt shy, not quite sure of herself.

Minnie said—I'm certain some of these will fit you. You're taller than I am, but then again they're not all mine. Some belonged to Boo.

Boo was the sister who had died very young, just failed away to scrapings up in the big front room with her favourite view of the monkey-puzzle tree. Poor Boo.

Minnie sighed, remembering, then became brisk.—But I insist. You must try them on. Here, and she thrust a trailing heap at her.

She held back a moment for the sake of appearances, then accepted shyly. Minnie was watching her with intensity, breathing a trifle heavily. Her cheeks looked unnaturally red as well. She realized with a shock that she had rouged her face when she was upstairs. What a curious old things she was, and what an odd day this had turned out to be.

—Go on, Hetty. Don't be bashful or prudish. Put them on, there's a good girl. There's nothing to stop you.

But there was, she felt it in her insides like a hard ball, embarrassment, strong and acute. How could she? She looked around the room for a screen of some kind, but there was none, and Minnie seemed set on having her way. So much for her own cleverness now. Could she ask Minnie to go outside? No, of course she couldn't, what a prize fool she'd look if she did. Seventeen, and too embarrassed to change in front of a silly old woman.

She began to slip off her clothes clumsily, on one foot, then on the other, over near the sideboard, keeping the horned and now silent gramophone on its stand between them. Minnie watched her throughout. Her fingers slipped and strained; the hooked fastenings on the old ball-gown seemed much more elaborate than when she'd first handled them earlier. Worst of all, she had this guilty feeling about undressing in the middle of the day in a downstairs room bright and lived-in. A bed would have made it more natural somehow . . .

At last she got the long fur-edged gown off and turned her

60

back, protecting, for a moment, her breasts. Her shoulders and the bare tops of her thighs were prickling. She couldn't face the old lady's eyes; she didn't have to look to know that keen gaze taking all of her in. Then she did a silly and further humiliating thing. Still facing the wall and holding one arm across her front, she stretched out the other arm, fingers turned and waiting to receive one of the garments strewn around Minnie – a ridiculous pose if ever there was one.

Her hot face stared back at her from the reflecting glass of a picture on the wall. It was a river scene with brown and white cows drinking at evening under willows. The water flowed across the painting and over her face, it seemed to her. She imagined her eyes and the shamed look in them just under the surface, drowning in her own embarrassment, then Minnie handed her something at last to cover her nakedness. It was the long brown skirt she had admired. Quickly she pulled it up over her legs and behind – those seemed the most vulnerable parts of her – and immediately felt easier.

Again she stretched out an arm, limp at the wrist this time, with something approaching composure, and received a silken bundle. Minnie laughed at her back and she joined in as she took the blouse and things from her. The game was resuming again. She had restored herself as mistress, but this time her maid was really waiting on her hand and foot. The blouse felt cool. It smelt of lavender and she eyed herself with satisfaction in the picture glass. Her bust was firm; twin peaks pointed out the silk. She blushed but longed for a mirror.

Minnie put on another record and the music was that moon thing by Debussy; she couldn't pronounce it, but it was dream-like and soft, just ideal for the mood she was in by now. More sherry was poured and drunk and she moved carelessly around the room pulling on long pale gloves.

Minnie cried out—Don't move! I shall be back in a tick. I have an inspiration, and rushed off upstairs.

It really meant nothing to her; she couldn't have cared less, she was deep in her own fantasies, queening it.

—Oh dear Lady Ermyntrude, this ball is so terribly tedious, don't you think, and the men are so frightfully dull. Too, too boring for words really, is what I say . . .

She giggled at that, using a real fan now and not the old

feather duster, then felt like saying something dirty in a loud voice in this prim and proper room, but couldn't remember a rhyme more shocking than:

—Your Highness Supreme, please pass me the cream.

You hairy old bugger, would you pass me the sugar.

Minnie returned, and she was transformed. The sight of her gave her something of a shock, for how could she have known what was in her mind and the fancy she was acting out on her own, for she was dressed as a servant from head to foot, white cap, tight dark bodice and white apron over a long skirt and buttoned boots; her feet looked so small in them, almost deformed. It was something she hadn't bargained for and it did give her a funny feeling.

Minnie curtsied and said—Now we are complete, now we are complete.

Odd wasn't the half of it. She found herself being led over to an armchair and her glass re-charged, and being attended by this stranger in maid's clothes. Things had taken a disturbing turn. She wanted to call a halt to it but couldn't, as this little old girl-woman in her rustling, starched apron and her painted cheeks fussed around her, opening boxes of beads and trinkets and putting them on her wrists and fingers and around her neck.

Those cold fingers on her skin made her withdraw further into herself but she bore it, allowed herself to be prettified, until at last Minnie cried out with great excitement—There! and held a hand-mirror up to her face.

Another start, for whose was this second foreign face staring at her from under the brim of a wide actress's hat, speckled feather and all, and then too the choker of pearls, three strands, tight as a minister's collar, and the earrings, black jet drops pulling down the tips of her ears? Before she could stop her Minnie had patted both her cheeks with a red powder and the transformation was complete. She rose from her chair, stately and more than a little theatrical, strange currents running through her.

Minnie cried—Bravo! clapping her hands and she heard her own voice ringing back with an *Ahem!* she remembered hearing once in some picture or other of high society. People in such circles frequently did clear their throats in that fashion; but

62

was it really her voice and was this really her now gliding over the carpet and holding herself in so stylishly?

—Oh Hetty, Hetty! cried Minnie in a transport.—I always said you had the stage in your blood. Who would have thought it? I feel so excited. Isn't this thrilling? Isn't it?

Silly old nanny-goat, she thought, as she admired herself in an oval mirror over the mantelpiece, but not all that silly really, for, *one of these days I will show all these galoots around here a touch of class, something to make them sit up and gape and choke on, all the things they've ever said about Hetty Quinn* – and she w as just runnng through a list of suitable stage names in her head, because Hetty Quinn was certainly not one to be considered for a moment, when Minnie gave a dreadful loud scream. Next minute she felt arms clutching her around the knees; she was almost brought down, and she struggled with the clinging figure while the cries continued.

—For God's sake, Minnie! she said, forgetting herself in the heat.—What's the matter with you?

Was this to be her punishment for all the airs and graces she had allowed herself, excitement proving too much for old Minnie? She even imagined a snapping sound, sign of the mind at last giving way.

—Now, Miss Maitland, you must get up. You must!

She felt so ridiculous now, her hat knocked over one eye, struggling in this daft get-up, while Minnie buried her head in the thick folds of her skirt.

—Please stand up!

The *please* was meant to take the hard edge off her voice and the cruel grip she had by this time on the old thing's shoulders, but what else could she do? On to the sofa she bundled her, more of a weight than she would have imagined, but still she covered her face like a child and no sense yet in all the gasps and cries.

—Oh Miss Maitland, this is not right. Tell me what ails you. Tell me, *please.*

But all she would do was give deep moaning sounds behind her hands and point at the window. She had been doing it all along, only she hadn't realized before that there was any method in all the arm wavings.

—Is there someone there? she asked, pulling herself up and away from her and crossing to the light.

—I can't see a soul. It must have been your imagination. You're overwrought.

She sounded like a nurse.

But Minnie groaned louder and kept pointing. Outside, the birds still sang undisturbed and the lawn, tussocky with neglect, ran clear to the fir trees beyond, as bare of life as always. It might have been a graveyard, this stretch at the side of the house, never a human sign, not a soul or movement . . .

—No, she said firmly.—Not a solitary soul, not one . . . We both need a cup of tea, that's what we need.

Minnie said quite clearly—I tell you he was there. It was him out there looking in. *Him.*

She had heard of cases like this, of old lonely people going gaga. This whole carry-on was beginning to make her feel distinctly creepy. Him. Who was *him* when he was at home?

—What are you talking about, Miss Maitland? Who did you see?

—Oh, he saw us, he saw us, I tell you! What will he think? So unseemly, oh so unseemly! And the moanings commenced again.—After all these years, all these years to see us—*me*, like this . . .

A glimmer was beginning to break, something faint, but distinctly sharp and bright like a candle flame at the end of a long hall. Could it be? Could it?

And just at that very moment the front door-bell rang. Someone standing out there had pulled the knob and its rusty wire out to full stretch and then let it suck back slowly on itself into the stone beside the jamb.

Minnie gave a short cry and passed out.

Sitting in the chair, with his knees high and pressed together, he thought busily – but not quite fast enough, he knew, for the events which he had set in motion. At any moment he felt he might literally be whirled off this speeding roundabout of sensations – thus his posture – and disintegrate in a fury of flying spare parts. So much for the more extreme fantasies of an old man, yet, no doubt about it, the feeling of vertigo was a definite one, not to be denied.

He hadn't even had the presence of mind to lodge the ash-plant he had cut himself on his journey out in the hall-way with the other household walking-sticks when he had been ushered in. It lay on the rich carpet at his feet. He looked down at it with rising distaste, worrying about a possible hiding-place behind a piece of furniture, until he realized that the maid, the girl – whoever, *whatever* she was – would be sure to miss it on her return. What a *faux-pas*. Behaviour no better than a cattle-drover's, and with a face to match, he felt sure, red and running, a character in the worst tradition of Samuel Lover, Handy Andy, bull in a tea-shop . . .

And the binoculars too, which he still wore around his neck, must appear quite ridiculous, dangling down as they did in his very lap. Not until then had the fact struck him about the only pose possible to carry off the wearing of such things. Why in god's name then did he continue to sit in this ridiculous sewing-chair, he asked himself? Why? And, most important of all, why hadn't he at the beginning simply merged into the growth outside, dropping behind a tree-trunk when she had first sighted him? Was it because of that feeling of nakedness without his masking glasses, eye to eye, both faces frozen in the terrible moment of discovery and then advancing instead of retreating, because of shock? Was that it? Going on until it was altogether too late? Yet three times he had pulled the bell

– the pressure it exerted was satisfying, almost muscular – *three times*, and in between the far-off delayed note dying to silence, total silence, the pull again. Almost a minute. And he had waited, *he had waited*. Or was it really because of what he had seen through the window, a tableau so bizarre that if he didn't seek investigation, its memory would haunt him, theory proliferating on theory, until life would be unbearable . . .

Sitting there like some grotesquely overgrown child, hands in lap, heels touching and waiting for the next twist of events, he reflected bitterly that spying habits only brought their own reward. The waiting was well-nigh unbearable. Better to flounder without warning than to anticipate. He wouldn't allow himself disturbing thoughts, though, about those areas which he had seen, so, for distraction, he eyed the furnishings, the decoration, the proportions of the room, its keepsakes and family photographs. Memories filtered into mind, times spent, meals taken, faces, voices, the sound of piano music, laughter and song, whispers . . . But steadily, despite all his control, the images swam back – in and out of focus – transposing themselves on the picture glass and on the gleaming face of furniture. The two women with their painted looks and open excited mouths, their gestures too, all exaggerated mime and knowing grimace, like something out of a silent film.

What in God's name had he witnessed then? The thing gripped him and in turn he determined to worry it until some meaning was forthcoming. He clenched teeth and fists and bored with his heels into the turkey-red pile as though to steel himself. Such things could not, should not, go unfathomed in this place, day and age. He was piqued, on his mettle, raw and red as any old cock-rooster . . .

In the middle of his rush of blood the door opened and the girl stood there. They looked at one another – silence for a moment – and he tried to move himself forward on the chair, something in the way of an acknowledgment really, but he was stuck fast between the sloping seat and the back of the infernal thing.

She observed his discomfiture with a half-smile. There were still slight traces of a cosmetic on her cheeks, so he hadn't completely imagined her earlier appearance, despite the fact that she had now changed her costume.

66

She said—Miss Maitland will be down presently. She has asked me to tell you that she's (her forehead contracted as she prepared to deliver the memorized phrase) she's a trifle out of sorts. Not herself.

Was she smiling? Had the girl a sense of humour? But the young face, quite pretty in a coarse dark way, snapped shut as once more she stared back at him.

His low position was a grave disadvantage. He would dearly have loved to rise up slowly and majestically at this stage to lean on his stick, stern patriarchal figure, and out-face her, but he knew the reality all too well. Red in the cheeks and dizzy, he would merely sway, a panting old bag of bones, further satisfaction for her and her youthful malice. *But, my dear, we've seen too many schoolroom skirmishes in our time, too many out-manoeuvrings from behind a desk for that . . .*

She said—Would you take a drink, Master Brown? And he detected capitulation, not only in her tone of voice – arch, yes, arch definitely now – but also in the phrasing of the question, an awkward country way of putting it, plus, of course, most telling of all, that final mode of address. How slow these people were to change the old tribal hierarchies . . .

—Thank you all the same, he said with coolness. But I hardly think so.

Then—Tell me, girl, what is your name?

He had her reddening now, shifting feet like any cowed scholar out at the front, just like the old days.

—Hetty. Hetty Quinn, she said.

One of the Quinns, so that's who you are, he thought, staring up at her with the old dead look; *and if I'm not mistaken, you're the wee by-blow who caused all the consternation – how many years ago was it now?*

—Tell me, Hetty Quinn. What age are you?

—Seventeen – sir.

Sir. She hated herself for saying that. He could read her like a book now. – Seventeen, he mused, knowing he made it sound dark, ripe with meaning.

She replied—Yes, sir, and hung her head.

He thought of her illegitimacy. Felt a touch of lust, linking it with his earlier and first sight of her in the wood that day. What was she doing there and why? That he sensed some association between the two outlandish happenings his glasses had picked out for him that day only increased his irritation. He couldn't abide mysteries.

—You come from the village, don't you?

—Yes, sir.

—And you walk all the way, I take it?

—Yes, sir.

—And do you take any . . . any short-cuts?

She looked at him and he recognized that sly, uncomprehending look which used to anger him in the old teaching days. Once they dived deep into their bolt-holes you could never get them out. A race of rabbits, coneys – that ancient word still in use in the parts, echoed in their Authorised Version . . .

—Never mind. Tell your mistress I shall be here, dismissing her curtly. (God forgive him his pride, he almost said, *you may leave the room.*) The door closed behind the firm young buttocks, the back stiff and stiffening, he suspected. He smiled to himself. Let her smart, the bold hussy. A humbling always was good for the young.

In better temper he gazed around Minnie's drawing-room. Nothing looked changed, either in arrangement or in that other subtler way that things have of seeming smaller, less vivid after so many years. Perhaps it was only when one left surroundings at an early age that they shrank in proportion to one's own physical growth, an *Alice in Wonderland* truism. The mind was a remarkable instrument, memory even more . . .

A line of carved elephants, Burmese and diminishing, marched along the top of the heavy sideboard. He remembered them and their arrangement, and the other Eastern knick-knacks as well, Benares brass-ware, teak, ivory and rattan placed around the room on little tables. In the far-off days he had looked on them as fascinating objects, exotica in a dull provincial setting. Now they seemed mere vulgar manifestations of the Empire. All these country houses crammed with stuff you couldn't give away at auctions.

But the books were still there, still ranked behind the high glass doors. The sun shone directly on them and eclipsed whole areas with its blaze – the Dickens, the Trollope and almost half of Thackeray were hidden. How he had lusted after those bindings and the thick feel of the pages. Secetly he had started his own collection of odd volumes picked up in the Smithfield markets of Belfast out of that envy, but knowing well that he would never achieve such splendid unthinking possession. The worm of envy had indeed burrowed deep in him in those days. All the damage it had done; waste of lives and living. This room where the worm had twisted deepest, effecting its cruellest inroads . . .

He saw the sherry bottle on its table, two glasses – a bottle, not a decanter – no pretence of respectability and, as the crude saying went, almost a dead man already. He shouldn't have come, he knew that now, should have held to his own safe track. There was pain here for him in every corner and article of the room.

He heard a swish of clothing outside the closed doors, then it ceased and he knew someone was standing out there steeling herself before entering. His own nerves needed calming, for he knew it was her and this sudden surge was something he hadn't bargained for. He panicked. He pulled himself up out of the chair to prepare himself. His temples pounded and he felt dizzy.

Minnie came into the room and they faced one another. *She must see it in my eyes,* he thought, but couldn't look away, *she must see it,* for if the room hadn't changed, she had; *by God, how you've changed, Minnie. Why should the house stay the same and you in the midst of it shrivel and age so?* He thought of the fruit and its stone, only a reversal. The flesh it withers, the stone it endures . . .

Almost as if they had collided, they began to recoil to different parts of the room, to sink down into facing chairs, and simultaneously all extraneous sounds – birds, a far-off aeroplane, a creaking gate in the garden, a loose strand of creeper stroking the outside pane – flooded into the room as if the walls had suddenly become porous. He felt himself choking. Something seemed to have risen to stick in his throat. He coughed once to relieve it, but it led to a paroxysm that brought water to his eyes. Through his tears he saw her terrified face, and he began to laugh through his snorts and gaspings in spite of himself.

She thinks I might have a seizure, collapse on the rug at her feet, he thought, and then the crowning irony – *She can't get over how old I look too!* It came like a cold douche, but only made him want to bray louder. *She thinks I'm a senile old wreck – one push and I'll fall over like a rickety gate.*

Her face was truly a study; the dabs of artificial colour on her cheeks hectic in contrast with the rest of her pallor. Poor Minnie, how he used to torment her with frights and sudden scares, preying on her nerves, until she would scream – *oh, why do you do it, why do you?*

He motioned towards the sherry, the not-to-be-denied gesture of a stricken man, and Minnie lurched at the bottle, pouring out a glass in the same jerky fashion, brief cascades of pale golden liquor which he watched gratefully. Then, obediently, she filled another for herself after a further wave of his hand. *Imperious old humbug,* he addressed himself, as the first sip rolled down his throat. Humbugger.

She watched his second choking fit with the same fright and he suddenly became weary of his game. Poor Minnie. Warmth – was it the sherry? – rose in him and reached out to her. A desire to press her knee, affectionate and eloquent squeeze renewing old bonds, seemed right, then didn't. Propriety. Both of them were gradually straightening now against their chairbacks. Propriety ...

He thought of a picture they might have sat for, of a type popular once upon a time, two old people sitting silently in a room, a swath of sunlight laid on the carpet between them, highlights on furniture, glass and winking fire-irons. *Dear Dead Days; Memories; When You And I Were Young.*

He took another swig at his glass, staring across. Her eyes were downcast, demure. *Tipplers* or *Their Shameful Secret?* She still brought out devils in him after all these years. Who would have thought it? He remembered another study he had seen, much reproduced, a man slumped over a table, bottle before him, a woman standing against the far wall, her back turned. *Ennui.* Every picture tells a story. They used to sit like that once, silent, without a word, in those awful last days when it was ending.

But, good God, they didn't have to repeat the past, their mistakes!

—Minnie, he said.

It came out like a bark, over-loud, explosive, and she started, spilling a little of her drink.

Appalled, he repeated her name, and this time it emerged as too soft, a word of love, binding. He shook his head like a water-dog.

—What I wanted to say was . . . but what did he want to say? —was . . . uh . . .

Too many things, that was it. *Make a start, you fool, a start, anywhere.*

—I would like to say that . . . uh, it was very civil of you to receive me . . . Civil.

Huffing and puffing now, was it, like some caricature of a colonel? Never himself. But at his age there was nothing left but to strike attitudes. He trained his eye on his glass, tilting it so that the oily liquid slid dangerously to the rim. She thought he was hinting at another drink and there was an embarrassed piece of business with her reaching forward with the bottle and he withholding his glass until the inevitable occurred and some drops fell on to the carpet. Really it was too absurd for words! *A Chapter Of Accidents.*

—Minnie, he said.—It's been a long time, and smiled.

His face felt as though it were made of cardboard, but at least he had gained a reaction, for he heard her murmur— Yes.

She seemed to be easing in her chair. It was to be a careful, coaxing operation, he could see that now, but then, why should he, he thought? The only good thing about getting old was that you could be as testy and truthful to people's faces as you liked. Dammit, they expected it from you. But he softened. Poor Minnie, or Minerva, as he used to call her, for she hated her name, common diminutive, her pet-name, as though she were one of the cats. Oh, there had been fire there once upon a time, spirit. Her green eyes would flash and she would stamp and fume and make threats – but to him alone, never to the old man, that silent-rolling bleak juggernaut. They would spike his wheels for him, so they would, whisper, whisper, leave him patrolling his rooms and passages alone, calling out as he rolled ceaselessly, hoarse and threatening, leave him, run away to-gether. *Lost Opportunities. Faded Dreams*

—Minerva, he heard himself say.—How many years has it

been? How many? – not really seeking an answer, merely lamenting the wasting away, the waste.

—Barbour, she said—Barbour, as though she would press her hand to his lips as she used to when he was too forceful.

Could the past be held in abeyance then, attitudes frozen, or was it only in his own imagination that these things occurred? He felt impatience, eager to put his whirling theories to the test. He leaned forward, gesturing in spite of himself with his glass.

—I wish I'd called on you before this time. I don't know why I didn't—

He stopped.

—Or rather I do know (he must weigh each syllable for truth) You know too (he wanted to band her feelings in with his, would she allow it, could she?) I think you do, yes, I think you do, yes, I think so, I do think so (her head was still lowered, he would have to drill with words into that thin crown, the hair was still glossy, cared for) I . . . uh, I mean, we – (he couldn't go on) What I want to say is . . .

Deepest humiliation; he felt exhausted, run out cruelly to the end of a tether. *Tongue-Tied.*

And so they sat there with bowed heads in the dying sunlight in the room, each studying their territory of carpet, black and tan hieroglyphs on red ground. The figures semed to possess a disturbing intensity. He was unable to place them in the larger repeating pattern, they throbbed with such brutal individuality. And, moreover, all the other things in the room, classed as a whole, appeared now to be conspiring to mock him as well. Under his brows he glowered with real hate at chair legs, beadings, bone-white castors, the coarse hessian tacked on the underside of chairs and settees. The pupils who stood before him dumbly like pillars, with bowed heads, while his tongue scourged them, he pondered, must have known something of the same baffled rage. If only floor-boards had a voice, what an outcry . . .

—Barbour, will you take tea?

Quiet voice driving a wedge into his preoccupations. *Will you take tea?* So the rest of the world carried on, the world of niceties, her world – but why should he pity her? What was so intolerable about fading away in a dusty museum? He nodded, but with not too much impatience, eager as he was to dive deeper into this latest speculation. Yes, was his own existence so superior? He seemed bent on comparisons, time-tables of risings and settings, dressings and undressings – when she reached out and shook a little brass hand-bell which rested on the table nearest her. The action was so sudden and for her so decisive that he stared at the gleaming object – it had human shape, a crinolined lady with the tiny clapper planted deep beneath its skirts – and then questioningly at Minnie herself. The cheeks looked flushed.

She rang the bell a second time, avoiding his gaze, then replaced it, cutting short its sound, exactly, he imagined, on its invisible circular resting place. He looked down at the tiny burnished features, the bosom, pinched waist and that swelling extravagance below hiding the mechanism. Had anyone realized the impropriety of burying the hard little kernel in there with such anatomical accuracy. A vulgar synonym came to mind – didn't they always? *Give us a luk at your rattley*. Poetry of the school-yard. Rattley. Rattle-box. If he weren't careful he would be swamped by images, each one more unspeakable than the last . . .

Outside the door they heard a cough and Minnie called out —Come, Hetty, in high, nervous fashion.

Her head was very erect. *A Formal Occasion*. He allowed himself to relax in his chair, feeling easier, less on show. The girl entered, staring questioningly at her mistress. He noted the glances passing between the two, not knowing or conspiratorial, as he would have been led to believe by what he had seen earlier, for now he knew they shared secrets, rather, the girl – Hetty, wasn't it – betrayed a kind of puzzled irritation. Her brow wrinkled and Minnie said emphatically—We should like some tea . . . please. Some tea.

Hetty looked at the bell on the table, then at Minnie, turned and walked out. The door closed with slightly more vehemence than was necessary, and it came to him that Minnie had been putting on airs for his benefit. *Lady Bountiful*.

A further cut for the young skivvy. *Resentment Below Stairs*. He felt himself warm again to the woman across the room, conscious of some kind of sacrifice she had made for him.

—You know you've changed very little.

A lie, but still . . . Minnie's cheeks took on colour. Could the old be said to blush?

In her lap her hands writhed momentarily. He noticed rings. Their quick glitter struck him. Unusual surely on those hands in this house where personal adornment had always been fiercely resisted. Hutton Maitland waged something approaching religious war on ostentation and the vanities of the spirit. *Jehovah In His Wheeled Chariot.* But the rings, the rouge, that earlier but still haunting glimpse . . . Once more the sensation of stumbling on to something outlandish. And the girl, her pique . . . What if? A new and dark interpretation of their relationship crossed his mind like a foul mist. No, no!

—Minerva (the name still sounded rusty, unused) Minerva, I—

He would make her reply this time. A question.

—Do you find much time for travelling? I mean venturing out and about?

She said—No, her gaze still lowered, fingers still entwining. Sparks of shine from the brilliants in her lap.

—Your rings, he said.

Up came her face and reaction was certainly there.

—What? she said, staring at him.

Recklessly—They look quite beautiful, such a show . . .

He forced a laugh. Did his teeth glare? He had a new and impossibly bright upper plate.

—Such splendour. I mean, I don't think I ever saw you wearing rings before. No, I am mistaken. There was one – a little gold signet, wasn't it?

An inspiration; he was beginning to sweat, wetness sliding down under his shirt.—Yes, I remember now. Your initials – but which finger, which finger was it?

He leaned forward and took her hand, loosening the fist and examining the palm intently for a moment as though he were a reader of life-lines and heart-lines and those other dried gullies of the skin.

—Such rings, he said.—Such rings. Quite splendid – an insane urge to lean over, screwing up an eye and miming a jeweller with his glass, tempted him. What had got hold of him this day? Surely not the effects of the single sherry. Now he was fondling her fingers quite unashamedly, savouring the

74

contrast of bright metal and hot skin, and babbling, no other word for it . . .

—Such a pretty stone this, a cornelian, isn't it, and of course this intricate silver one, a puzzle-ring, I think it's termed? Turkish. Dear me, what a hoard of useless information one collects over the years without realizing it, and jewellery of all things. Jewellery. One of the trickier words to spell, I remember, yes, one to catch them out with – like – like, fascination, or, or . . .

—Isthmus, she said quietly.

He looked at her. She was smiling. A weak and timid smile, but still a smile.

He said—Possession.

—Ocean, she returned.

—Thistle!

—Thorough.

—Through.

They laughed together and he still had hold of her hand when Hetty pushed the door open without knocking and came into the room.

—Ah, tea! he said, keeping his grip firm despite the look on the girl's face and the fluttering attempt at withdrawal in the thin fingers clasped in his. Certainly he wasn't going to relinquish any of his hard-won ground now. And not to any sour-faced chit with her rattling and her disapproving and sniffing airs.

—Thank you, he said. The Cup That Cheers! dismissing her grandly as though the house was his.

He looked around him . . . and it might well have been his too – if he had played his cards right (a cold phrase). Would he really have had to surrender all that much to old Dadda Maitland and his tyranny, over the waiting years? At the time – then – he had thought so. Now he wasn't so sure if the loss would have been all that noticeable. But past was past and disinterment a fruitless exercise . . .

They took tea and he eyed her over the fine rim of his china cup. She bore his glances better now, occasionally smiling when their eyes met, no longer fidgeting. Well-being filled him; that and a vague warm sentimentality, which he knew was leading him on to a rush of confidences. He wanted to engulf her, tell her all in his mind, like some child inordinately grateful for what in reality, he supposed, amounted to a relatively small mercy.

—I've been out walking—he announced.

Again that barking abruptness.

—Every day, if the weather's suitable, I go walking. It's something I've grown accustomed to.

—You look very healthy, she said, and his foolish old heart fluttered.

—There are times when I feel I know every stone and plant on my travels. Of course the area is a small one, a few square miles only, but I flatter myself that no one else can know it quite so well.

Should he tell her about the journal? Would she understand such a thing?

—I've been compiling something in the form of a study of the locality – past as well as present. Nothing too ambitious, just a few notes, jottings really . . .

Mute Inglorious Milton.

She said—But you must publish what you've written. It would be something of value.

He was about to say, *do you really*, then stopped himself. He sipped tea instead, staring down into the pale liquid. That mock-modest phrase to be delivered with lowered eyes, and then the disgusting parade of *oh I couldn't*s etcetera to follow. And so the moment passed. What a pathetic mollusc he was, to be sure, played upon at will by these tidal pulls, self-awareness sucking at him.

Minnie said—I always felt you had a talent in that direction – Barbour. Your letters . . .

She stopped, blushing.

He looked at her carefully. Did she still have them? After all these years. Tied with ribbon?

There was a silence, both of them studying their tea-cups intently. The quotations from Browning. God help him but he had encouraged a fantasy that she was Elizabeth and he the passionate poet, both of them beset by an identical restriction. *Minnie! Minnie!* came old Barrett-Maitland's voice, *Where are you?* Hunting them down, wrists like a navvy's, whirling his hissing rubber wheels along. *Answer me, girl! Where are you?*

His own hand over her mouth in the greenhouse. *Don't. Just this once*, but tears sliding down wetting his fingers. *Here I am, dadda! Here I am!*

He finished his tea and stood up, avoiding her eyes, knowing that open defenceless look now too well.—Well, it's been most pleasant. Most pleasant. But I must be going. I don't want to outstay my welcome.

Meaningless, polite babble. Anything to deflect that yearning. Those faces on the largest of advertising hoardings, eyes following, mouths engulfing . . .

He moved closer to the door.

—This way. Come this way, she said, pointing to the central and tallest window. He had forgotten about the terrace. To think that once he had known this house as intimately as –

She was struggling with the handle. He stepped forward briskly to help. Their bodies brushed. Perfume. What else? The odour of old wardrobes, cachous . . .

—There we are. A little stiff with un-use, that's all . . . *A Man About The House.*

The day was in decline, sun dropping, but the birds as frantic as ever. This must constitute a paradise for them, he thought, as he eyed the wildness, the tangled stocks and canes in the old fruit-garden. He breathed in deeply and at his elbow she echoed him.

—Remember? she said. Soft and yearning again.

Earlier he had been the one who had sought confrontation.

Nothing had changed, when he thought about it. In the past hadn't he always made the running, then pulled back and she had carried on, willing racehorse always, but for that single throttling exception. And wasn't that in fact the reason he had pressed, so eagerly, so cruelly, on that part of her, knowing that she could never give way to him? All those years using the old man as his scapegoat. The cruellest age this one without doubt. One entered the place without illusions and it looked as though the exit was to be little different.

On the terrace he took out the binoculars and slowly began raking the distance, left to right, a controlled sweep that brought his back around to her. He needed to be hidden, to think his private thoughts, eyes masked now by the cold circles of metal, face and front averted. His voice continued though. Pleasantries to outwit and evade.

—Three boys working in a hayfield, he heard himself say – and I can see the very perspiration on their bodies. One of them is making the others laugh. If one could only read lips – what power . . .

She cried out suddenly, impulsively:

—Let me look! Oh please, *please*, clapping her hands.

The sound disturbed; he felt trapped behind his lenses. It was as though he had been wrenched back to an earlier time and a young girl was clamouring at his elbow. The illusion died when he took the glasses from his eyes and handed them over. He watched her aiming at the spot between the trees, watched her, seeing a thin ageing woman, shaking a little, hair escaping from its flattened grey cap, mottled stretched skin on knuckles, furrows in the cheeks. Almost greedily he regarded those blemishes, her stance, the antique clothes, as though now he had come to her at last after all this time his curiosity could not be appeased. So much conjecture to be equated. The vacuum of years to be filled.

He needed to continue in the company of this woman from his past, not just now, today, but again and again. How often and how soon couldn't be decided quickly.

Then she cried out again, startlingly, swinging around, binoculars dropping to the limit of their straps. Her face was white.

—Oh, she whispered.—They looked straight at me. Into my very eyes. Do you think they can see us up here?

—Nonsense, he said taking her arm.—Not at all. How on earth could they?

Night

1

—In a small private room at the rear of a downtown dive and beer-parlour somewhere on the West Side sit the three men who are the principal actors in our drama. Within twenty-four hours these same three men and their exploits will be front page news, and every law-enforcement officer in the forty-eight states will be on the look out for anyone answering their descriptions. Harvey 'The Horse' Gault, so-called because of his superhuman strength; male, Caucasian, six feet, one hundred and ninety-two pounds – this man is dangerous, repeat dangerous; Frankie-Boy Glass, 'The Professor', one hundred and fifty pounds, slight build, has a nervous cough and reads a lot; Mack 'Diamond Legs' McFarlane, the brains of the outfit, tall, good-looking, witty, debonair, a first-class ballroom dancer and dangerously attractive to women ...

Their laughs washing away the rest of Mack's preposterous mimicry, a great hoot combining with the thump of their by now empty glasses on the surface of the wet table. Harvey shouts out to the hatch in the corner:—Maggie! Something similar—and her put-upon but smiling face appears briefly in the frame.

How long would it be, he wondered, glancing around, before they abused their privilege of drinking in this woman's kitchen with its black and silver range, its ticking clocks and delph dogs. He caught the eye of one of them – King Charles' favourite breed. After another few drinks the ranged canines on the mantelpiece would begin to stare down at their antics with disapproval. He had the feeling that if hooliganism were ever to break out here in this low-ceilinged place it would involve one or all of Maggie's prized dogs. The idea made him smile with a certain amount of malice.

—And what is the deep one amused at? Secrets? Eh? Eh? Mack, with head cocked to one side watching him, gleam in the eye but no ill-will or cruel sting – as yet. He stared back coolly. Wonderful what stiffening there was in a couple of bolted whiskeys with slow beer chasers. Then, echoing Mack's own Hollywood newsreel delivery, he announced in his own turn to the room:

—Presenting another case from the confidential files of the F.B.I., the implacable foe of all American enemies!

And their favourite quote:

—Now it can be told!

(Scenes in his head from that last episode they had all gone to see – Broderick Crawford, staccato and brutish, with his foil, the perpetually worried Lloyd Nolan.)

Then the other two roared approval with more beating on the mahogany and he felt pleased and as usual more than surprised that he had carried it off so well.

In the Saturday-night cinema they liked to startle the people around by joining in with the dialogue on the screen, particularly the commentaries. Mack could send out an uncanny impersonation by pinching his nostrils. He himself had never felt completely in tune with the sport. Detection worried him. The old man shooting the beam of his torch into the faces along the ninepenny benches might easily find him mouthing and come for him. He flailed without warning, a war veteran with shell-shock; the three of them his only real adversaries.

Not that he feared the stroke of the long silvery torch, that was for the children in the front rows; no, it would be the humiliation of the discovery of his age and identity. He felt sensitive about being still at college, and teachers-to-be didn't go in for rowdiness on such a level, at least not while they were sober anyway.

—A wee drink for the young master?

Mack again whispering in his ear. Their eyes met. Glasses were lifted – the little whiskey ones first – and drained with a shudder and a gasp. Medicinal almost, that first draught, but it soon burned and spread in their veins, stoking up the fires for the night ahead.

Friday night. Pay-night. Everyone got paid tonight. The public house was full of men burning up wages, all a little delirious with the thick feel of folded notes; one at a time peeled off, waved in the air or stuck forcibly on to the wet bar or the old woman's tray. He noticed the way they handled their money. Not a miser among them tonight, all full of bravado, not one who covered his hand, drawing each single out as if it was his last and only ace. Getting poetic again, he thought ... But, through the hatch in the bar he saw a red-faced labourer gesturing with a pound, folded like a spill. Money to burn. Another man jostling to pay first actually threw his note, crushed into a ball, to the old woman who was serving. The episode seemed miraculous, happening like that before his eyes, as though he had willed it. He realized that he was getting drunk.

Harvey wanted them all to sing.

—Come on then, boys, what about it?

Earnestly, his face glossy as a pippin, grip encircling his glass of Tennent's.—Just a wee verse or two.

Mack caught his eye. *Just a wee verse or two.*

Poor Harvey, with his old-fashioned, country way of putting things. His clothes too. A hairy green sports-jacket (*Thorn-Proof*), flannel trousers equally impenetrable, with turn-ups, and of course the open-necked white shirt, collar scrupulously folded over and down almost as though it had been welded on to the thick tweed of his jacket. He had a silver badge in his lapel which said *Leyland Motors* and his hair was spiky with hair-cream.

A bitter truth indeed that his appearance might damage any chances they might have of picking up some decent women later at the dance. Not that the local talent would be all that devastating. It was only a nine to twelve hop in the local Orange Hall after all, but occasionally out of the night would blow in a giggling and heavily made-up bunch of girls from the city, to inflame and excite. He could almost smell their perfume now and the drink on the breath of the boldest and best-looking as the two of them clung together in the Ladies' Choice ...

Harvey said—What about *Me And My Shadow, All Alone And Feeling Blue?* and began to hum the opening bars as encouragement. But they merely regarded him coldly until he faltered, then dipped mouth and nose into the froth of his lager. Poor Harvey. A voice as flat as a corncrake's, irritating them whenever he and Mack wanted to harmonize. Usually by dint of sarcasm, unspoken for the most part, they were able to keep him silent, but when a mood of heavy gaiety took him – as now – helped on by the drink, he would insist on joining in. Poor Harvey.

Mack got up, making for the toilet outside in the yard, and the two of them were left to drink in silence.

—I wonder what sort of shape we'll all be in, in the morning. Out in the hay, I mean—he said cheerfully, for want of something to say. Harvey looked at him with that same black incomprehension that he himself had assumed a moment ago. Menace seemed to flow when you were alone with him. He wondered if it was the same with Mack. Hardly, he suspected. And he would never find out either. You didn't put things like that into words, especially to Mack. Often he debated why the three of them should ever have teamed up in the first place; an odd alliance, certainly not friends in the accepted sense of the word, but perhaps he expected too much, especially after a few whiskeys . . .

He hummed a bar or two to himself – *Dear Old Pals* – and felt better immediately, ironical and self-mocking once more.

—My round, mates—and bounced on thick crêpe soles up to the hatch.

The crowded bar beyond opened up before him – a panorama – as he leaned in on the shelf fastidiously, elbow propped on a dry island in the midst of the interlocking rings of beer and water. There lay their score, that is if anyone wanted to keep count. On the facing wall he could just make out his reflection in a fly-blown mirror advertising a long since defunct brand of pot-still whiskey. Head and shoulders seem to swim on the faded silvering among the curlicues and ornate lettering.

Beneath the mirror sat two old men in a daze of drink staring straight ahead of them. He watched his own face in the glass above theirs. Alertness and a sly smile – not altogether to his taste – above those two expressionless ovals. One with a moustache, heavy and drooping. The sort to be brushed across and down compulsively with the back of the hand. His grandfather had one, stained brown, a fine dew on the hairs around the mouth. It gave him the look of a brigand, a foreign human exhibit in his chair by the open fire of his wee house all day and every day. His face became as black as the chimney breast.

84

Senile inertia. Old men were sad, especially old men in pubs on a Friday night with no money to throw around them. He would have liked to have offered, through Maggie, to set them up a round, but hadn't the courage. Always afraid of drawing attention. Keeping himself to himself.

—Maggie, you have a customer! Thon young fella's tongue is hanging out.

Eyes in the bar beyond directed to him as a big man in bib-and-brace overalls and a knitted cap raises his voice.

He felt himself going red at the laughter, good-humoured though it was, hanging in the hatch, turned in a moment into a grinning cock-shot. All his preening in the mirror too. His appearance of which he was so proud a second ago, hair growing out (just right) of his crew-cut; maroon shirt; tie, pale with its Windsor knot, flat and firm; the off-white sports coat matching tie – shoulders in reflection as broad as Mature's or Mitchum's – now was too eye-catching, even effeminate – that worst of crimes – for this place and these men.

He wasn't known here, never would be. A typical whim of Mack's to cycle up to this hill pub tonight where they drank in the kitchen only occasionally and at closing time the three of them would free-wheel abreast downhill, drunk and hallooing, all the way to the village and dance.

Behind him Harvey called out—What's keeping you? and he turned to him, growling.

—Ach, keep your bloody hair on!

The other two laughed at his rage, not knowing its cause, and of course he had to join in, healed suddenly by the daftness of it all. And over the drinks which had miraculously appeared at his worst moment there at the hatch they began a giggling fit out of nothing at all which went on and on.

Mack started doing his imitations, a gallery of the local eccentrics they all knew well. This time, Frank Cooley muttering and snorting to himself out among the pigs at slop-time – they recognized the resemblance in sound startlingly for the first time. The one called *Exchange & Mart*, because of his mania for coupon-clipping the small print bargains from that periodical. His cottage almost a warehouse for Admiralty compasses and binoculars, army surplus water-bottles, haversacks, jack-knives, mess tins, stoves and clothing from every theatre of war – his own uniform was a German battle-dress, an Australian bush-hat and R.A.F. flying boots, winter and summer. The bicycle-mad McKibbin family, grown men, racing about the roads in ragged convoy honking and accelerating vocally; their crisis came during the week of the Isle of Man T.T. Races, days and nights given over to stripping, painting and polishing their ancient machines. One would be out and about on a peaceful stretch of country road in early July when quite suddenly a sound like swarming bees would swell out of nowhere and next moment the McKibbins would be on top of you, heads lowered, rumps up, legs pumping, wailing nasally, Geoff Duke or some of the current Italian aces to a man. Nothing or no one could injure that dream, each cruel trick or gibe rebounding from their shell of fantasy – one of the wonders of the locality, a legend.

All these people with their delusions – but then everybody had them, hadn't they? Their own circle for instance ... He looked at Harvey's red laughing face. What did he dream at night up in the big grey house on the hill? Himself as movie strong man perhaps, Lex Barker getting all the Janes, smiting him and Mack, whenever they had been at their most wounding – or did someone like Harvey have more earth-bound fancies, Master at The Craigs, for instance, ordering schemes of drainage and husbandry, lording it over the menials or even – wilder – wasting his inheritance on parties, women, a succession of white cars, all on approval, sitting in the yard for the well-doing Presbyterian neighbours to shake their heads over?

Yes, they all had their dreams, had to have them. He himself. A troop of private-eyes for him, jazzmen, champion boxers in the top weights, submarine captains, gamblers and gigolos – he wasn't one hundred per cent sure what that last implied, but it sounded good and if it meant having any amount of women, well he would go along with that, pencil-line moustache and all ...

—Hey, you! Make a name for yourself! Your round!

Mack being admonished now by Harvey with heavy jocularity. And Mack was certainly inclined to meanness, holding back to the last noisy draining of glasses, a habit that irritated, particularly when drinking speed must be maintained. Vague resentments could be stirred up out of such delays, unfair motives inferred. He had seen it happen before, the screw turning blacker and deeper as the night wore on, all the more damaging because the feeling must never be aired, too shaming an accusation ever to put into words, small-minded, the original meanness somehow transferring itself.

But Mack merely laughed (he felt relieved) and went to take his place at the hatch.

Crossing the floor, he added one further and final pantomime for their benefit, cheeks distended, right elbow flapping, while fingering a tune in front of his stomach. They recognized who it was immediately, of course, down to the very strut of the slightly bowed legs, that head held back, the solemnity of bearing and expression. Jim Gillespie, The Piper In The Corn. His own invention that, and pretty good, after he had seen him one day practising his airs out in the fields. He was moving at a slow marching step through the thistles in full kiltie uniform – he had just joined a band – and overflowed with the serious-ness of his new honour. Calling up the other two, he had watched him through the hedge, enjoying the sight to the full. They had split themselves. About their own age he was, a red-haired stocky villager, something of a simpleton. Oh God, The Piper In The Corn! They laughed and laughed until they nearly threw up, gas and hiccups choking them. Christ almighty, what an eejit, what a right bloody eejit . . .

Maggie came in to wipe the table, smiling apologetically, in the midst of their uproar, a faded wan woman who seemed to bend at every whim of her customers.

—No trouble now. We want no trouble, was the phrase most frequent on her lips, a whispered remonstrance which summed up her philosophy of life, helpless and hopeless in the face of events. Her husband was dead, killed by drink. He had left her the pub but the only change came in the inscription above the door, her name over his in new script. A woman who had succumbed, our Maggie, he thought, as her damp clout circled their table. They had lifted glasses obediently and she kept murmuring her gratitude as she wiped. A smell of stale beer and dishwater hung about her, the apron stiff and spotted with stains, falling down straight to her knees, as she touched them occasionally with her moving body.

There were stories. It was hard to associate this tired creature with the tales of lust in circulation, of customers sitting each other out long after closing-time for the prize of a night in her bed, but . . . what if he slid a hand in and up under the apron as she bent across, no one to know but her, and she might allow it, free access, as she prolonged her rubbing on the table-top, enjoying his touch, face as expressionless as a cat's, the perfect sensual woman, the one he had dreamed of, inaccessible up to now, and here she was all along waiting . . . It took a certain kind of sagacity to scent depths like that in a woman – women – drilling through to the nakedness beneath, knowing the magic touch, word or look that did the trick . . . an art . . .

Across the table from him, smiling into his beer, sat such an artist. It wouldn't surprise him in the least to find that Mack had been one of those lucky leavers, hammering home the bolt in more senses than one after all the lights had finally gone out in the pub. Mack, secretive about his conquests, coming and going on certain nights with only a smile for them, whenever they questioned him afterwards. Smiling, always smiling . . .

Harvey was talking loudly now, his tongue loosened by the drink, boastfully about men of sport – his own theories about the American Lee Savold and why he was sure to be toppled. He had no left hand. Up against a good stylish boxer, he wouldn't stand a chance, jab, jab, jab . . . With fist clenched, he punched the air a foot in front of Mack's grin.

Mack said slyly—Like Bruce Woodcock for instance? And seemed to invite that mimed punch, but raising his glass to his lips at just the right moment. *Never hit a man with a drink in his hand.* Where did they get these ridiculous unwritten codes of behaviour from? Not that Harvey would ever hit Mack, glass or no glass. Mack knew it, Harvey knew it and he knew it.

Conversation resumed on these lines. With boxing and boxers out – their only sporting interest it seemed – topics swung half-heartedly between film stars and singers. Did Jo Stafford spell her Christian name with an 'e' or not? He lost interest. There seemed no place for anything he might have to say between Harvey's angry assertions and Mack's fly contradictions.

Earlier he had noticed something swelling Harvey's jacket-pocket, a book or a folded magazine of some sort, and gradually it had been working its way upwards, pushing back the flap as he twisted his body to and fro, while he argued the toss. Carefully moving his hand over, he waited now until he could take a grip on its wadded leaves, then withdraw it with all the pickpocket's daring that the drink had engendered.

He felt a sweet triumph at his prize, opening it just sufficiently in his lap to recognize what it was, for there she was, lying in the surf, head back, breasts bare, waves foaming over her goose-pimpled thighs, an eddy at their convergence drawing the eye to the suggestion of something barely submerged, weedy, awash. His eyes strained in the bad light. Then:

—What the hell do you think you're at? And Harvey was snatching for his dirty book back across the table.

A glass almost toppled but was saved by Mack taking in the situation at a glance, now on his feet, gesturing for the catch. The *Lilliput* flew to him, was held, shook out in the air derisively for a moment like a piece of washing for all now to see.

—Oh horny Harvey. Isn't Harvey horny and so quiet about it too.

Then blonde Miss Mermaid sailed back to him again and he held her between finger and thumb.

—Dirty, dirty, dirty.

—Yes, dirty Harvey. Harvey's not a nice boy. I wonder what Maggie would say if she had a wee dekko. Eh, Harvey?

—Eh, Harvey?

—*Give me the fucking thing, will you?*

—Oh, so that's what it's for?

Back to Mack again.

The inside spread fluttered to the floor, another sea-nymph presenting her bum this time to the camera – he would have liked to have had a long look in peace himself at all that wet rounded flesh, felt sympathy for poor old Harvey, remembering the mail-order catalogue slipped guiltily under a cushion at home, big smiling women modelling peach-coloured knickers – then Harvey caught him with a half-blow, half-shove of his body and he was falling backwards into a stack of chairs in the corner.

More conscious of the noise of the clashing bentwood than anything else, it was a moment before it registered with him that Harvey was now crouched, fists half-up, glaring at him in a new way which left no doubt what he was in for. He felt sick, frightened and bruised all in one second. Also an overwhelming sense of unfairness. Why should it have to be me? he thought, but of course knowing that it had. And just a second before, fellow-feeling, sympathy, no less.

They looked at one another, he trying to postpone the moment of truth the barest second more by scrabbling just enough to make it look plausible among the shining coils of legs and backs of chairs all shift and slide, Harvey swelling up and out, red, inflamed. The strike when it came would be colossal, obliterating, he thought, not to be parried, his blood and brains flying. And he would have to rise at this precise point to face it, before falling just once like a bag of blocks. Honour demanded it. *Honour*. As if all three of them didn't know already how shit-scared he really was – but Mack, *oh – what a friend we have in Maa-ick* – reached and pulled down an imaginary mike from the open sky over Madison Square Gardens.

—In the red corner, folks, at one hundred and fifty pounds, that immaculate little lightweight from our home state, the plucky, the indomitable, folks – Glover Boy Glass! And in the green corner, Hurricane Harve, top contender for the Golden Graip contest, King of the Haymakers, Lord of the – and then a halt, flow snapped off with a venom that shocked both of them – Oh fuck it, yes, fuck it! Why should I bother my arse? Go ahead, fight away, be big men, why should I always have to – always be the one, always have to – oh, forget it, for-*get* it!

The room was ripped by the outburst, but the silence following, paining worse, much worse.

Mack drained on his glass with brutal relish, a sound to further humiliate. They both looked at him, hating the bastard. *The bastard.* He raised his eyes to theirs daring them. *Come on, both of you, come on. Any time.* Why didn't they, he asked himself, still stretched in his limbo between floor and the air, oh yes, why not hurl themselves on to him, smash him in turn into the tangle of chairs, mingle his arms and legs with those wooden ones? Yes, *smash him.*

Then the blood seemed to fall away from his brain; he closed his grip, raised himself, dusted jacket, trousers, shirt-front, slowly and fastidiously, went on brushing and nipping pieces of fluff between finger and thumb, for ever it seemed, his head bowed to the task, on and on and on . . .

Maggie entered, perturbed, anxious, fluttering her poor wash-wrinkled hands.

—No trouble now. Not in this house. Please, no trouble, young lads.

Mack stirred himself, went to her, hands on her shoulders.

—Everything's under control. As right as rain. We're just about to leave. This very minute. One last wee favour, Maggie. Two dozen beer in a bag. Okay?

She left to get their carry-out and the three of them drained glasses without looking at one another. The lager, still gassy, stung his throat, made him choke. He heard Mack laugh; he smiled himself, grateful, his head still averted, then the beers arrived in a thick brown paper-bag, folded over at the top for a grip . . .

Outside, the darkness of the night surprised him. Their bodies chilled rapidly, sweat drying. It would be cold, free-wheeling down all that way, even with their coats pulled across and up to their necks.

Mack hoisted the bag into the front carrier of his bike – it was one belonging to the village post-office which he'd 'borrowed' – then they swung legs up and over and they were off under the stars, hay-smells coming at them in waves. The whole countryside, it seemed, was under cut grass.

Mack sang out—All together now, boys . . . and abreast, wheels racing, wind in the face:

—*Me and my shadow, Walkin' 'long the Aven-oo, Me and my shadow, All alone and feelin' blue* . . .

The fire hadn't been lit all day.

On rising early, he had carefully built it, layer by layer, a regular habit, hard twists from the local newspaper, kindling, coal, a sprinkle of paraffin to soak in and stain; at first it wet the coals to black brilliants. It was one of the delights of his day, a comfort awaiting him, the flames springing up from the grate at his touch when the light started to go. But he had been pacing like a caged thing since well after dusk unable to put a match to it.

His indecision and restlessness were new to him. He felt as though some rare malady had struck him, a rage in the veins without precedent. Occasionally he would even clap hand to brow, holding it there, to test his temperature. His tongue, when he could still see a reflection, had seemed no paler than usual. He listened to his heart, felt for it beneath his clothing. Why was it that all pulse seemed to disappear the moment one touched the skin, the spread fingers searching blindly? It was as though the organ, listened for, felt the creeping hand and perversely stilled its speed.

How ridiculous to be in such a turmoil, he told himself, as he walked about, then sat down, walked again. Only women in their middle years were supposed to have 'the hot flushes'.

It was a term picked up from his niece. She cooked for him and mended his clothes with sullen application. Her house was a quarter of a mile away; he had his meals there, silent affairs fraught with resentment. Alex, the husband, munched strongly with head lowered, a man whose sole aim in life was to labour without giving offence, a harnessed being who would drop one day where he stood without cry or protest. *A well-doing man, harmless soul* – people would say of him, and then think no more about the matter. Martha would survive him of course. A heartless word *survive*, *outlive*, even more so, possibly more

92

appropriate, his niece being the sort of woman she was. He anticipated her mood the following day when he turned up, having missed his supper this evening. Martyrdom slightly lining her brow, sighing reproaches as the dishes would be laid down with more vehemence than usual, before the two men.

Once – a long time ago – he had tried to make his break for independence. Self-sufficiency, he argued, was perfectly reasonable in his own case. He ticked off a catalogue for her of his surviving (the word again!) faculties. She sat, or rather now that he remembered it, she was on her feet baking, always baking, like all her kind, the only form of eloquence known to them. It was probably her bannocks that snared poor Alex in the first place. He did feel a little peckish after all . . . But what was it she said – what was it? Something irrefutable – about a man and his 'needs'. As if she would know anything about that.

He thought of the two of them lying in their bed right now. They retired early, a great saver of the lamp-oil, so it was; any lust in that lanky, work-wracked body by her side snuffed all those nights over the long years as surely as finger and thumb turned out their single household Aladdin. But he must light his own lamp. It might help to slow down at least this frenzy in his thinking, this darting of ideas. Minnows.

He found the lamp in the scullery, shook it to see if it needed oil – it seemed half full – then put a match to the wick and slipped on the globe. The lamp felt chill to the touch, slightly steamed. Carrying it before him, he moved into the main room, noting how the dark corners flew to meet the light, then sank into gloom again as he finally decided on the placing of it. Beside the battery wireless-set on the dresser. Should he light the fire after all? The room needed the comfort of red flames; the lamp's bilious glare was a heartless thing. It made the place look like a shed – *cold nights with the Tilley on a nail waiting for the cow to calve, the best milker's eye rolling as big as a saucer up to the light, weary vigil* . . .

Now where did that come from? The farm. His father's. Shed, yes, shed. Word association. The mind was like a deep pool; memories humped beneath the surface, waiting to be tickled to the top. Or gaffed. His days and nights spent angling obsessively. *The Compleat* – Izaak Walton was there in the corner beside – squinting at the spines – Jefferies' *The Story Of My Heart*. He was a cataloguist as well. Yes, he could say he was a neat, tidy sort of a Christian. No descent into disorder for him. Breakfast things – one bowl, one spoon, one mug, one tea-spoon, one knife – washed and dried after use, then racked; bed made; room aired; chamber-pot emptied, ashes raked, fire built, and at the back where no one could see the rug flapped. It cracked like a whip, roosting birds, magpies mostly – always the first to be abroad he'd noticed – scattering at the sound. *One for sorrow, two for joy, three for a—*

A man and his needs. His were simple, spare; they seemed to dwindle as one aged. Reduced at last to filling the belly and emptying bladder and bowels. God spare him that. There were tales of old people being found like animals in a stall. First thing to be done was wash them (curious the priority) scrub them down, ignore their cries as the layers came off. Not easy to acquire that patina, year after year of wood smoke, dried soap scum, tobacco juice – tears too. And the final result – a being fit to meet his Maker, clean and Protestant looking.

He thought of Martha his niece. Why couldn't she have been young and pretty and a bit feckless as nieces should be instead of – Ludicrous to have a middle-aged woman, heavy on her feet, a moustache too, for a niece. Her hands would show no mercy if his time ever came, scrubbing his limbs, nether parts too. Only doing her Christian duty, while he fought feebly, second and final humiliating childhood on him at last. It was hard to be an aged hell-raiser.

Now a great melancholy oppressed him, a nameless weight. Taking the lamp in his hand, he moved about the room in a haphazard fashion, for want of something to occupy himself. The light from the globe, a wavering circle traced on the low wooden ceiling, kept pace with him. There was a slight smell of paraffin from his hand, the right one holding the lamp. The weight seemed to press heavier.

There was a man who lived by himself further along the road, Davy Cowan, half his age, but a desperate case already. One passed by and he would be groaning to himself inside the darkness of his cottage, or his face would swim out of the gloom above his half-door, eyes fastened on one. He tried to avoid walking that way if he could help it. Wrestling with devils or one particular one, more like it. One's very own personal incubus. That was a fearful activity. No rest, there. For the wicked . . .

He himself hadn't been to the church for almost a half-year. A gradual, and it ought to be admitted, cowardly withdrawal from attendance at the Meeting House on the hill ever since his retirement. Cowardly in that he hadn't made the break sudden, irrevocable; no, an occasional Sunday appearance, token gesture to that fierce congregation with their drilling eyes. *Ardens Sed Virens*. The Bush that burned – symbol stamped, carved and embroidered throughout that place. It met one's eyes at every turn, even hanging on a velvet, tasselled square like a red tongue out of the pulpit bible, unquenched like the people in the pews. Oh a scorching race, a torch to the back-slider in their midst. Thank God, at least he had been spared any chiding visits from the minister or even a delegation of elders, as he would have been if he weren't the Master. His learning still protected, it seemed; a leeway offered to eccentricity, culled from book-knowledge.

Sunday mornings he spent in his bed listening to the traffic of the faithful on their way up the road to the church among the trees. No bell warned the countryside (it was a fiercely nonconformist congregation) and he endured those feet and wheels and horses outside his window until he knew it was noon by the silence, and then a wind-blown fragment of the first sung psalm or paraphrase came drifting down to him. At that point he would leap from his bed, dress hurriedly and engage in his morning routine, as though the worshippers on the hill might at any moment cut short their praise and descend on him to bring a judgment on his lapses. An image of them surrounding his house, spreading out into the fields, up into the very trees, to bell him, hymnal exhortations falling like rain, continued to disturb him – an idiocy.

But why that particular image, recurring as it did? In his researches into the oldest of the church records there had been elements, vague references, maddening because the writer had his own idea of what should be reported in detail and what shouldn't, which echoed in some curious way his very own experience. Presbytery reports, confrontation between vestry and local fornicators, men who ploughed on the Sabbath, drunkards, loose-livers, blasphemers, once a suspected warlock

95

and his witch-wife – they had been commonplace. Did the past then hold the key to the present? Were these hazy dreams, shifting shapes inside his head, the fumes from a pit choked with forgotten names and actions and their motives? Had one only to wait until the cycle started up again? He thought of his journal, notes towards an understanding of what was and is, never will be – no, enough there to be going on with – but just notes, nothing more, jottings, scraps; and he would probably never get around to reading all he had written in those five books over there on the second shelf anyway.

Leaning across he took out the clutch of blue-black notebooks, held them between extended forefinger and thumb. What a narrow compass really for so much effort. How his handwriting had changed. Pages fell open, he riffled through them; the ink in the early entries seemed to be rusting already. Those loops and serifs – he had been teaching then, his copperplate still a model, but lately . . . Did his hand now betray a gathering unsureness, a raggedness of purpose? His runes there between stiff dark covers. Universal secrets laid down with an old narrow nib – Conway Stewart his pen, gold clip, mottled barrel blue as a wren's egg.

At that moment he heard something, no more than a faint movement in the distance; nothing really probably, because every sound seemed to carry at night in these quiet parts. He would lie awake listening to sheep in the fields, owls and other night predators, even the diminished but still audible upset outside the distant village public house at closing-time. Almost every sound carried in the dark nights, but this . . .

Without further speculation, he snuffed out the lamp, one blow on his cupped palm atop the globe, then listened. His heart thumped. No need now to search for its pulse.

The footsteps came closer – recognizably footsteps now – and he waited for them to pass by outside, heavy, plodding, a man's – some farm-worker returning home late – the studs of his boots ringing occasionally on the metalled road. In the darkness he leaned towards the door, listening. The sound ceased opposite the front gate, silence, then he heard the catch being lifted and the man, whoever he was, began crunching over the gravel, heading for the front door. He shivered in panic – *was the bar across, key turned in the lock?* Who could it be?

He hung there and the feet came nearer, and now a worse dread entered into him, because this intruder had not stopped before the door but was instead moving around the side of the house, circumventing it stealthily. He had heard of robberies, solitary violent acts. The local paper reported them regularly in detail and almost invariably the victims were old people living alone, like him. Had some sullen brute singled him out for his one outrage, unthinking and motiveless, for surely no one could imagine that he had a hoard? Ridiculous though it was, the psychology of the man and his act engaged him as he quaked there. Precious seconds flew yet here he was tracing out in his mind possible resentments, inadequacies – perhaps a disfigure-ment or speech defect, humiliation by some woman, or women, one of his old pupils even – it was impossible at times not to bait the unfortunate . . .

A light suddenly shone on the window-glass outside. Could it be a burglar? Surely no burglar, however amateurish, would carry a lamp – a lamp, mark you, not a torch. He suspected a hurricane, held at head level. Its rays pierced the gap in the curtains, and he shrank away into another corner of the room. The edge of the dresser caught him in the small of the back – curious phrase – my God, at a time like this he could still . . .

A hand touched the glass; he gasped; scratching began. Odder still, this was the sound someone made to attract another's attention, surreptitious, like a tossed handful of gravel on an upper pane. Then distinctly a voice, a carrying whisper. His name.

—Barbour!

It came again. *Good God, it was Alex!*

—Barbour, can you hear me? It's me.

What did the fool want? At this hour. He couldn't move, he knew he should, but couldn't.

—Are you still up? Barbour!

Stay where you are, he told himself. *Doggo. He'll go away. Have to. Let him talk himself into an understanding.*

—Are you in bed?

Ah, there it was. A long silence now. He could almost hear the mind at work out there, ponderously.

—Barbour!

And more tapping, a sound that went through him, couldn't

be withstood much longer. He felt he might in a moment shriek out, go bursting into the air outside, his clothes were stifling, clinging to him in moist layers.

—Barbour!

Weakening perhaps? Did he detect that?

The light moved suddenly from the glass; he was in total darkness again, an easier feeling. His pulse slowed until he realized that Alex was going to try the back door at any moment. And there it was, a tentative lift at the latch, up, then down, up, then faster, staccato now, drilling at the nerves. My God, was there to be no peace for a man, was he to be badgered without mercy into the very grave by Samaritans?

He felt murderous; the thought of discharging a gun, if he had one, into that shaking door and into his tormentor was suddenly very sweet, both barrels peppering the wood to shreds, and then through to the fool on the other side. What judge wouldn't acquit him? A fellow-feeling perhaps. Men of their age had a right to privacy, sanctuary, the repelling of boarders.

—Are you in bed, Barbour?

Faint, dying, for some odd reason.

And then miraculously he heard him withdraw, moving back the way he had come. A light passed the window, disappeared, the latch of the gate clicked once and the heavy boots moved off down the road. Reprieved. He sank into a chair, wiping his brow, siege over. Thought – reflective, more evenly paced – filtered back. Poor Alex, yes, poor Alex, once more – for how would he ever be able to appease his Martha, convince her that he had carried out orders with more than ordinary zeal? The catechism, endless, endless . . . *But did you do this, did you say that, was there, wasn't there . . .?* ending up with, *oh I knew I should have done the job myself . . . I might have known . . .* Married to a man-child, hopeless and helpless.

Did he ever have dreams of revenge, he wondered, he – Alex, felling and slitting, suspending the reality of his trade – he butchered pigs for the neighbourhood – that screaming snout changed in the moment he swung his sledge to her scalp, parting in her hair drawn geometrically as though with the very edge of his own blade . . .? What a depth of violence he had stirring in him this evening. Blood and maiming. A

98

red cloud coming over his mind, a lust to run amok, to punish, avenge . . .

He was pacing up and down again, still in the dark, a short passage between the furniture imprinted on his memory; he could find it, pace it out, wheel and turn with his eyes shut, doubling the darkness. His foot caught a chair leg and he staggered, only just saving himself from a fall. Pride. Did the body's equilibrium then become disturbed when one covered the eyes? He had heard that the sense of taste was affected as well, drinkers being humiliatingly confused, a favourite bar-room trick. Had blind men also then to adjust their gait, unconsciously correcting that veer? So if a man suddenly, miraculously recovered his sight he would go tottering, the earth seeming to slant away beneath him, a possibly far worse sensation . . .

He was thinking too much, too fast again. The lamp was close at hand. Careful not to burn himself on the still hot globe, using his handkerchief, he lit it for the second time that night. The flame rose gently to a careful height – it wouldn't do to betray his presence just yet – and the room came to life again, furniture humping in corners, gleams on veneer, brass handles, the silvering of mirrors. This way and that he swung the lamp softly, his gaze fastening on each piece as the rays struck it, then glanced off. There, the sideboard, fretted overmantel, door handles shaped like hanging acorns; a bookcase that revolved; a chesterfield sofa upholstered to an amazing tautness like a sleek brown seal – it withstood the body with almost wilful energy – two chairs in matching leatherette; the table with folding leaves to seat ten; the standing bookcase with the glass front – double-doored; sundry pieces – coal scuttle, fire brasses, the American clock on the wall, pictures of Kerry and Hebridean scenery (little difference really), a foot-stool, brown dying plants in pots (three on a table under the window), a family Bible with its limp, protruding marker. Pot-pourri . . .

They all seemed drained of any life or personality they might once have had, enfeebled. Their sadness pierced him, self-pity prickling his eyes. He wept a little standing there with the lamp still held high. When he'd gone, all this furniture would be strewn around some auction room, people prodding and testing, upending, scanning for worm-holes – as if he'd ever noticed – and then scattered into different homes, parlours and rooms, attics, hallways. The life cycle of household effects, much greater than any human span.

Good God, Barbour Brown, he admonished himself, *you sound just like the Reverend Mahood and one of his sermons, metaphors racked to breaking point.*

—Brethren, have you ever considered the message – God's Divine Message – contained in even the humblest of objects, the most ordinary of domestic chattels . . .

He mouthed for a little while, lamp left down on the sideboard, miming that pulpit manner, hands on lapels, lower lip protruded, occasionally plucking an ear-lobe, walking, pointing up to the gallery. Fourth-rate theatricals. The performance pleased him, tickled was a better word, quite restored in fact to the earlier balance of spirit. There was great balm in ridicule; wonderfully healing. Took the sting out of things, relieved pressures, lanced the boil, the bile. Hadn't he seen people transformed by a single dry thrust from a wit in a corner at a social or a church meeting, changed in an instant from a roomful of blocks to a mischievous, rippling gathering, eyes alight. Oh the greatest recreation in the word surely, hunting the scapegoat. A national sport no less, practised by all ages; local champions lovingly nurtured, their best barbs cherished in the folk-memory. *But do you mind the time so-and-so said this, and then your man said, and then he said, and then, and then* . . . What an infinite capacity for rancour, the people of this Valley had, *his* Valley, yes, his Valley, and his people too, for no matter how apart he would try to hoist himself, surveyor through the hole in the hedge that he was, with his glasses and his notebooks, he had the same nose for weakness, those same appetites. Hadn't he managed to protect himself all of his years in the schoolroom with his wit, surrounded by the ready laughers? There were times he believed that satire was the only idiom they understood, those sons and daughters of the soil, sitting there in rows grinning while one of their number stood out with hanging head. Teaching had nurtured his talent for derision.

It had always been there of course . . . He remembered early days; soirées, picnics, the Sunday School excursions to Portrush or Castlerock, sprawled in the dunes, while the surf murmured and each naughty observation leisurely followed the next. *Oh, Barbour Brown, I'm sore with laughing. If you don't give over I'm sure I'll be sick.* The ladies. In a clump on their own plaid travelling rug at a little distance, but within ear-shot. Busying themselves with the contents of the wicker baskets. Minnie. Saving him the choicest morsels, the last chicken leg wrapped in a napkin. Minnie, yes, Minnie, for he couldn't put her out of mind much longer, not for much longer. Out of sight, out of –? No, not after today ... Still, he permitted himself a last little fling of nostalgia, a bon-bon of memory before facing up to thoughts of her – now.

A photograph swam up, a group taken at the seaside, all those summers ago, the men dark-faced, with folded arms staring arrogantly into the lens, the women at their feet with spread skirts as though growing there out of the sand like some curious species with human heads – female, sun-hats and parasols. Himself. He had his moustache then. Gave him a slightly raffish look, 'a proper caution'. The photograph was upstairs somewhere, in a box with all the other snapshots, memorabilia, but he couldn't be bothered, too much trouble to go raking among them and it would mean getting up stiff from the floor hours later after losing himself in all those albums of sepia relics. But his friends, in the photographs, he remembered ... Teddy Topping, played cricket for Ireland, a careless, easy athlete, always a grin; Harold Duff, a banjoist; fat young Charlie Laird in love with Hazel McFadden – what prodigies of weight-reducing he endured for his beloved, exercising in shorts and a zephyr at dawn (she married a dentist from Larne); 'Dusty' Miller killed on the Somme; Sam Gribben, too.

The Somme. So many of his friends' names in the Deaths column of *The Ballymena Observer*. Three pages of obituaries, and nearly every house full of women in black dresses for months. He had a faulty ticker, or so the doctors told him at the time. It saved him from the worst horrors, namely the maiming, blinding or choking to death in the Belgian mud-holes. He had only read about it, of course, they didn't talk about it much when they came home, that shell-shocked generation, fit for nothing but Outdoor Relief, as it was called. A nice irony in those words somehow ...

But those earlier times, days and nights of banter and singing and gramophone parties, good times slipping easily past before the War came and changed it all. Men together, yes, he missed that . . . In his arm-chair he put his head back, remembering . . .

The house was very still, almost as though it were watching him, holding its breath. It enclosed him and his thoughts, but lightly now. He felt it all around him. It withdrew at times, at others contracted – almost valvular.

Through the walls he heard a sound, somewhere in the distance, then approaching quite fast, voices raised in song, young people on bicycles racing downhill past the house. Now they had passed; he heard the wheels whirr, their singing, loud and careless, some popular thing, one of the boys (how many of them were there?) worked his bell rhythmically. Into the distance. Young voices dying. He felt sad again. He wondered where they were going, what schemes they had laid, waiting for them, that marvellous flush of blood, youth . . .

The fire was still unlit. There it sat – how could a fire be *unlit*? More riddles. That was all he did these days and nights, riddling, turning thoughts over and over, inside and out. His mind worked like a rabbit chewing on leaves of cabbage. A ruminant? Or was that only . . .? *Stop it, Barbour Brown, or your brain will come to pieces like the insides of a demented watch* . . .

He had a bottle of whiskey somewhere – or a half – purchased a long time ago and dipped into occasionally for a punch when he had a cold or a thimbleful held in the side of his mouth when toothache struck. Getting drunk, or something milder, suddenly seemed irresistibly attractive. He moved from his chair purposefully before the scheme had time to disintegrate, opening the door of the sideboard, the carved acorn felt cool to the touch, a satisfying teat, and laid hands on the bottle of Bushmills at the back. Without hesitating, he uncorked it and raised it to his lips. For the merest second he held the liquor in his mouth, an ample slug, still time to spray it out and so pull back from his course whatever it was, but then he swallowed, the whiskey slid down, he staggered a bit from the effect, his route was set. Another drink, easier this time, then another not so great, a trickle of warmth thin and spicy; he

marvelled at his capacity for the stuff. Certainly revelatory . . .
Minnie . . .

He made himself comfortable, bottle within reach on one of
his ridiculous little tables that nested together. Its top seemed
paper-thin, hardly wood at all. Still, the square bottle, uncorked, sat there secure, amber in the lamplight. He took
another swallow. Minnie . . . Her face, poor sad face, was
rising in his thoughts as though out of water, down deep but
rising . . . Minnie . . . Another sip. He had judged her harshly
for her indulgence. Her *vice*, he had considered it, the very
thing he was doing now himself. Minnie. Poor, careworn
Minnie. How could he have been so superior, sitting there
with a ramrod for a spine – his bones now melted agreeably –
how could he? Minnie. Unfeeling, he had been to her, yes,
that, despite his pride in being a sensitive man all these years,
aware, attuned. But only to himself, oh only to his own merest
shiver of mood, never to hers, no, only to himself. Selfish,
inward-looking. A misanthrope. A schoolroom word. Kept
recurring in Meanings. Year after year perfecting the state;
constructing this shell for himself, from the inside out – like an
igloo – yes, yes, the image took hold, yes, – ice-block after ice-
block fitting, then slowly coalescing until only a last aperture
remained to be filled.

He drank.

Was there still time to clamber up into the air and out?
The whiskey warmed and wormed its way down and then – it
too – up and out like a slowly bursting flower. He laughed
aloud at the extravagance of his thoughts, but seriously, seriously
now – was it too late? Talking now to this other stranger
who shared him. *Is it too late, damn you?* A burst of anger directed
at –! *Come out, wherever you are.* He shook the bottle at a shadowy
corner of the room. *Coo-ee!* No, enough of that, enough . . .

He rose carefully, chastened, feeling a little foolish as well,
but with a decision, yes, he would do it. No turning back, not
this time. The idea spread through him. Borne in the blood?
Sped by the spirits? The lamp flared just once as he grasped it,
then it straightened up, firm, aloft in his new grip. Was it too
late?

He was moving to go upstairs, to the wardrobe where his
pale suit with the pearl buttons hung against the inner wall.

Too late? Time, on two levels, years as well as the daily movement on the clock's face, informed the question. But the suit, yes, the suit! Symbolic. Her face, when she saw it again. White knight on his charger. When he had dressed he would get out the old bicycle. Only last week he had noted that it was still roadworthy ...

The band was playing a quickstep when she arrived at the Hall. She and Teresa Mullan. They could hear it coming out of the open windows. All the way up the street it had met them, getting louder and louder, *Cherokee*, old as the hills like the band, but it promised excitement, quicksteps always did somehow, and she imagined the Hall crammed and everyone dancing at a great rate. Teresa giggled with her and she gave her arm a quick squeeze as they ran up the steps together.

—Is there a big crowd, Bertie? she asked old man McCrory, a shade breathlessly.

He sat just inside the doorway; in front of him on a card-table the biscuit tin for the money and a big roll of pink tickets. He tore off two, saying—A brave few. But anyway, sure it won't be long in filling up, and in her haste to get in through that inner closed door to where the music thumped and couples spun she hardly took notice of what he said.

She might have known of course he would delude her with his double-talk, for when she and Teresa had pushed past and in, good money paid over and retreat cut off behind them, the Hall yawned, not a sinner on the bumpy glistening floor, just a few lost souls sitting in each corner and all staring at them in their finery. She clutched Teresa and they moved crabwise until the edge of a form brushed the back of her silk stockings. Why did people gape at you so? But then there was little refinement among this pitiful crew, she told herself, middle-aged, courting couples for the most part, down from the hills, by the look of them. And what made it worse of course was that this lot never got up to dance, were never known to, they just came for the supper and the chance to gawk, passing remarks to one another about the dancers behind their hands.

But now that she felt more composed in herself, she stared back; it was difficult to pick a target, because so many eyes from so many quarters were fastened on them, but she gave a fat woman, younger than the rest, red dress, and frizzed hair, as good as she got. She tried to be hurtful in her appraisal, gazing fixedly at the woman's perm, then at her frock with the cardigan draped over her bare shoulders in what she imagined was the height of sophistication, then down at the stockings, thick and a bilious tan, and last and worst of all the shoes – maroon patent with crossed straps.

She pretended to laugh then to Teresa, her hand cupping her mouth, gay and ladylike. *Oh, poor thing, such a get-up!* But Teresa looked at her as if she were crazy and edged along the bench. She could have strangled her. But then of course she might have known that Teresa would behave in that way. The place made her nervous, being what she was. Not that anyone would pass any remarks here, the Mullans being the only Catholic family for miles around, but there was always that wee uneasiness at finding herself inside the Orange Hall. Most of the time it seemed to her to be quite needless, some-thing out of the dark ages, an old feeling running deep which she couldn't share or comprehend even, but there were other times when she forced herself to understand, especially when people around her, her 'own sort', talked about Catholics in that way they did. Her father, for instance . . .

She felt a sudden rush of loyalty for Teresa, her very best friend, sitting there beside her with her knees together, two hands clasped as if she were in church. Poor dote, maybe she did think, God help her wit, that there was something sacred about this place after all, you never could tell. How good she was, how clean and neat – not a bit like Catholics were supposed to be, always smelling fresh. Mrs Mullan kept them all well turned out, one couldn't deny it, even though there were seven of them. Made all their own clothes too, every stitch, down to their very vests. The Mullan children hated those because they were made out of flour-bags, oh, washed and ironed of course, and beautifully finished off on Mrs Mullan's treadle Singer, but one of them still had the blackbird on it, faint but recognizable; the brand was Early-Riser. They all had to wear it but the girls would cry bitterly whenever it came round to their turn. Teresa of course was the eldest – her own age – so perhaps she hadn't to any longer. Should she mention it, just to give them

106

both a good giggle, anything to take their minds off this dreary place and these people? On second thoughts, no, she might be offended. She knew herself the shame of hand-me-downs. Some day she and Teresa Mullan would tell them all what to do with their cast-offs.

In one of her favourite day-dreams now she made room for her dear friend, for instead of just she alone riding in furs and luxury in the back of the big car she saw the two of them lying back and having the great laugh together. *Drive a little slower, Ponsonby, I wish to take a look at my old home. Teresa, darling, how did we ever put up with it as long as we did? How on earth did we?* And she would advise her on what to wear, clothes and jewellery, perfume as well – she would be able to speak French by then – and tell her how to do her hair. Teresa would need all the advice she could get. Poor Teresa, it was awful to be as poor as she was and the eldest of a big family . . .

Just then, miracle of miracles, Frizzie Lizzie in the red frock rose to dance with her partner. They were the only couple on the floor and the man held her with his big hands, the two of them standing there, with that look of painful concentration on his face, waiting until he got on to the beat. It was an Olde-Tyme waltz; once settled into the rhythm, you revolved until you stopped from dizziness, round and round, spinning, held out, almost floating off the floor. It looked beautiful in the pictures, Cornel Wilde and Ann Blyth at the Palace Ball, but it never ever lived up to expectation. She usually refused, if someone asked her. Fright took hold because of the way the men became excited, the heat of their bodies, their eyes and faces, as they spun faster and faster, laughing at her cries.

The couple danced awkwardly, not looking at one another, around the edges of the floor. The man had a white carnation in his buttonhole. She supposed they had been to a wedding earlier in the day. The band played – a medley of three tunes – and not once did the woman in red nor the man holding her exchange a word or a smile. Each time they passed them sitting on their form against the back wall, they presented their faces in turn as they went past like two dead things.

A weight seemed to press on her. She couldn't even enjoy ridiculing them any longer. If she could only learn not to build things up so; far more sensible to anticipate the run of things, accept all that a dance in a place like this entailed – but that wasn't true – she was arguing with herself in her head as the music beat on for the engaged couple – not true at all, because she remembered times, indeed she did, when she could hardly wait for each dance to finish and the next begin, and in the same instant yearn for time to run slow almost to stopping-point. Nights when the band took on a lease of life, laughing among themselves at people rushing to dance, the men pushed out in a big lump at the door, eyeing every girl in the place, a hundred looks a minute, hungry for a whirl, a touch, anything, burning, half-mad.

—Sssst . . .

Teresa was whispering to her; she had something to say, something too good to keep to herself, despite her nervousness.

—The Well-Dressed Man. He's been seen again. Isn't it awful? Oh, Hetty, what would you do if he jumped out on you in one of them dark places?

—Well-Dressed Man indeed! He'd get the right dressing-down from me, I can tell you.

She put on a fierce face and voice for the other's benefit, but of course couldn't keep it up, had to giggle out loud at the poor dope and her expression.

Poor Teresa, she'd believe anything. Tell her any old string of rubbish about some ghost or banshee or other and she would sit by the fire quaking all night, afraid to budge, her eyes staring in her head. Catholics of course were well-known to be a super-stitious crowd, always crossing themselves and muttering to a lot of statues. Mrs Mullan would even turn the holy pictures to the wall if she heard bad language on the street.

The dance ended and the couple returned to their place along the wall. Then there was a lull as the band lit up cig-arettes and talked among themselves. She wondered what time it was; she hadn't a watch, neither had Teresa.

—But, Hetty, would you really stand up to him? Would you?

She felt the plucking at her frock, the soft press of the other's arm on hers. Poor dote. Eyes big as plates and those freckles she was always trying to scrub off, and the party dress her mother had made her out of a length of blue and white curtain material that the doctor's wife didn't want.

—Now, listen to me and pay heed, just in case it ever happens to you, because it might, you never know – (she couldn't resist it, although it wasn't right) – All you have to do is stand your ground and defy them to do their worst. Because you know they're as scared as you are, maybe more so. Just stand there and look them straight in the eye and then say – she whispered it, giggling – Come one step further and I'll prune your Willy John for you with this knife I've got here.

Teresa's mouth opened and closed; her face went pale, then red, pale again. Oh so innocent, such a child. She had tried at times, to tell her a few things but always gave it up as a bad job. The shock would have been too much anyhow, for despite her head being stuffed with 'mortal sins', as she called them, she wouldn't know one if it came up and sat down next to her.

Inside her own handbag was the little notebook that Minnie Maitland had once given her when she had thought – they had both thought – she was leaving to go to the city to find a new life. Minnie had been full of embarrassment pressing it into her hand at the last minute, and although it had all been a false alarm, something of a joke as well, neither of them had referred to it again. It contained advice in Minnie's funny crabbed handwriting on how a young girl should take care of herself, about her periods and suchlike, and how she should never let any man 'fondle her in the wrong places'. If he did that he didn't love you, so Minnie said, or wrote, rather. She could never imagine Minnie saying any of those things, never. And it was funny, because reading the words – just like the writing in a school copybook – the shock was somehow greater, it seemed to dart into you more; she could remember it still, the feeling as she sat on the ditch that day on her way home. She couldn't help herself, she had to finish every word, perched there at the side of the road in a quiet private place. And then getting up with her eyes blinding, and her limbs stiff and damp, excited in a funny way, unsatisfied, as if she wanted to go on turning the pages on and on and on . . .

She felt affected now in that same way, here in the Hall, as the band played another number, lost to all around her, feeling, remembering . . .

Her legs quivered a little, a quick tremble underneath her smoothed-down frock. She touched her thighs just once. It

stopped. The field earlier, the heat, smell and itch of the hay
... All day she had repressed it; it went down like something
under water, but she knew it would rise again – it did now.
She felt sickish, stomach sliding, remembering the three
touching her in 'the wrong places'. How little Minnie knew.
She shut her eyes and ears like those three brass monkeys on
her mantelpiece. Oh yes, it was all right for the likes of her going
her own sheltered ways and writing down advice on how to
behave oneself with 'the male sex'. No one had ever pulled
her down in broad daylight with their rough hands tearing
and tearing and fingers poking. She pressed her thighs tighter
together as though to squeeze out the memory. What would it
be like, she wondered, cutting it? Would it slice off clean, or
would you have to saw at it like an old root?

—Ladies and Gentlemen, the next dance will be a Ladies'
Choice.

The drummer was winking at the others in the band as much
as to say, 'Some hope', then he rattled his sticks and they
started to play *Oh, Lady, Be Good*. There was the leader, who was
blind, on the piano-keyed accordion; a fat, bald bus-conductor
called Eddie Smith playing the fiddle – he sometimes sang; a
saxophone player she hadn't seen before, and of course the
drummer. A lot of girls thought he was the last word, clean-cut
with dark, curly hair, a sort of John Garfield type, and he
fancied himself no end. Some girls were easily pleased.

> *I'm just a Babe who's lost in a wood,*
> *Oh, lady, be good*
> *To me.*

Her feet jigged under the bench as the music swept on to an
empty hall. Oh, how she loved dancing. The rhythm gave her
goose flesh. It came and went on her skin and was delicious.
Would Teresa ever dance with her, she wondered; it seemed a
sin to sit this one out; she would lead and Teresa follow, but
oh, what was the use, she knew what the answer would be.
She seemed destined to be stuck with other people and their
backward ways. They caged her in, indeed they did, not only
the people but the place, this old Hall with its Lodge banners
on the walls and dusty red, white and blue streamers looping
and crossing above her head and outside the village and beyond

that, the Valley itself, hills on either horizon. All these things tightened around her, tight wee place, tight wee people, tight, tight, *tight* . . .

Teresa was looking at her oddly again; she must have been saying it out loud. They all thought she was a bit mental anyway. They did. Wild, headstrong. She knew the words, knew what they thought of her – old Harper the teacher, women in the village, the Minister that time he rebuked her for laughing in church – her father, yes, him – wouldn't he have the pink fit if he knew she was wearing make-up and this dress?

Paint and powder, powder and paint. You're on the right road. A huer. Nothing surer. On the right road.

She must make certain to get back before he came home from Ballyclare. He always went on Saturday nights, riding there and back on his bicycle, a regular thing, winter and summer. Weather never deterred him. What would? She supposed he must look forward to his few bottles of stout, but she couldn't imagine him there in the company of other men, drinking and talking, laughing. Never. Couldn't imagine him doing anything like anyone else. Even . . .

That time she had burst in on him in the privy with his trousers down around his ankles. Luckily he was sitting sunk deep in the seat, covered that part of him. It still gave her a funny feeling. Shivers. His legs were so white and thin, like bleached sticks. Were all men's the same? Horrible, pale and unhealthy looking. How could you love any man if his legs were like that? Beside yours in bed on the honeymoon. She couldn't understand why her brain should be so active tonight. Such strange thoughts. It was a funny thing really, all these people in this place, all with different secret ideas racing through their heads and no one to know but themselves.

—Knock, knock . . .

Teresa looked at her as if this time she had really gone mental.

She repeated it – a sudden whim, no rhyme or reason to it, just something that came to her lips, and daft, here with the band playing and the people around the walls with their straight faces.

—Who's there?

No laughing, just an agonized face. God wasn't Teresa Mullan a right drip! – Yvonne.

—Yvonne who?

—Yvonne your knickers, your da's coming.

Why did she say these things? *Why?* As soon as they came out they turned to ashes in her mouth. A foul taste.

She laughed, she had to do something. Those big, stupid cow-eyes. What a drip, what a drip. She wanted to nip her until she screamed. *What's 'pin' spelt backwards?* She must watch herself. The urge was almost more than she could control.

The band finished the number. They looked weary now. She supposed even they lost heart playing to an empty floor, taking it personally, no one to appreciate their music, rattle, bang and scrape though it was. Now they would start having longer breaks, deserting the stage with their instruments sitting about on the chairs for up to ten minutes at a time making the place seem even more forsaken than it was. On the face of the big drum was lettered in red, *The Merry Macks*. She should have paid more attention to the posters, *Music By The Merry Macks*, along the bottom in small print a warning of what to expect.

The band went out through a door at the side of the stage. She knew it led to a kitchen where the women were preparing the supper, laying out egg and ham sandwiches and pastries on bakers' trays, and boiling up the big brown pots of tea that scalded the roof of your mouth if you weren't careful. She didn't feel a bit hungry though, just resentful that still another part of the short night was to be further wasted on eating and drinking.

But then at that precise moment – her lowest point – a diversion, *the* diversion occurred. The door opened with some force and into the Hall came four young strangers. Laughing, all chewing gum, and unmistakably townies by their clothes, gaberdine suits and suede shoes with those thick crêpe soles – their faces fell the instant they saw the bare floor, the band-stand and what passed for a crowd sitting around the walls dumbly watching them. They hung there for a moment and she could almost read their thoughts.

She tried not to stare as brutally as everyone else, indeed she glanced off to the side a little trying to be aloof, but her heart thumped as she felt a hot wash of blood on her cheeks and neck. Teresa was gaping like any common fool and how she

112

wished for a more sophisticated friend, particularly at a time like this, because wasn't the tall dark one in the nigger suit and the blue knitted tie the most gorgeous fellow she had ever seen. She wasn't looking; her eyes were settled for want of somewhere to land on a banner high up on one of the side walls. Queen Victoria was pictured handing a bible with a gold key on its bright open pages to a kneeling man. The man was bald; something which made the scene wrong. She couldn't fit a man like that into history somehow. But that was only a sideways leap away from what her attention really craved. Like all the rest of them, despise them as she would, she longed to stare at the four surveying the Hall and the prospects. She sat there with her hands pressed together, knees too, waiting for the dark good-looking one to notice her. She would know all right.

Then the door beside the stage opened and the band came out, still laughing among themselves. They seemed to spend their time laughing when they weren't playing, and even then they were always winking across to one another. She wondered what sort of a joke it was that could be stretched out all night between four grown men that way.

Events from that point on seemed to pick up speed, for no sooner had the band started to play again than three other newcomers arrived, but girls this time. She had seen them before, a trio of cheap specimens from Larne, smoking and laughing and sending their made-up eyes running around the Hall. *Hussies*, she thought, tightening in on herself, back stiff as a poker.

At her side, Teresa stared harder than ever, and she bit her lip with the effort not to leave a mark on her. She felt like going home that instant. Nothing seemed ever to go right, nothing. She just knew now if she stayed, her place would be in this corner all night beside Teresa Mullan, with her mouth open. For the first time she noticed the awful dress she was wearing. Worst of all, when she glanced down at her own, it seemed almost as dowdy. She wanted to tear it off and rip it into pieces, but not here – somewhere quiet and away where she could yell to her heart's content, like out in the fields deep in the country, and roll over and over in the grass, scoring the ground with her nails. It was the second time that day she had felt the urge, unexplained and a bit frightening. Maybe she was going mental, like all the people said she was, after all this time, catching up on her because if you believed something when people kept telling you you were often enough, it would happen.

A voice spoke to her.

—Would you like to dance?

She looked up, still with the mad fancies in her head, and it was *his* face looking down at her, and he had got rid of his chewing-gum and all she could think was that was nice of him.

Then they were dancing, without her even knowing whether she had said yes or not. She had this awful strong desire to close her eyes, make it all the more intense like the way it could be in bed underneath the bed-clothes, when everything was blotted out, and you could only smell, and hear your own blood pumping. It would just be the sound of the music and her hand in his with his right one pressing her gently in the small of her back. His palm felt dry and cool and he wasn't clutching or squeezing or trying to feel you through your thin dress an inch at a time up to the straps of your brassiere or down to the elastic of your knickers. The urge to dance blind was much greater now, to sharpen all of her experience into one hard little lump, something about the size of a boiled sweet. A strange nonsense, but she saw it like that. She would swallow it, have all of it in one go. A brandy-ball. She smiled to herself. The name always sounded indecent. A Minnie-word. And he must have felt her face move for he said quietly—What's the joke?

He wouldn't understand of course – who would? He would only think her a bit touched, like all the rest of them, but then again he might not; he looked different, felt and smelt too – some sort of lotion and a slight hint of drink, but not that awful Guinness smell, like sour milk, and the brown ring around the mouth.

It would be nice to say things straight out for a change – just once – the private things, and have someone listen all through to all of them, even the ones you daren't mention. Instead of which she found herself whispering to mirrors behind locked doors, or calling out in the middle of McGookin's wood, bad filthy things to the trees, shouting down into black holes in the trunks. When she was younger she used to post 'letters' through those same holes, thick wooden lips, rubbed smooth, the bark pulled back like real mouths.

114

—Well? Are you going to keep it all to yourself? What's the joke?

He hadn't that thin sing-song accent that townies had; something a shade better off, you could tell. She said:

—That's for me to know and you to find out, isn't it? And instantly wanted to die on the spot. The cleverness of it, head to one side, and the cheeky Miss Smartie-Pants grin. *What made her come out with it like that? What in God's name?*

And now the damage was done; she could tell that by his silence and the way he was dancing, holding her as if she had turned to a plank of wood. She felt she would trip over her own feet at any moment; the music blared in her ears as they went past the stage, suddenly extra loud, and she was positive that the drummer was winking and pointing them out to the rest of the band. *God*, she prayed, *let me not disgrace myself by falling, and let the dance end quickly, please Lord, I don't ask you for much, you know that, just this one thing . . .*

The first number ended and they stood side by side facing the platform, awkward like two sentries, and not as much as a look or a word between them and the drummer took his time before hitting the cymbals to start the second tune. And then the same grinning jack-ass was doing something smart with his drumsticks, *rat-tat-tat* on the round things that looked like coconuts, and before she knew what was afoot the other few dancers were thinning off the floor and they were left now forced to face one another and he was saying—Can you do the rumba?

Nothing in her life up to then, it seemed to her, had been so terrible as this moment. All eyes on her, thoughts like knives piercing her and how could she either go through with it or walk off the floor? How? All that ran through her head was— *They've got an awful lot of coffee in Brazil,* as the music brayed out reminding her all the more strongly of her humiliation, because it played only for them.

He took her hand then, but she still couldn't bring herself to look him in the face. He said—It's the same as the fox-trot, only slower. We'll help each other through it, and she was sure that she was in love with him already, as he took her and moved her strongly but gently off and into the rhythm.

It was as if they were in a bubble, floating free, in and around each other, all mixed up, legs and arms and cheeks touching.

115

The 'sinful thoughts' that Minnie had warned her about rose in her thick and fast, but she wanted to hold them in her head, enjoying each to the full, sorry to feel it slide away before another took its place. She gave herself to them completely, the way she would give herself to him if he asked her. Right this minute if he asked her, she would leave with him, without a backward glance, or one single regret. *She would, she would, oh indeed she would* . . .

—Will you keep me the next dance?

The music still played, his voice seemed to come from very far away, and she came back to reality, blushing as she remembered what she had been thinking about.

—Oh yes – she said straight out, and she meant it, indeed had to hold back from saying, *every dance, if you like*, for there was still that tiny safeguard at the back of her mind, slipped away in there by Minnie at some time or other like a letter or a note behind a clock.

She held up her head now, looking about her proudly as they swept around the Hall. The tango was a dance she could do well. Its dash had always appealed to her and she was glad she had pestered old 'Cookie' Hughes who fancied himself as a ballroom expert to teach her its steps. *Jealousy, you conquered me, jealousy*, oh what lovely music it was and she had never heard an accordion played so well. Look at their faces, sour as crabs, as they rushed at her, then retreated, as he directed their pace so cleverly and manfully, just stopping short of the wall and all those feet on each run.

It was surprising how many people had come into the Hall by now. A night for them all to remember and talk about. The night Hetty Quinn bloomed before their very eyes. She began to look around her boldly, out and over his shoulder now, judging and observing.

Mr and Mrs 'Pooshie' Patton from Hillhead, never missed a hooley, he more of an old woman than she, panting home from his day's work to tell the latest bit of oily gossip (it was him they called 'Pooshie', not the wife) the Gourley sisters, two peroxide queens who'd never got over the times they'd had with the G.I.'s, only officers were good enough for them in those days (some said they went out with darkies too) but Elmer and Byron and all the others never sent for them to go out to their big ranches, no sir-ee, they were still here in Tardree, with all their glamour and dyed hair. She gave them a pitying look as she sailed past; they'd never get a man now, never. And over there in a corner with all the young girls around him was the ageing village Romeo, Albert Higgins, who worked at the creamery. They said he wrote away to the Lonely Hearts advertisements in the paper. *Well set-up bachelor with own place, wishes to meet refined lady of similar means with a view to companionship and eventual matrimony.* They found out it was him when Sadie Brown replied to his Box No. in *The Belfast Telegraph.* It was hard to keep it to themselves; the letter he wrote back was such a scream. She whispered a bit of it to herself that she'd memorized before Sadie Brown lost her nerve and threw it into the river in pieces so that no one could ever put it together again. *A feeling for the finer things in life, reading, travel and listening to symphony concerts on the wireless* . . .

As she danced past all of them, she felt so superior, privileged, that all her life was before her and anything could happen. It lay in front of her, stretched out, a road that went on and on like the one in the school reader starting off thick and broad and disappearing into a point at the top of the page, curling and dipping with men and animals in fields along the way and farms and castles with enchanted woods and blue smoke rising out of the middle of them . . .

Someone standing near the door called out:

—Hello, Hetty, in a bold, loud voice, and she felt herself go stiff in his arms.

He noticed it because he said—Who's that? The boy friend, is it? and she said—Oh, it's nobody at all, but couldn't get herself to laugh and so make it convincing, and she thought, *oh, my God, I'm being punished for my pride,* because there he was, that creature Mack, grinning along with the other two.

She had her back to them now but knew they were watching and making cracks to one another, drunk too by the cut of them, and what must he be thinking as the tango rushed on to its close? All her schemes and dreams would die with the music, she felt certain of that now, all of them.

He said—Remember. The next dance is mine, but she knew he didn't mean it. What else could he say?

They parted and she went back to her place beside Teresa.

117

Her head was full of heat and noise and Teresa was looking at her as if her face was on fire. It felt like it, but she was past caring. Straight ahead of her she gazed, neither to left nor right, hearing no one, hearing nothing. If she could only stay like that, untouched, unmoved, until she gathered enough strength to get up and go home on her own, and then creep into bed and burrow deep down beneath the blankets. That warm, lined cave seemed the only place left to her now holding out any last hope of comfort.

But Teresa was pulling at her, full of excitement. It was as if it had all been happening to Teresa and not to her.

—Oh, my God! he's coming over again! Hetty. *Hetty.*

She felt the tug moving her back and forth on the seat, but was too tired to resist or be annoyed, be anything other than a sack of potatoes. Who would want to dance with a sack of spuds, she asked herself in a daze, but he did, it seemed, and for the second time she was in his arms sweeping around the floor which someone had just sprinkled with white flakes of wax out of a tin a moment before. She watched it disappear beneath the feet of the dancers. It went like snow off a ditch, because there were many quick-stepping, all anxious to wipe out the memory of the tango. They bumped into her, but it hardly seemed to matter, she just hung her head and watched the feet coming and going down there as if they weren't attached to anything or anybody. An expression kept coming into her head, *the shock proved too much for her,* that Minnie used a lot. If she really did throw a fit here in the middle of Tardree Orange Hall, tearing out her hair by the roots and screeching, wouldn't it serve them all right – *them* being everybody, even her partner, for again she felt bruised and afflicted from all quarters that long weary live-long day.

Suddenly they stopped, or rather he halted for some reason, out on the edge of the floor. Someone was blocking their progress. Mack's hateful smiling face was there, fat moon-face; she saw his two cronies at his shoulder and he was saying in that polite voice that could never take her in for a moment— It's an Excuse-Me, and her partner with his arm holding her around the waist was considering and she knew so well that he was going to yield. She knew it.

In that instant she felt as if a red curtain was passing down over her eyes. The heat struck her and she started yelling without control. She could hear her own voice giving out loud and long, without any break in the things she was saying, as if it was some other person and not her that was scalding Mack McFarlane – and a part of her marvelled at the easy way they flowed out of her and from where she knew not, such a casting-up. She called him for all the names she could think of – *fat pig, dirty dog, scabby head, porridge-face* – things you could hear any day of the week in the school-yard and he only threw back his head, and laughed, enjoying it. But that made her all the more determined to sting, mad as a bee. Now she called him *a lowdown country shite*, and she felt her partner shrink away, but what did she care for any of them, they were all scum, the lot of them with their wee thing between their legs they were so proud of.

She said—And you would put it where I wouldn't put the end of my walking-stick, and that was a rare one, for the smile was going off his kisser now and his fine friends' for that matter too. (Their turn would come in a minute or two, never fear.) Sure had he ever told them how he used to sneak around the backs of the houses after dark to get a good dekko at daft Maisie Parkes getting ready for bed, had he told them that, because everyone knew that all Mack McFarlane was ever any good for was looking up the wee girls' clothes at school, and had he also told them about how he was never done tormenting her to go out with him, had he told his cronies that? It wasn't so completely accurate – perhaps he had asked her once or twice, once certainly, that day up at the old lime-kiln – but it hit hard, she could see that by his face. He moved at her, white as a sheet, and her partner said—Now push off, mac, not knowing it was his name and she shouted out too.

—Yes, push off, you fat fucker you! And she had used the word. It had slipped out unawares and the last one of her lady-like airs had flown along with it. But it still felt good saying it.

Then Frank Glass tried to butt in and she turned on him —And you can keep your trap shut, Frank Glass, because I have one or two home truths I could broadcast about you as well, you creepy wee book-worm you, and she had, that time she and Roberta Brownlees had spied on him down at the weir, playing with his thing, while he kept looking at a photograph in his other hand.

It was funny how they were all coming back to her, these things, and they were too good to waste. She must get them all out. She would make them sorry, that trio, they had ever taken their liberties with her. Her blood boiled and she stamped her foot, lost to all around her.

Frank Glass stuttered—There's someone at the door looking for you, and she knew it hadn't come out the way he wanted it to, for she cut the feet from him, you see. His dial was a picture, torn as he was between fright that she'd affront him and a grinning cleverness. She took her time about heeding what he'd said, expecting some trick or other, but then she looked and *oh God above*, her limbs turned to jelly, for it was *him* standing there with his old cap hanging off the side of his head, and under his arm a bloodstained, brown-paper parcel of butcher's meat from Ballyclare.

He hadn't seen her yet. His eyes, blurry with drink, were peering hard into each knot of people on the floor. *Oh, how could he do this to me*, was her first thought, and then terror took hold as she remembered the weight of his hand from the past. *Powder and paint, paint and powder*, as he whaled into her with the strap he sharpened his razor on. It hung under the stairs on a nail and her dearest wish was to take it from that place and hurl it into the deepest and fiercest part of the Moylena.

Never for one instant taking her eyes off him – oh, the picture of him swaying there with his old steak and sausages under his arm and his old eyes screwed up in the poor light – she moved back and away in among the dancers.

Her partner called out —Hetty! just once to her.

Later the sound of her name like that from him was to stay with her, but she had no choice but to go, no word to anyone, to him or even poor Teresa, still sitting there unawares; she just slid through the dancers looking for the side-door by the platform. It was lucky she hadn't a coat with her but it wouldn't have mattered anyway, she would have left it behind, such a panic was hammering in her breast.

When she reached the door, like a fool she looked back, just to make sure her escape was secure. She couldn't see him at first through the dancers, then suddenly a way was cleared between them, and he was looking straight at her down that long avenue. He raised his fist and the sodden parcel fell to the floor. She turned and ran down the steps in among the women making the tea in the back kitchen.

They called out after her as she gained the street door. Some of them knew her. All would know of her disgrace before that night was out. The whole world would know, the whole wide world, and she had nowhere to hide from them. She just ran and ran, mad, mental Hetty Quinn, down the village street under the moon like the wild thing she was.

2

Mack was keeping up an impossible pace, even though his bike was the oldest and heaviest of the three, a red roadster taken from the post-office. Its wide tyres bit into the cinders with venom as, coat-tails flying, he flew along what was little wider than a cat-walk by the river, the two of them closely following. Harvey held the middle position and he brought up the rear. He had no intention of having his new Raleigh Sprint crushed between these two maniacs, both bent on some private joint destruction, for that seemed clear now with every thrust of the pedals, every corner grazed, Mack piling hazard on hazard.

He had left the dance-hall without a word soon after the row, not a backward look, a hint, nothing, face like stone, a little paler than usual, but not much, ignoring them. They went after him – was he sick? – listened, but no tell-tale sound, only the band inside, then he came round the side of the Hall, head down, legs pumping and they scattered in time. Into the middle of the road he tore – they heard his grunt as the wheels made the drop from the pavement to tarmacadam – then hard left down the hill to the village. They followed, not even taking the time to light up, police barracks or no police barracks, and Mack was doing his level best to lose them, once he knew they were on his tail.

He streaked up the narrow entry beside Carlisle's shop, across Joe McBride's precious timber-yard where a sheet of corrugated roofing rattled under them – a light came on at a top window, then, sly bastard that he was, back over the tin again, a shout from the window, they might have had a charge shot into them, *them*, not Mack, oh no, and that was only the beginning. He led them through somebody's chicken-run, the soft hen-shit slowing them almost to a standstill, Mack labouring like them, in slow-motion only a couple of bicycle lengths away, then Harvey toppled into a coop and the whole shebang went over, Harvey shouting out: —I'll stretch your fucking neck for you! as he fell.

They heard Mack give a laugh and the chase was on again as their wheels caught. But the laugh was short and bitter, and it was no game Mack was playing now, like so many of his private amusements, because when it came to him that he wasn't going to shake them off, a hard vicious mood took over, evident in every twist and turn he now dared them to imitate. The moon rode above, lighting up their path, and it made the dark places only darker. Each time his front wheel crossed a blind threshold, Harvey being swallowed up ahead, his mouth went dry and his body sweated, the handlebars burning into his palms. He visualized the grip melting to a squalid mess – he had bound the tubing lovingly with tape in the fashion of the aces, until it felt right, layer upon layer. All of the bike, every part of his beloved Raleigh – was being abused.

Then they hit the river-pad, three bumps on to the hard packed cinders from the track that circled the allotments, and his wheels – narrow alloy rims, tubular tyres pumped solid, Dunlop radials with their yellow ribbon – hissed out their own pure sound. He held back deliberately to relish the tone, nothing like it really, even with the other two, head down, backside high and folded around the hard cutaway Brooks saddle, legs down, up and around, feet and ankles clipped and circling, just that small powerful diameter down there centred on the gear wheel, surging him along, as though from a hose. Wembley Stadium under the arc-lamps, phalanx of riders swooping up, down and around over the banked hardwood, the same hiss only fifty-fold and seven days of it. Fausto Coppi falling from cold Alp to the heat of siesta fifty kilometres an hour down the white winding ribbon, legs like oiled wood, freewheeling straight to the French Mayor's kiss, flowers, cheers, the yellow jersey . . .

The river sped past. It reflected the moon which hardly seemed to move. There was a smell of roots washed and steeped below water, then left bare. The level had dropped nearly a foot this last fortnight in the heatwave. The village people talked of typhoid to frighten the children from bathing. They said the same things every summer. It would be nice to swim now. Soft brown kisses . . .

He heard Harvey give a cry ahead, for Mack had trapped

himself – no escape once this pounded black ribbon of clinker ran out against the wall of the turbine-house up in front. The roar of the fall which powered the mill was getting louder every second. In a moment spray would fall, a mist on their skin. Harvey shouted out a second time, quickening his pace. *Tally-ho, Mack.* He pressed down on his own pedals. *Into the river with him*, he caught himself thinking, straining closer. A leg and an arm apiece and then in with him, flying free-fall and slowed for them to enjoy. He was biting his lip, muttering to himself, as bad as Harvey. The bike felt as though it might well collapse too within his surrounding grip, hands and inner thighs pressing, pressing as he willed it along. Just like Harvey and his rages against his lumps of farm iron.

They sprinted on and the water roar boomed louder. Spray was wetting now. The noise of the place and that downward plunge like a terrifying falling curtain had always made him afraid, tons of water endlessly plummeting. He could see his own head bobbing there in the foam beneath the drop before being rammed under for eternity. Did Mack know? It was hard to see what he was up to ahead, for Harvey's travelling bulk was squarely in front. Slowing, he moved over as close as he dared to the edge of the path, containing his wheels to a mere strip.

Yes, by God, indeed he had run out to the end of his tether, for he was dismounting, looking over his shoulder at them – the avengers! He hummed a martial blast. In with him, plump and spread-eagled, oh, in with him! But, *Christ, what was this*, for doors did open for Mack, and one did now – there was the alley he had forgotten about running between mill and turbine-house, causeway for rats and the deaf old man who tended the machinery and Mack was disappearing up it at a run, pushing his bicycle in front.

Harvey yelped—After the get! After him! and collided with the wall. He swung his machine back like a scythe, both wheels clearing the ground, then in a rage he flung it into the mouth of the passage-way. The narrow walls held it upright but the handlebars were facing out.

—Bike, bloody bike! Harvey shouted, and began manhandling it, too furious to heed the damage he was causing, as he scraped along the brick.

—Bike, bloody bike! he could be heard shouting, as he disappeared.

He held his own machine at rest for a moment, waiting, listening to the water, for it would be like being trapped with a bull in that tunnel to follow straight after.

He moved in. It was slippery underfoot with the oily waste from the turbines. Once his hand touched the damp wall and he recoiled. What was he doing anyway on nights like these forcing through traps and holes at the whim of others? Always the smiling and the pretence. Perhaps the others had a nickname for him, Smiler, behind his back. He had never forgotten, or forgiven, a woman teacher who had once stood him out for 'smirking'. The word came to denote some facial deformity he had been unaware of until then, and in a moment there was the certainty that everyone else had known about it all along, like bad breath or dandruff, but much worse, much worse . . .

He heard Harvey give another cry of rage up ahead and he pushed on and out into the open to see what was happening now. All he wanted was for this to be ended. His mind felt like a shrinking ball, inward turning. *Hedgehog,* he thought.

Mack had found a way across the river at its fastest, most dangerous point, for it ran, the colour of steel, in and through the teeth of the flood-gates, and there he was, bicycle held aloft, footing it across a bridge no wider than a shelf. He remembered in an instant the feel of it beneath bare feet when he was younger, pierced grid, smooth and treacherous, and the water rushing with a hiss just below, and the eel that lived down there too, relishing the pull and suck, as thick as a man's arm, big, bluish monster to give him nightmares, *no, enough was enough, he wasn't going across there, not he.* Harvey leaped on to the foot-bridge, up and down like a madman, to shake and rattle it, up and down he went, and Mack hung frozen in the middle, one arm wrapped around his post-office bike, the other holding on to the old warped wood. The metal under his feet bounded with a noise like thunder, and Harvey howled like a dog. Din of madness. The moon had affected them. Three loonies abroad under its pulling rays, faces painted silver and Mack's face palest of all as he was shaken. *Find a way out of this, Mack.* The cast-iron rang, the structure swayed, and Mack bounced like a—

—Pea on a drum! he yelled. Pea on a drum! Harvey and

he chanting it together with glee, faster and faster, as Mack's head shivered round towards them – their clockwork man. He heard himself laughing.

—Pee on the drum! His own command now, and no one to know but he its indignity, and Mack's eyes were fastened on them as they searched his looks for a sign. But there was nothing in the round white face, nothing in the eyes. They glittered, that's all, hard as stone, so, *sink you, Mack, hard man, let's see you dance even faster.* He laid down his own bicycle on the grass, stepping forward.

Then Mack gave out a loud cry, holding them still, thoughts forming up against his, barest fraction of time.

—*Yeeoow!*

His yell came again, warning, and slowly he was taking away his grip from the wooden supports until he stood, both hands holding the bicycle out over the racing flow. And he dropped it in. The red bicycle went under like a stone. Through the sound of the water they all heard it bumping and grinding, muffled, down there, deep and lost for ever. Joe Gorman's post-office bike, with the straps hanging down from the front carrier, the one he wheeled out every morning and returned each night with the straps down, the pump carried away in his inside coat pocket for safe keeping.

—*Who the hell do you think you are?* Harvey's roar, and Harvey himself, always too late, too slow with things.

But, unhurried, Mack was walking across to the other side, then climbing the slope leading up and away from this deadly place. They watched him. He went up the hill, bent over, clutching the grass, the colour of frost in the moonlight. Chill handfuls.

At the top he stood, surveying them, legs spread.

—Okay, wise guys.

Voice of the young Cagney drifting out over their own neck of the woods. Night and the country sleeping. Only the three of them abroad and nothing or no one to curb a solitary one of their outrages. His blood stirred. All was lit, bright and spacious, waiting for cameras to roll.

He called out—Mount up! and moved forward, carrying his bicycle on one shoulder, Cagney ousted by John Wayne, and Mack laughed above him and he prickled with pleasure.

Harvey exploded—*Ach, for fuck's sake!* on the far bank and they both laughed. Poor old Harvey, the reluctant dog-soldier as always.

Near the top of the slope he took Mack's proffered hand, no resentment of that magnanimity in the—Here, grab a fin—and was heaved to level ground.

Below, Harvey toiled upwards and they burst out laughing again, equals now. It was a sentimental moment, at least he felt that, and kept his head turned away, no one to read his expression or see water in his eyes.

Harvey's head rose over the brow of the hill. He was blowing and muttering, his bike was the heaviest after all, a solid Humber, black with fine green and gold lines and a Sturmey Archer three-speed gear. In top he could surge along with slow thrusts, no elegance of course, he pedalled with the heart of the foot, a brutal movement that made him wince, legs like thick pistons, farmyard shafts pumping straight up and down in their tweed. But the Humber was for usage, nothing more, like a wheel-barrow, indeed it was kept out in the barn at The Craigs, growing a fine coat of dust that fell from the hay-loft overhead – the saddle the only part of it to ever receive any attention, a rub of Harvey's hand, and then on to it with a leap and a grunt. Now he was bent over its bar and panting.

—Oh, I'm buggered, he groaned.—Purely buggered, and they joined in laughing at his expense once more.

Something very refreshing in all this, disarming, pleasing, they both felt it – he knew it. Poor old Harvey, hung over the bar of his bike, and squinting from one to the other now, trying to comprehend what it was in him, that was setting them off, and beginning to be pleased himself, for a crooked light was coming, wolfish old glimmer of a grin.

—Pair of pricks, he growled. Pair of pricks, and it was the last straw, that and his expression, and he and Mack had to hold their ribs in and yell. Oh, Harvey, Harvey, you and your hair, and your big red clock, and that sports coat weighing a ton, and your open-necked shirt, the triangle of hankie, and your shoes, oh your shoes – did shops still sell shoes like those?

It was a mad moment, a good one too, one they would recall

in later times with a, *Do you remember the night Mack dropped Joe Gorman's bicycle into the Race,* only that wasn't funny now. But it would be. But this was funny now, oh God, yes. His side hurt and there was a sour taste in his mouth. Laughed himself sick, he thought, or dirtied himself, that old schoolroom gentility. He tightened his rear end. Diarrhoea. They never dared setting that spelling at school. He wouldn't either – though it was the daddy of them all.

—Here, Harvey! shouted Mack, recovered, his old bossy self once more.

—Here—gesturing—let me on to your bar.

—Yes. he heard his own voice—Let Mack on to the bar of your bike, and it wasn't sucking up. Harvey eyed them. It wasn't. Still the self-confidence of an equal.

—Come on, Harvey.

Chivvying the child.

—The night is young! Mack declaimed, another quote from the silver screen.

—*And you are beautiful!*

They laughed together and Harvey made room, sitting back on his saddle, thighs spread. He looked happy again – open to any scheme.

They were on the high wide and empty road and corncrakes were busy not far off in the fields. The scent came in waves. Others had been toiling in the hay that day as well. It was hard to realize that anyone else had been engaged like them. Just the three of them in the big Field raking and forking out the dry hay, no one else nowhere, not here, not anywhere in the world. You were like an ant, deep in your scheme of things, nothing but the touch and smell of what was near, tiny stamping ground, then it could come over you, unsettling like now, how much more of everything there was.

They wobbled on their bikes, figures of eight on the lonely white road, a little delirious, yelling nonsense. Mack's legs were thrust out, Harvey steering their double weight. It was as though they had all been re-charged with the drink, but that was at the bottom of the river now, down there among the straining water-weed. Harvey's face glistened with effort in the brightness of the moon. Once more pitting himself, but everything he did was like that, a task confronted, then wor-

128

ried through strongly to conclusion – everything. How clear at such times were the motives of the others.

He threw back his head and howled. The others joined him, all three now baying richly to the moon. Mack started in on an old ballad, voice quavering to the twists and turns of the bicycle. It went like:

> Four and twenty virgins,
> Went to Ballynure,
> And when the ball was over
> There were four and twenty fewer.

And it made them feel like rollicking blades, their laughter a warning to any girl they might come across, dear help her in her little cotton socks, dear help her, for they were the Terrible Three abroad and bent on devilment.

Mack cried out:

—They went that-a-way! and both bikes moved together to roll abreast down the road in the direction of his pointing hand. Past cottages where the lights had all gone out, past a farmyard where a dog grew frantic at their noise, hurling himself against a gate to reach them, Mack led and song followed song.

> Oh but it's great, after being out late
> Walking my baby back home;
> Arm in arm, over meadow and farm,
> Walking my baby back home . . .

They were free-wheeling, breeze on their faces, and that was the one that changed his mood for him . . . *And she gets her talcum all over my vest . . .*

—*It's the American word for waistcoat,* he said once unwisely, and Mack bantered straight off, *You don't say. Did you hear that, Harvey, did you know that?* but that wasn't why he felt this way, now and unexpectedly, it was another and different wriggling worm of memory. The wind blew on his face and hands and through his hair and sought out the parts of him that were sweating, and he was melancholy in an instant, feeling deprived of something, yet not knowing what it was. But the song had done it to him, of course. The words and all they evoked.

He thought of the ball of mirrors revolving high above the travelling heads, and all around faces and bare shoulders patched with bright lozenges, then going into darkness again as the spread of light moved on. He looked up at that ball, saw the single beam strike, then spill down, thickening and speeding. To watch it flood the floor caused dizziness. Instead you shut your eyes, moving in as close to your partner as she would allow you in the darkness, but closer, tighter always in the dark, imagining that the wash of blue and green and silver light when it came must be cold on the skin, while the band pumped out slowly and richly, *Harlem Nocturne* – the Stan Kenton arrangement – saxophones up and outwards, flaring bells of the horns . . . Yes, the band, best and a joy to watch always, but especially in the dimness as they rose and fell in ranks to play, brass and reeds, turn and turn about. Light from their stands on their faces as they concentrated, reading. A hand would move into the glow, turning over, and suddenly that hand – illuminated like that, perhaps a silver wrist-watch or ring, big and with a stone usually on the little finger, because they affected everything American – would be magical, not for any words to describe, just fixed in the imagination for ever, and no telling why . . .

And now he thought of a girl, for that was what the words of the song were always about, not *the* girl, in his case just any girl, but then again she had to be like this and to feel like that and move in the dark as they danced, bare arms, shoulders and neck, and down low on her spine his hand resting, while just that fraction away, which he could never bring himself to travel, but perhaps might some night, she flexed and tightened beneath thin silk. And that was an even more astounding thing than the sight of the lit hand, the sense of her moving like that so close, such a miracle of softness yet firmness and never still . . .

Only instead of all that in the big domed ballroom up at the Zoo and pleasure-grounds among the Belfast suburbs what had they got for themselves on this night of nights? Dues of three corner-boys kicking their heels whilst hating themselves as much as those clodhoppers on the floor. Bile in the mouth and in the mind and always the wasted opportunity.

So he thought then of Hetty Quinn as the bicycles continued to roll onwards through the night, his head bent low over the handlebars. Her dress, and its fine slithery feel those hours much earlier. To dance with her in the dark, for sometimes they did dim the lights even in Tardree. So much he wanted to say to her, explain, as they moved together and closer as words went home. Words, yes, but she'd called him a *book-worm*. That's what his words meant to her, in spite of any fire he might charge them with.

Hetty Quinn. That dress and the shoes and the red lips and her hair spun out like a fine bush, and the way she moved her body as she danced. All their eyes on her and all of them thinking the same thing. *We touched you and we know you, our hands have been over you and we'll never forget, you'll never be a mystery again. Whenever you see us you'll know what we know and that we know.* And then when she turned on them like that, eyes alight in her head, the feeling of shock, *but don't you know that you are ours now, that we have power over you, we broke through and plundered, we did.* But she wouldn't allow them their right, she might easily have shouted out—*You don't own me!* instead of all those other things. It was a phrase he had heard often, or if he hadn't, it was familiar ... *Do you think you own me?* A series of angry women had used it, perhaps always, and he felt as he pushed the bicycle along that he'd come on a great truth. It hung in his head but unsteadily and out of focus. If only he could hold on to it and always have it ready for reference, but then each time was different and each woman with it.

When he was with the other two they swopped generalizations endlessly – he as well sometimes – secret lore, the right and wrong way of it, just do this, say that, touch her in that place while doing, saying this. They theorized passionately over drink about it, while Mack smiled, occasionally ridiculing some of Harvey's wilder statements. Harvey favoured the farm-yard approach naturally, seizing and mounting without preliminary. They both suspected his to have been very raw encounters with a raw kind of woman. (Had he ever faced *her*, they wondered secretly, that girl up at the farm?)

And Mack of course was dark, as always, about any of his experiences. Just a smile, a quip, the manipulation of the debate so that they exposed themselves and their fantasies, and his, if they existed at all, fell further and deeper away. Except tonight, of course; for that had been a glimpse in the dance-hall of something he had been unable to keep from them. Hetty and what she'd said. The cool Mack, above it all, as original as some sort of diamond, had actually pressed Hetty Quinn to go out with him and she'd refused – Mack who had never been turned down, or rather never allowed such a situation to arise, the great Mack singing away now as he was carried onwards into the night. Oblivious. No idea in his head of what *he* was thinking here at the rear, what knowledge was stored away in this head and of the time coming when it might be used against him along with all those other slow-accumulating fragments. Out in a boiling flood, or singly at bewildering speed to sap and then finally demolish? The second of course. A great day for the book-worms. Hetty's word. How she could wound with one word, but then he was easy meat, his plating riddled with so many holes he was like a colander. There was a time when it seemed he was alternately blushing or going pale, off and on – that time, a light bulb. That was what being a book-worm did to you or for you – easy images, but always in the head. His dream, a time coming when they would crash straight from his lips, dazzling all, then just that select few, the poets, other wits, but always the older appreciative woman, always her. *Oh, Joan Crawford, where are you?*

Harvey cried out—Watch where you're going! Do you want to put us in the ditch or what?

In his dreaming he had pressed too close, nudging the wheel in front. Harvey wobbled across the road and Mack commented drily—I told him to give it up, so I did. It'll be the white stick for our friend any of these days now.

Harvey guffawed.

—Yeah, I don't care if I do go blind.

—Very funny, he returned, and Mack was watching him, thought-reader on the bar of the other's bike. He looked like a fat, obscene infant, just a short body, his head barely reaching Harvey's chest, leg-less too.

Very funny, yes, very, very droll, he thought.

And hardly aware, he countered musically—I dream of Hetty with the light brown—expecting another and much louder guffaw.

Instead, Mack spoke with an edge to his voice.

—Pull up. And then stronger—Pull up, damn you, Harvey! and the bicycle swayed to a halt.

Oh my God, he thought to himself, *now I'm for it, and for the second time this night as well. It's to be blood and wrestling here in this lonely place with Harvey holding the bikes.*

Mack dusted down his trouser legs a little piece away from him in the roadway, just like in a movie, deliberate and unhurried, while he gripped his machine tightly, hoping in some way that it might stave off the inevitable – *never hit a man when he's—*

Harvey said—Why don't you pair grow up?

Sweet respite.

Mack looked at him, then—Keep your neb out, old hand. Savvy?

It was between the two of them for a second now, wills locked; although he knew who must win; why should Harvey care?

So if he was for it, he was for it. Still he held on to the sweating saddle and handlebars, braced and praying, not too hysterically, just that it might happen quick when it, whatever *it* was, did come.

Harvey spoke out again—Don't you think there's been enough bloody carry-on for one night? Quite cool in tone. Remarkable that.

Mack sneered.—Carry-on? I'm afraid I don't quite follow you. Bloody carry-on? spacing the last words.

Harvey said—Now, don't push your luck. Just don't push your luck, and he sounded hard and threatening, looked it too in that moment, leaning over his old Humber Sports, looking straight at the other.

The temptation was strong to butt in now, join forces with him, but something warned him against it, and the hunch was right, for, in the continuing silence, Harvey muttered once more—Don't push your luck, that's all, and the balance of power had returned to Mack, Harvey out of words and back to his old knots again. He would crave something to grip and knead just now, and the bicycle would probably do as well as anything, for it was nearest and under his hands.

The moon was still in the same place, heavy, immovable. It lit up the fields around, flat coating of light on the hay-rows, and in other fields the mounds with their shadows. No sound anywhere, just the three of them becalmed in the middle of this sleeping landscape. Did the others feel it? They seemed to,

133

because they hadn't shifted or spoken, just waiting and listening. He heard himself sigh out loud, deep and long and then nervously.

—Let's call it a day. What about it? he said.

The others looked at him as though yawning already, but then Mack, a new and suddenly revived Mack and, thank God, already forgetting what had been happening, *had* happened, said—No. One last bit of sport. The finishing touch.

He faced them in the moonlight, sly grin starting, hands in his pocket and tie loosened.

—Let's go up to old Minnie's.

—What for? asked Harvey.

—Give her a scare. Scare the shit out of her.

Harvey laughed.

—Three colours of shit, and then at last it was his turn to chip in.

—No, three *shades* of shit.

And they all began laughing at the sound of it, and he was back in his old place again. Word-spinner.

—She has a pear-tree, said Harvey.

—Better still, said Mack.—Better still, my boy.

The laughing became louder, no one lagging, strong and confident and all fully restored.

Then he saw a light in the distance. He was the first to notice it bobbing in the dark places of the road, too slow for a motor-cycle, no sound as well, and not steady as on the front of a travelling push-bike.

—Look there! Coming up Blayney's Hill. Somebody with a torch.

Mack said—Let's see who it is. Get down behind the ditch. And—uh, hold your fire, men.

Harvey and he, they giggled . . . Good old Mack, trust him, as they lifted their machines up and over.

They lay and waited in the dry bottom of the ditch, spaced out and silent, while a little beyond in the field their still turning spokes glinted silver. It felt good to lie there, cheeks close to the side of the bank and the smell of the grasses growing. One needed closeness with the ground. That thought came to him. As today when he had lain stretched out, feeling he was melting, down through the roots deeper and deeper, and then

134

next moment as though the earth was entering through and into him.

The three of them lay there, and presently the sound of a voice came to them, still low and indistinct, but strengthening and overlaid with the clicking of a gear-wheel, slow turn of the rims as whoever it was walked his bicycle nearer. This mystery man was talking to himself, and they looked at one another, hugging in their glee. They strained towards the approaching murmur, heads lifted from the grass.

—Who the hell is it? whispered Harvey.

Both turned on him, hissing—Be quiet!

And now they could hear phrases and words, the monologue of an old man. Returning home drunk, he thought, telling them all where to get off after a night in the pub, that's the way it would be and weren't they the three royal cunts tuning in to his privacies. But then he stiffened like the others, as keen as any. The night-walker had stopped a little way off to rest after his climb. He breathed in and out heavily, a rasp in his throat, then spat.

—Pardonnez-moi, they heard him wheeze, then laugh at his own refinement.

They looked at one another in their dry trough, dying to raise their heads but not daring to. This was no labourer weaving home to a sleeping wife and brood.

The man, mere feet away, said distinctly:

> 'Twas brillig and the slithy toves
> Did gyre and gimble in the wabe,
> All mimsy were the borogoves . . .

He heard himself whisper—*And the mome raths outgrabe*, knowing that Mack and Harvey were staring at him and it was the best thing that could have happened to him that long day and night.

Then the mystery man, still invisible, sang a verse or two of:

> Who were you with last night?
> Out in the pale moonlight –

an uncanny imitation of one of those old cracked voices that came from some thick black disc with the dog revolving at its centre.

135

A burst of fellow-feeling for the man then – whoever he was – out there on the roadway, thinking aloud and oblivious to all but each fancy in his head. He seemed a rare old bird. He wouldn't mind knowing him, pleased with himself for recognizing the progression his mind made as the moon flooded down.

Harvey stirred at his side, *but he mustn't make a noise*. He put his hand out to restrain him and Harvey looked at him strangely. Mack was watching too. They couldn't understand, not even Mack, with all his sly putting of two and two together, would never understand, neither of them, stretched there at his side. It was a funny moment and anything could have happened, but it didn't, and marvellously the old man, out on the road, mounted his bicycle and rode on. He was humming to himself. Some other old song.

Mack waited until all sound, man and machine, had died away, then rolled over on to his back.

—Give us one of your fags, Harvey, he said.

They lay beside him with their hands under their heads, like three soldiers in a trench, while he puffed smoke. Then he said —Do you know who that old goat reminds me of?

They waited.

He said—The Professor here. An older version of course, but definitely young Frankie boy. Definitely.

Then, savagely, and hurling his lighted cigarette up and over the field as far as it would go, he said—Now for that other old cod. Let's go. You bums.

They were waiting up for her, her mother touching the bars of the grate every so often, and Bertha with her nose in the *Red Letter*, but looking up irritated each time she fidgeted with the poker. Then she would scold in that way of hers; but she couldn't hear a sound, just her lips moving, not even the clock on the wall, its pendulum silently stroking away, because she was out at the back looking in at the two of them through the scullery window.

She could smell the damp smell of the water-barrel and ashes and the Lusks' old tom-cat. She put her hand into the cool soft rain-water up to her wrist for no reason except something to detain her, for she'd every intention of rushing in to them in her state, but then when she had looked at them sitting there by the fire, waiting up for her, she had held back. The way they looked made what was about to happen to her seem much worse, as though they were strangers and wouldn't care about her and her troubles.

Her mother kept raising her head to look at the wag-at-the-wall. Worrying, always worrying. And Bertha again scolded silently. But then they all did, God forgive them. *Poor old Sadie* (she called her that to herself sometimes) *no one ever gets close to you to comfort you because you are always glancing about in a panic in case someone's tea isn't ready, or his shirt or Madge's good chemise isn't ironed.* Madge and him. The two privileged ones and always in league. No one would ever raise a word against Madge in his house, not if she stayed out until first light. Last night she had come in at three in the morning wakening her with her noise across the room, feeling her way about, hiccuping and once worse, and when she'd spoken out—Who's there? just for something to say in the dark, the voice came back at her—Who do you think? *Big Aggie's man!* cutting her to the quick.

She really hated her and her ways, and the bulk of her over

137

in the far bed tossing about and groaning in her sleep. If some of her fancy men could only see her then. She had a vision – strong at times – of suddenly switching on a light overhead in the small hours, exposing her for what she really was, sprawled there with her mouth open, fat arms and legs indecently bare and curlers in her hair. There were some things about other women she couldn't stand, the deceit, the sluttishness among themselves, when a man couldn't see them. She would always care for her appearance, for herself and for no other. No switching off and on for some poor thing just because he wore trousers. Angry in an instant because of her thoughts she plunged down into the top part of her dress, pulling out the tissue paper she'd placed there, and flung it from her. Two pathetic scraps moulded to her shape lay before her on the ground. Then one blew away and she shivered in the following wind. The coolness brought her back to her senses, reminding her of where she was and of how she mustn't be seen here.

She cried, *dear God, help me to get out of this thing and I'll be good for the rest of my days, because I haven't the courage to go in there and face them and him, him, most of all, when he comes back the worse for drink and looking for me and even if I did get into bed with the lights out, he would still come up the stairs after me because he did see me, I know he did* . . . She could anticipate the look on his face plainly as he grabbed for her hair, because that would draw him in his drunken state. When he was sober he would growl about her clothes and her silk stockings. For some reason those seemed to upset him more than bare legs ever did. Madge would yawn before the fire with her great shins and thighs growing mottled, shameless, exposing herself, and he wouldn't pass a remark, but her stockings set him on edge and of course her hair and the way it sat out after brushing as if she could help what Nature had given her . . .

There was a noise at the far end of the entry and her blood went cold. Someone was coming, a man with heavy steps on the cinders, by the sound of it, talking to himself as he put one boot in front of the other carefully, but at the same time making a great crunching of the dry pieces of burnt coke underfoot. (They tipped it there out of carts from the mill, then spread it with shovels, so thick that the back doors wouldn't open outwards. Cinders in the summer, snow in the winter.) Why did she think things like this when the steps were coming closer all the time, and if it was *him* then she was in for it. The back door would crash on its hinges and he would pick her out easily in the light from the scullery window. *Oh daddy, don't, please don't, daddy* . . . The humiliation of calling him that, the lie in it too, as the arm went up over her. His smell too, tobacco and the curds of shaving soap, and the drink turned sour in him and on his breath. Why did he have to be like every stepfather she'd ever read about in books or seen in films? Charles Laughton, the worse for drink . . .

The footsteps stopped and she listened, a hand to her heart. He was listening too, was that it, turning his head from side to side out there, cunning as any old animal. She looked about her for a place to hide, but there was nowhere except the coal-house, and to be caught in that narrow black place was too terrible even to consider. She couldn't go in and she couldn't go out and she felt the beginnings of panic, her two hands tightening into knots on the iron rim of the water-barrel.

Then she heard a new sound from out there, wherever he had halted, and at first couldn't make out what it was, a kind of hissing, starting off low and then getting stronger. It seemed to have great force behind it and then, oh, it struck home to her what it was, and her temper and shame rushed up in her, for the thought of him making his water up against the back brick wall of one of the neighbour's houses, like some dog with its leg lifted, outraged her more than anything could or would. Heedless she rushed from the yard punching the door ahead of her with all her force – it flew back with a noise to waken the dead – grabbed a handful of cinders up and flung it blindly in an instant in the direction of the continuing sound, shouting out

—Take that, you dirty, filthy pig!

The stones, dry and spiky to her palms, flew up, then dropped to rattle down off a sloping tin roof, but she didn't wait to appreciate her aim, she was off running at top speed up the entry and away from her deed.

She ran and she ran away from the village until the stitch in her side became too painful. Her breath came in gasps as she rested against the wall beyond all the houses where the three-cornered plantation skirted the castle demesne. There was safety here – for the moment anyway – the high stone at her back, Lord Upton's trees beyond and the smaller trees planted by the council in front, hiding her from the road.

She had often played here when she was younger, at wee houses among the roots, with pieces of glass and broken delph which they would wash and dry for their own best china. It seemed so far away now, the games and the imagination and the long bright summer days among the trees, each day after school, or from morning to night in the holidays. The moon shone down and it would be lovely to step in there and play again. *This is my parlour, and that's yours, and this stump here is the table, and look, I'll spread my hanky and then we'll set it with the tea-service we only bring out on Sundays for visitors.* Even then it was lying and make-believe, for they never had any visitors at home, nor had they good china or cutlery left past either. She remembered a Coronation plate *he* once smashed in a fit of rage. Her mother had a few things hid away, little cheap pieces of glass she'd bought from pack-men at the door, but they never saw the light of day because of him and his jealousy of anything that was nice or different.

An owl hooted behind the wall somewhere in among the dark trees, and she shivered. His eyes like coals. She was cold again, brought back to the present and her plight, for she couldn't stay out all night here, or anywhere else for that matter. Dead in the morning, stiff as a board, and then they'd be sorry . . . But there she went again. Where could she find safety for the night, this night only, because in the early morning, she'd decided this, she'd creep back to the house for her clothes and the money she had saved, almost four pounds now, notes and change, hid away inside the brass bed-knob. It screwed off and was hollow inside. She'd have to creep up the stairs while they were still asleep, even her mother. No creaks, not a sound when she opened the wardrobe door, and she'd have to be extra careful of the wire coat-hangers. There was an old khaki bag belonging to her brother Sonny when he came home from the prisoner-of-war camp. She would put all her things into that. He would never deny her anything.

She thought of him now over in Watford with his German bride. The day he came back, almost a year after the war had finished. *I've got somebody with me, da. I couldn't leave her behind. She was good to me, ma.* And all of them looking at her. The funny clothes, men's shoes and a soldier's pullover, and brown woollen stockings. *She can't speak English, da.* And then *him* saying loudly, *Take her back home. Or marry her.*

Four pounds would surely get her across to England and she could stay with Sonny, just for a little while anyway, until she got settled, for Helga was funny, very possessive and jealous, yes, even of his own sister. She and Sonny, they used to talk together in German in front of the others and you could tell it was about them. Her English didn't seem to improve much, and there were nights when she could be heard crying in her bed in the next room. And then the two of them went to England and Helga was laughing and her mother was crying. Sonny was always the favourite and she still kept all his letters from that Stalag place and the photograph of him in the Irish Guards football team that beat the Germans in the camp. So it couldn't have been all that bad, not like all those films about torture, and tunnels and things. There were times when she wished she had been one of those girls the Gestapo captured, riding bicycles and taking messages about when the parachutists would be dropping. There was that film with Lilli Palmer in it –

Behind the wall among the trees a terrible sound of animals fighting broke out suddenly. She held on to the stone while it raged – two creatures at one another's throats – then there was an awful silence, and then crunching. Bones and fur, she thought, and felt sick. She clapped her hands to scare it away, but the sound continued in spite of her. In there, after dark, things took their own course. And maybe it was the same everywhere, all over. She felt like the only person abroad. Everyone else was behind closed doors, in their beds, or poking the last dying coals in the grate.

But maybe there was one window somewhere she could look through – not her own – where the people looked as though when her knock came, their faces wouldn't be alarmed, and they wouldn't run to put the light out. She thought of Mrs Mullan. Would she take her in? Many's a time she'd been entertained in that spotless kitchen, so different from her own, though only three doors down, but then three doors down wasn't far enough away from the trouble *he* would create if ever he found out she had taken refuge there. Especially in the house of one of *them*, he would say, with all their heathen images on the walls. His worst time of course was always at the Twelfth of July when he'd take his drums out and, with the other men, beat them down at the weir or by the side of Semple's pub. Mrs Mullan always got her headaches then, she'd noticed, and stayed indoors with brown paper soaked in vinegar across her brows. She was as touchy as an old bear. Remember that time she had poured the piss-pot over Bertha's head and her father had wanted to fight wee Jimmy Mullan who was a harmless being, but then they always did say that Catholic women were more bitter than the men . . . No, she couldn't knock on that door.

She began to think more desperately, any alternative now, because it seemed to be getting colder and later every second. The castle clock must surely strike soon and tell her the time, but then if it struck only once she wouldn't know if it was half-twelve or one. But why was she so worried about time anyway, because it didn't matter how late it was, she couldn't go back home, even if she wanted to, could never, after what she'd done to him there in the entry, her own father, or what passed for one. *The old devil*, she thought. *I'm not sorry, I'm not.*

She began to laugh, couldn't help it, at the idea of the stones falling down around him like hail. The shock there must have been on his sourpuss, and – the giggling became stronger – wetting his trousers, yes, that as well. What an odd creature she was, one minute crying, the next laughing. She wiped her eyes. Tears both times. Maybe you went through things every few years. Attacks. She knew a lot of women of all ages who were bad with their nerves, dizzy spells and the waterworks. She laughed again, thinking of his waterworks, then, serious, she thought of the time when she had first taken the curse. That was when she was fourteen, so did they come every three years or so? Life would be a torment if you had to look forward to that every so often. Oh, but if only she knew more, then it wouldn't be so bad, but this series of mysteries, each one striking her unprepared, made it unbearable. And books were worthless, because even when she was able to get her hands on something medical, none of the knowledge inside seemed to be about you and your particular condition. You only ended up imagining you had all the symptoms and diseases ever invented, awful things you daren't mention to people, let alone pronounce. Once she had reconciled herself to having Rowley's Vesicular something or other. She found that underneath a diagram of the chest, with the bad bits marked in blue, and went around for weeks imagining her lungs turning more and more the same colour. Each time she spat out she expected to see the worst, ink, then she forgot about it and she was cured. A silly bitch that's what she was, just as people kept telling her, but what you had to do was keep quiet, never answer them back, until one day you weren't one any longer. They all knew it, and you knew it, but, God, up there, *how long have you got to wait?*

She could see the full moon through the trees, hardly moving. It looked so close, big as a pancake, another mystery. Right at this moment it was pulling the tides – that was from the reader, *Wonders Of The Living World* – and affecting some people's brains too, but she hadn't got that from any schoolbook, that was common knowledge. It was strange to think of. Men and women too, lying in their beds, with that light shining in on them, so soft and silvery and innocent, yet doing things to them they couldn't help or understand. Bela Lugosi with a face like chalk, and his awful black lips.

Her skin started going bumpy and she felt shivery again. What a night she'd picked on to go roaming.

She began to tap-dance on that little cleared space under the castle wall, to take her mind off horrors, forward and back, *by the light,* tap tap tapetty, tap, *of the silvery moon,* tappetty, tap, tap, tap, *I love to spoon* . . . an odd old-fashioned word that which some people still used. Barney McCoubrey, sitting outside his cottage, on the bus-seat he'd let into the bank – he looked as if he was growing out of the grass – and calling out to the courting couples as they passed him, *Off for a wee bit of spoonin' eh, is that it? Eh? Eh?*

Up the Whinny Hill they would all go, linked, when it grew dusk, to their own place on the bank to lie there and do *it,* or not, as the case may be. You could always tell the ones who did from the things found afterwards. Frank Preston, his sister Beattie and herself would examine each bay the next morning on the way to school. *Here's one!* Frank would yell and hold the pale limp thing up between finger and thumb. She and Beattie would shrink away, squealing, as he waved it at them. *The man puts it on his finger before putting it in there to feel about, you know.* Frank was older than they were, so they took his word for it.

How innocent then she was. If only they were all true still, all those childish silly things they believed in and whispered to each other in the school lavatories, instead of it being just like the animals in the farmyard up at Gault's. That time Harvey had called her out to the barn when one of the sows was being served by Alex Thompson's big prize black boar, and she had gone like a fool into the middle of it all, that awful squealing and grunting and the foaming screwing thing that the boar was trying to put into the other pig. She'd never be able to forget that or forgive Harvey and old Alex either for the grins on their faces as they watched her. She picked up a bucket and flung it at Harvey, but the two of them had got their satisfaction and then she cried afterwards out in the chicken-house. But they couldn't make her do that now, no siree, not one of that same pack of blackguards.

She had her ways of getting her own back, so she had, on Master Harvey Gault. Her own special wee way. Loosening the bolts on his bed once, but he never mentioned it, and she wasn't there to hear it collapse in the middle of the night. Apple cores, stones, worms and black beetles and once a tin of itching powder slipped into the same bed, but that wasn't remarked upon either. She had to be extra careful of course, for he knew she made all the beds; Lizzie wasn't allowed to do any jobs up-stairs or in the parlour downstairs because of breakage. Work-ing in the big old dark rooms – the blinds must always be kept drawn because the sun might fade the carpets – was something she'd hated at first. Picking up Harvey's dropped clothes, breathing in his smells, shaking out his dirt from his sheets – it was no wonder he didn't notice her little surprises – became after a time nothing to her beside the power she had in knowing their secrets. For instance, under his mattress Harvey kept dirty books, and a full packet of those same balloon things which Frank Preston used to wave about on the Whinny Hill. She noticed with delight and satisfaction that he had never used a single one. But at the same time it meant that if she ever pricked a pin-hole in each of the three, as the worst spite she could possibly think of paying him, it wouldn't do her much

144

good anyhow. But patiently she had been able to piece together things about all of them, just by keeping her eyes open as she moved about in the gloom among the old furniture and the photographs of all the generations of Gaults on the walls. Nothing they owned of course was a patch on any single item Minnie had in her place. Minnie was a lady and the Gaults nothing but a crowd of clayhawks. Coarse they were, and everything in the house took after them, even the very chamber pots beneath the beds she despised, after having seen the delicate and pink-patterned one at Hollybush House.

The castle clock chimed a sudden single note and she jumped. It was so loud, just as if it was in her ear, and yet she knew where it came from and how far away, there in the tower where the pigeons nested. But was it twelve-thirty or one? There was no way to tell, not even if she waited for the next stroke. And what was the sense in waiting here any longer, in this place? She could go on now that she'd rested. There was nothing to detain her in this place. Except that it did hide her, the wall at her back, grey stone and nearly double her height, and the trees in front in the little plantation where she used to play. It did seem smaller though as if they had trimmed away more and more of it since then, a little piece every year, until there would be nothing left. There was one old thick tree where they used to hide things. You put your hand in if you were the one after eeny meeny minie mo and you held your breath every time waiting for it to be grabbed by a goblin. Sometimes you pretended it had got you and you screamed. The others ran off and then you laughed.

She couldn't remember its whereabouts, that old tree with the hole in it. Could it be over on the far side near the road, or was it close to this? Stepping in amongst the trunks she glanced around her but didn't see it for some time, because she was looking for one much bigger, as she had remembered it. Then she came upon it and had to stoop low before slipping a hand, just about, into its blackness. There was water in the hollow there out of sight, and old brown leaves, cold and slimy, met her touch like dead things. She pulled her hand out in a rush, almost didn't make it at first because of the tight fit, and gave a cry; then she was free and panting, still crouched and looking up at the sky through branches.

Not a star was out; the moon, it seemed to her, had banished every single one of them, its light was so great. She wiped her fingers on her dress. The shock and the chill wet feel had certainly killed any further dreaming of babes in the wood. She felt very old and resolved in her mind now. Outside these trees and away from the walls the open fields were as bright as day, she told herself. Moving across them in the moonlight would be like walking over grass at noon, no shadows to disturb her, and no harm could come to her in such openness. She thought of haystacks and burrowing deep into the side of one, but it was too early in the season, the crops still lay flat. But she would start travelling anyway, and as she went between the rows it would come to her where to go.

Soon she was trudging in a straight line, hedge to hedge, over Dickey's field, the big one that lay beside the road. There was a faint dampness on the stalks underfoot but she paid no heed, just kept travelling. Her mind became fixed on the next objective, namely the stile on the distant facing side, eyes holding it; then she had reached it, was astride and over and on to the next dark gap diagonally across from her this time. And so she proceeded across many fields until she realized how far she'd come and, more important, that her thoughts had held still all that time. She was no closer to deciding where to find a place of safety; she might just walk on for ever until she came to the sea. It was a romantic idea, heading over hills and valleys until there it would be, with the sun coming up and across, if it was very clear, the shores of Scotland. Like something out of a story-book, only she was too old for such things, and now that she'd stopped moving her brains were working again. Where was she anyway? Over there in the dip were the trees she'd started from – the castle clock-tower was clear as well – and down there the river, silvery, and ahead was a great rising hedge, as high as a house, and dark. It looked familiar yet not, as though she knew it from its far side and not this, but that size and the holes in its base as big as herself had a ring somehow.

Then she saw something lying sunk in the grass in the shadows. She took a step closer and it was an enamelled bucket with a dark rim, blue, although she couldn't see that, but she knew it anyway because it was the feeding-bucket for the hens. She had walked clear all the way to the Gaults, coming up on

146

the back of their haggard, because that's what was on the other side of the big windbreak hedge, the haggard.

Amazement filled her, for it was as if she had been walking in her sleep, but why should she be drawn to this place? There was nothing here for her, not even one haystack to shelter in, because the ground there through the gaps she knew was littered with circles of bare stones and thorns and nothing else, waiting for the new harvest to rise up on their foundations.

She moved closer to the hedge, peered through bare branches and saw the wide swept yard beyond, bright in the moonlight. Nothing moved, and nothing disturbed that flat floor, not one solitary article left out to mar it. Mr Gault was very very particular and inspected it each night when milking was done before dismissing Frank, which was usually late.

Poor old Cooley, he was worked like an animal; precious time ever left to himself. But she was nearly positive she had seen his face pressed to a pane earlier tonight at the Hall. He was given to that, when dances were on. Too shy to ever venture inside, he would watch through the windows with the children, as the dancers did their bit out on the floor. She felt sorry for him most of the time, but these were nights when she would have gladly let him dance with her in spite of the ridicule, that's if he had ever been able to screw his courage up to come in. And the thing that pierced her most too was him scrubbing himself out at the pump in the farmyard on such nights, with his rag of a towel tucked in over his collar, and all to what purpose? Just to perch outside in the cold on an old window-sill with a lot of youngsters, and him a grown man, although a bit soft in the head. But if he was, she argued fiercely to herself, it was other people that had driven him to it, never letting him alone, with their tricks and tormenting. She had often wondered how he had got to the state he was in, always trembling and talking to himself, what he had been like when he was younger. Some said it was shell-shock in the last war but she had never been able to get him to mention it, because they did have conversations together – of a sort. She knew he liked her, would do anything for her, and she liked him too, poor old Frank with his shaky hands. He was worth a dozen of that other bunch who abused him, so he was.

She could see where he slept, through that door there up the

147

steps, above the potato-house, just an old shed with the straw thick on the floor. Once she had gone up to see if there was anything she could do for him, perhaps tidy up, some little thing to surprise him, but when she saw the place she knew there was nothing. It was so sad and bare with only a few little things laid out beside the mattress on a tea-chest, with its silver paper still sticking out from under it. There was an old nursery alarm clock that didn't go, with a picture of Donald Duck on it, a piece of broken mirror, a cup with no handle, a razor and a wobbling brush, and a photo of a dog in a cart. That's all he had in the world, she told herself, not another solitary thing, and nearly all broken or useless. It made her want to cry. She picked a bunch of primroses out in the fields, put them in water in a washed jam-jar and placed it among his treasures. He never mentioned it of course, in case he might be laughed at, and she didn't either but she knew he knew and that was enough.

She thought of that tiny posy now, withered, turned to dust, but still there on the tea-chest, for she felt certain he would never throw it out. Poor old Frank, he was up there now; she could tell, even though no light showed beneath the door – the Gaults would never let him have a lamp in case he burnt the place down. Why didn't she creep across the yard, tiptoe up the stone steps to his door and knock very lightly, hardly a sound at all, but he would hear it, for she was certain he would be a light sleeper. Why didn't she, because if anyone would befriend her this night it would be him, old Frank. Why hadn't she thought of it before?

Stooping, she went through the hedge and then across the haggard, picking her way with care among the stones and the cut thorn and whin bushes, laid out ready for the building of the corn stacks. There wasn't a sound, not even from the animals all asleep, and the high windows of the house were dark. She crossed the swept yard; it was bone dry like a floor and wide, much wider it seemed, under moonlight, and at last she was at the foot of the steps. She started to climb, holding her breath, and keeping close to the wall because there was no hand-rail. *Whitewash will be all over my frock*, she was thinking, for she rubbed against it, afraid of the drop, and poor old Cooley, why hadn't he had his brains dashed out long ago; then almost at the last step, her foot raised, there burst out, at her it seemed, and just as if it was holding in too until she had reached the top, from behind the closed door, there arose that awful, gurgling sound which she would never forget, like an animal choking, and so loud as if the whole world must hear it, and lights go on and windows open and voices ring out.

She clapped her hands over her two ears, and of course lost her balance. The fall to the yard below knocked all the breath and the sense out of her too, but she still had made a lot of noise. All three dogs tied for the night in their barrels, Gyp, Prince, even old Spot, went wild and tore out as far as their chains would allow. They didn't seem to recognize her, and, God knows, she had been the only one to feed and water them this past two years, but this was no time to feel hurt by a thing like that, for a lamp had been lit in the main bedroom and Mr Gault she knew kept a double-barrel on the landing.

She took to her heels, back the way she had come, nerves in pieces and her heart beating wildly. She felt sick as well and knew that it wouldn't be long before she would be limping, for something had given a crack when she fell. Then she was in the fields again, and as lost as ever. The dogs still barked but it was all behind her now.

Thinking came back as she slowed her pace over the wet grass, for the dew had started to fall, so suddenly she noted, coming down like a curtain to drench everything in its path, even her hair, but that could be sweat. Or perspiration. *Gentlemen sweat, but ladies perspire.* One of Minnie's sayings. Minnie in bed now with that cap she wore and her white cotton gloves. Those gloves were a mystery all right, no rhyme or reason to them, just Minnie Maitland and one of her odder notions about skin-care. Hollybush House and the sleeping Minnie must be over there, or rather, no, over there. The trees would tell her because they were different from all the others, Christmas trees the year round. She swung slowly about in the middle of the field, looking for their shapes against the sky. They would stand out like the ones they used to cut out of green shiny paper in school. And there they were, too, pointed and sharp, and in their heart would be the house, safe from harm, and in her bed, Minnie, safe as well, with all the doors barred. How she envied her.

149

She felt sorry for herself and began to cry a little, standing there with the damp getting into her shoes. Double pneumonia would serve them right, so it would; her last moments passed in an oxygen tent with that same crowd all around, trying to get her forgiveness, but would she open her eyes to please them, not likely . . .

As she looked at the trees she seemed to see a light shining faintly through. Could it be the moon, reflecting on one of the upstairs windows? Her eyes strained and then the moon went behind a cloud, so she knew it must be a light after all. Minnie was still awake!

She started to run, praying that she would get there before that lamp went out, her mind fixed on it, sitting there on the marble-top beside the bed. She could see that deep blue glass bowl with the wick dropping straight into the oil, the brass base, the globe with its flame turned down to a pale glow. Then Minnie's gloved hand reached out and she called out —*Wait! Wait!* as she ran. The light still shone.

Other thoughts were in her head now. Cooley and his snoring, because that's all it was really, only it didn't sound like that, something worse, like an animal dying. And if she had knocked, gone in, what would it have been like? The rest of the night, his eyes on her, then looking away, worse and worse, not knowing what to think or do because she had confused him, put him in a state, and maybe he might think she was encouraging him, a girl coming up to where he lay at night, late like that, whispering at his door to be let in.

She ran faster and heard the noise her wet feet were making through the grass. Behind her there would be a trail, silvery in the moonlight, like snail tracks. It would be easy to follow, but she didn't look back, just thought about something different. Into her head came the tree and the hole, the one earlier, then the one much earlier than that, when she was young, and played under the leaves in summer with the others. Her hand would slip in and down out of sight and it was always dry then inside, always dry, always, in those days . . .

Many summers ago the party of archaeologists had come from the city and laid out their encampment on the side of the hill. Digging had begun, the turf stripped carefully first from the domed mound on the summit. They were as delicate as surgeons, cutting downwards on a shaved and carefully outlined plan of operation. The three labourers hired by the day by the Welsh professor for the less precise spadework talked about it in the pub. People came to watch and conjecture – at a distance. They itched to penetrate that thin ring of beech trees hiding the mystery. Beyond on the tonsured bulge, the young people knelt and worked with trowels in the dry soil. But what were they after? What had they found?

Rumour grew. One of the labourers quit the job, the other two followed him down to the pub for good a day later. It was July, the time of marching and reaffirmation of the ancient loyalties. The second week was coming and yet these strangers worked on. Did they know about the holiday or, more to the point, did they even care? At night singing could be heard coming from the tents. The sound seemed to mock the other heavier sound beating through the countryside as the men perfected their drumming for 'the big day'.

One morning there was a Union Jack flying from the tallest tree on the site. The children in his class talked gleefully about it and kept looking through the windows up at the hill. They were restless and difficult to restrain because they knew the holidays were near; sullen too, he always remarked.

The flag on the hill held all eyes and thoughts as each hot heavy day rolled on. When he got up in the morning he would go first to his own bedroom window and look across the fields to see if it was still there, or had been tampered with, for whoever had climbed up the biggest beech in the dead of night had unconsciously lashed the pole at a slant. That symbol high

151

above all heads held now a far greater power because of its very lop-sided swagger. Although he never involved himself in local affairs – they were all too seasonal and predictable in his book; he preferred even then to stand aside and watch – there was a current running which disturbed him. He found himself praying (too strong a word, but what other?) that there would be no storm, for if that pole ever came down . . .

On the last afternoon of school he went up to the site. He came through the trees silently on to grass to find all those bent backs among the excavations; no sound except the *chink* of the hand-tools and larks overhead. The old fort had always been a sanctuary for wild birds and their nests, a place shared only with the ancient dead and underground people. He saw the soil heaped up and the digging scars and the way the place had been taken possession of, haversacks and measuring rods thrust into mounds, clothing, kettles and cooking-stoves. Resentment stirred in him; as unreasoning, he told himself later, as that the Valley people felt out of their old sullen moulds. But now, at this time, he thought, would these diggers put everything back the way they had found it, a tidy suturing after all the surgery. . . ?

He stopped a little way off, standing his ground, waiting. What would he say, why had he come anyway?

The tall Welshman saw him and came down. It was a perfect day, he remembered, blue sky and massed pure clouds, the birds and Cabbage White butterflies moving about in the air. He and the Professor walked along talking, mainly about the neolithic sherds and arrowheads they were bringing up. Already some bowl and beaker fragments had been sent off to be reassembled. A speculative date was mentioned – 1750 B.C. – and Iberian influences. The Professor spoke about a great remorseless tide of cultures spreading westward, even to this remote place, century after century, techniques and new ideas. He himself mentioned the stand certain local Jacobins had taken on the precise spot after the failed revolt of 'ninety-eight – an event some of the older people still talked about. Ideas spread faster in those days, political ideas. They both looked up at the straining flag in silence. The fabric occasionally cracked out.

The Professor said—Symbols and symbolism. Always with us, as they moved away.

152

He took his leave then, handshakes passing, was asked if he would like to come again, help with the discoveries; they all had a feeling that something important was waiting down there. He said his vacation had now begun, he would be delighted to offer his services. It was just before the Great War, he was thirty or thereabouts and could dig with the best of them ...

Next morning when he looked up at the hill and its treed crown he saw an amazing sight, and, as he shaved, he kept breaking off to laugh in the mirror at his own lathered reflection, because nothing quite like this had ever happened before. *Two* flags were flying now. And each day that passed saw yet another, until the far-off shock of green resembled nothing so much as a growing, waving pin-cushion, liberally pricked with loyal emblems.

But by that time, of course, he was on the hill himself, a fellow-conspirator, working in the pits and trenches, sharing the food and the jokes, especially that single and colossal one which renewed itself with such great good humour each time they took it in turn to climb high with the next flag. His turn came too – at the end – and they called up to him on the highest, most dangerous fork. He was a little drunk at the time, he recalled, but felt his claim was strongest to that last and what must be crowning stroke.

The Valley was spread out below and before him as it had never been before. He rocked gently high in his bower and knew that this time he had beaten them, all of them out there toiling and plotting; but, this time, *they* had been outwitted, their own tradition turned in their faces. But then he felt hollow, as he remained perched up there, leaves brushing his face. The rising banter made the feeling worse. Voices of the foreigner. They were no real part of him, his friends of a moment before. He took a last look, then began the climb downwards. The feeling passed ...

All of that so many years ago, and nothing now to remind him of that summer but some photographs and a single fragment of a pot he had kept. It still bore the thumbprint of the Stone Age man who had made it. That seemed miraculous to him then and he had to have it. The photographs were mostly of picnic parties on the hill, his friends of one short season stretched carelessly with bottles and glasses in their hands.

153

Drinking, singing, and the short passionate liaisons that the days and nights encouraged, much wit and nicknaming, practical joking. He seemed to himself younger each morning in the looking-glass. A moustache and side-whiskers appeared. The students and their life intoxicated; he became one of them; began a brief affair with a girl, who introduced him to the novels of H. G. Wells. He was unfaithful to Minnie that summer and she wept at his off-hand manner on the few occasions he dragged himself to see her up at Hollybush House.

The other girl's name was Dorothy – Dot, everyone called her; so different from Minnie, a whirlwind of energies and the new ideas. She had great plans, he remembered. While he lay sprawled on the grass after the day's digging, heavy and dull as a draught animal, she would talk about life and literature and the changes coming. Then she would laugh at his face and embrace him with a rush, putting his head in her lap. Heat seemed to rise from her always. Later when they wrestled moistly in her tent a little apart from the others he would stifle her cries. She was only the second woman he had ever been with; the first was a whore in Amelia Street in Belfast, after a drunken farewell party on the packet boat.

But of course it had to end, just as the summer ended, and the hill closed its wounds and the wild things returned to nest and burrow, just as though nothing had ever taken place. All silent and dead again before he had a chance to become restless enough to pull up roots, cut connections. Instead, of course, he stayed on, letting the weather and the seasons flow over him like a gatepost, or old walls in some field, leaning a little more each year, growing a little crazier with time too.

He belched loudly, breaking the reverie. One could do things like that, living alone. Not all the time of course, because that would dull the pleasure. But, much worse, might easily encourage a slackening in personal habits. He was very conscious of such a danger, for there were others, living solitary lives like his, whose hold had loosened. Their habits were common knowledge, their houses filthy hovels, where they moved from bed to fireside to table and back again, hardly ever putting smoked faces out of doors. And their inertia had reaped its own reward, for didn't they all end up the victims of every bored yahoo who thought it the finest sport in the world to stuff a few sods down a chimney at Hallowe'en – any dark night for that matter?

Still, he belched again, then followed it with a rapidly breaking cluster of farts. The little fusillade made a brave sound in the open air, sharp and satisfying to his ears; daring too. Leaning on the handlebars of his bicycle on that stretch of road that skirted the old sleeping fort and its dead, he thought, *that will put an end to any further long-windedness*, then laughed at his own small joke. Gleefully he shook the handlebars – applause, applause – and his light wavered about the roadway.

There was no need for the lamp really, for the moon was full and high and his own glimmer scarcely registered. The jet behind the glass made a tiny companionable hiss, for it was an old-fashioned carbide lamp of some silvery metal with an inset lozenge of red glass in its dome. The ruby glowed steadily. The whole apparatus must be as old as he was. Indeed he had forgotten it ever existed until he started rummaging about in the coal-house and lo, there it was up on a shelf with a tin of the white powder still by its side. Gas was given off when water was added and then controlled by a knurled screw. Quite marvellous really, how the complete process of loading, priming and lighting had come back to him after all these years. He did it all without thinking, just like a school experiment. His fingers smelled of the powder . . .

Above on the hill a night creature gave a thin cry, a single sound, then silence among the trees. Badgers and foxes had been seen there. Their lairs ran deep among the bones of their ancient hunters, the bones he had also patiently uncovered that summer long ago. Camel-hair brushes were what they used on the most fragile pieces. There was one tiny skull he found, almost perfect, fitting into his cupped hand, with a neat hole in the cranium. Downward axe-blow, sending a soul into the nether world, for the Professor believed these people, squatting on their burial mounds, had fears of the deep earth-forces. Sacrificial offering, then cremation to placate the lower reaches. Blood and ash. He had held the skull most carefully. Such fragility, and he had been moved by the thought of that child, its short life, the end when it came almost casually. Like one of his own pupils. That little pale creature in the Junior School with the face and eyes of

155

an Arthur Rackham changeling. He would watch her through the glassed-off partition playing with her blocks and her worms of Plasticine. Such delicacy of features, hands and feet and hair so fine, a true faery child. He wanted to touch her, cradle her, but the nearest he ever came to it was when he went next door and gruffly catechized the Infants' class about the alphabet, the Godhead and the multiplication table. There was the true trinity all right, for these sons and daughters of the Valley.

Later he did let his hand fall lightly on her head as he moved up and down the rows of scaled-down desks. That tiny, warm pulsing scalp. Its vulnerability made him afraid. He went back next door and bully-ragged for a good half hour before he could calm himself.

But the child continued to haunt him. He would see her in the playground every day, crouched where the walls met, nibbling at crusts like a little creature too sensitive for its own good. His too – because the obsession grew; swung between an aching desire to fondle and a new urge to hurt in some way. Luckily she left the neighbourhood and the school before she could move up into his class. The episode had been disturbing. He had put it out of his head, but it would swim up – like now. A thing like that didn't bear too much examination, particularly for someone in his position. But even now it still wrung him, the unmentionable all these years later, all these years . . .

A stanza came to him. Out loud he recited:

> *Still she haunts me, phantomwise,*
> *Alice moving under skies,*
> *Never seen by waking eyes,*

because who was there to hear but the deep dead and the night predators?

Too much of a coincidence if that child's name was the same; but why was it his favourite piece of verse anyway, and why his favourite author, that other lonely gent, fond, as well, of young limbs? It was all a puzzle, despite his constant delving and dipping into memories and old scenes.

As he often did he went back over the path of his thoughts – the child in the schoolyard leading to the prehistoric one, then farther to those days under the sun on the hill; but abruptly he took hold on his meanderings, as roughly as he now shook the

156

handlebars of his bicycle. No, no, he was both romantic and a fool then, his head softened by all the misty illustrations in the reading-books he doled out; legendary nonsense in the print, matched by the drawings of ravens and thickets and the godlike ones wandering there. That skull he had dusted out was the skull of some creature, naked and matted, half-human, half-pig, rooting for acorns and white grubs up there, not the young Bran or Finn or Cuchulainn. And he was an old goat who liked nothing better than to watch young girls as they bared their bums in the middle of a wood or behind a hedge.

Aha! did that shock you, Master Barbour Brown, with your wee row of fountain-pens clipped in your waistcoat pocket, and sometimes the short cane up your sleeve too, chill against the forearm as you went up and down between the desks, stepping it out, battening down the lust in your heart with every drill-sergeant's stamp on the bare wooden boards . . . Long days in the class-room with thoughts sprouting like tubers in a hot-house. The senior girls burgeoning too before your very eyes. That shameless one just under your high desk, twisting and writhing about on her buttocks, breasts on her like a grown woman; arun with perspiration; heat and the odours of the estuary rising from her.

Now, why couldn't he remember that girl Hetty? She must have gone to the school when he was in charge, and she certainly possessed those same coarse dark looks which caused him to shiver on hot summer days of flimsy dresses and bare legs and arms. As he had shivered earlier today on his bank with glasses trained. But then she would have been too young to be in his class. Moved up most probably when Harper took over. What a scourge she would have been though, 'an occasion of sin', as the Catholics carefully put it, each and every day under his glance in Tardree First National School. No, he couldn't place her. She had receded from memory like any of a number of faces from those group photographs which he still had about the place.

At the end of every June the little cripple would arrive with camera, tripod and thick velvet cloth, then stand in the playground, favouring his bad leg, until he had assembled the School – Infants to sit on the gravel, Senior Infants on a bench behind, then the rest of the School standing in rows behind that,

Miss Cunningham the Assistant, at the left, himself on the right. Baby faces at the bottom, most of them smiling up innocently, then the gradation of expression through self-consciousness to that heavy, sullen immobility carried by all the biggest boys, ranged out from his shoulder. Every picture tells a story. Every one of those photographs did, at any rate, for there it was, a record for all who would see it, the face of the Valley and its generations. Oh, such a hardness setting in; seriousness of purpose and a life of labour ahead, and they embraced it, could hardly wait to age, be 'well-doing', add their own row of little faces to the bottom of the picture. And then those faces changed in their turn, moved upwards then disappeared out of the back row while he never shifted, year after year, summer after summer . . .

Miss Cunningham got stouter, had one child, then another, began to grow grey, a dull woman eternally knitting. She was always called Miss Cunningham even when she got married. It didn't seem to matter.

He prayed she would leave, take up child-bearing full-time so that a new young piece would be appointed. Someone like that girl Dot was who he had in mind, someone progressive, flighty, and who wore silk stockings and flesh-coloured cami-knickers. He saw those so precisely in his mind's eye as she strained upwards with her pointer to tap the Polar Cap where the bears come from.

—My dear Miss Abercrombie, allow me to offer this stool, that you may reach that map with greater ease . . .

—Oh Master Brown, you're terribly considerate, really you are. I'm so inexperienced, really I am . . .

What an old cesspool his mind had become over the years; but he had to admit that he did enjoy trawling in its depths. Flickers of guilt might still arise but they were so much rarer now. Perhaps this was the happy age after all and not those summers when his face in the photographs betrayed how truly reined in he held himself.

He really did feel fine – now, brought back to the present and this moonlit road, abroad with his blood beating strongly and calmly, his skin so dry and cool. The clicking of the free-wheel soothed as he walked along. The pedals kept their position so perfectly, the whole machine almost buoyant on its firm cushions of air. How clearly he was experiencing things! He could almost believe he had insight into the very density and odour of that air he had pumped earlier into the tyres. It smelled of rubber now of course, those old slack skins lying so long against the rims; dry rust – his fingers reacted – fresh chalk from the valves – to that as well – a whiff of oil . . .

His escapade this night was proving illuminating, a revelation indeed. Master of his own destiny and destination too. Did that lamp in the upper window still shine? Earlier he had seen it, a pinprick of light among the trees. Then he'd lost it, recovered it, lost it again as his wheels followed the road.

He mounted the machine again. Such ease, almost elegance of action having stayed with him all these years, waiting there in the sinews. Quite remarkable how memory was stored in the body as well as the brain, for it was automatic, this left foot on the pedal, the push off and away, then the slow almost lazy lift of the other leg up and over. Settling on the saddle – he had just floated his coat-tails out from him – he fastened the top button only of his pale suit. He was off and pedalling easily, just enough to give momentum . . .

And now he was that wraith again, speeding silently through the night. Minnie awaited him, her knight errant come at last to rescue her after this long, long time. She had lit her lamp, kept it there as a sign all those years in that mullioned window under the eaves. Rapunzel brushing her hair, oh, a lifetime of strokes, and why should she change her habit now? But their tryst beckoned . . .

He began to move faster, felt the air on his face and clenched hands. His jacket filled, flapped a little. What a stroke the suit was, though. He exulted in it. The lotion he had patted on cheeks and temples earlier had lost none of its pungency. He felt bathed too in an almost wicked anticipation, for, whisper it, Barbour Brown's intentions were not quite so chivalrous by this time. Strange twists of imagination were moving him now; the oddest of things happening inside that house once he had entered, taken off his bicycle-clips, stood there listening to the clocks and the silence. His voice will begin whispering her name; she doesn't answer at first, but hear him she does, lying up there with a smile beginning. She giggles once, then puts her hand before her mouth. Her eyes glitter, cheeks bright as flame, for the cosmetics she wore earlier are still there as if she knew quite well he would come prowling, seeking her . . . but of course she knows, hasn't she been stretched out for hours on the counterpane awaiting him, gently smiling mannequin?

He begins his ascent of the stairs, stopping to listen on every second tread. Such thick, soft carpeting held by brass rods. Their gleam guides. He is certain he can hear her heartbeat now, his own too. The old house begins to fill with the sound. That pulsing is not yet in unison but it will be, oh, yes, it will be soon . . .

He reaches the landing. The slow stealth to her door, hand on that cool knob, then the turning – careful, careful . . . The door opens, he is inside in the darkness, but the lamp is quenched. *She is not there.* He stands a moment. Why? What? Her perfume is everywhere, a heavy musk. Such an odour conjures up her lying there only a moment before, outlandishly dressed. All this oddness excites. Rustling garments, scents, gongs, tiny silver bells. His head is filled to bursting point, whirling. Then he hears her laugh behind him, and that is a chime too, outside the room somewhere, somewhere in the house . . .

Their game of hide and seek begins. It begins and as it does all ensuing events also commence to speed up, as if his imagination is cranking faster. The two of them skip from room to room, closet to wardrobe to cupboard under the stairs, jerkily, like characters in a penny pier-machine. And so with impatience he now winds those images past, quick, quick jinking blurs . . . can't wait to reach the final tableau . . . every picture tells a story . . . can't in truth contain himself, cannot wait, cannot wait . . .

He is riding his bicycle, slow turn of the feet, slower turn of the rear wheel and inside his head that other flywheel. The fancy distracts only momentarily, because the last frame is there, held, and the two characters in dumb-show joined at last. In the half-light of the wide hall down there below on the floor on the Chinese rugs they fumble and pull at one another. Shoes are being kicked off, the constricting garments of late middle age loosened in a giggling frenzy. All this is shocking enough to the viewer with his eye pressed to the peep-show, but there is one final scandalous touch. Old Hutton Maitland him-

160

self looks down on it all, for the couple grapple and writhe almost directly below his framed and family portrait. And of course he, or his imagination rather, has added that to the scenario, just had to, bubbling up from the deep, that final grotesquerie. Still it does, did have, a certain flourish, like the sweep at the tail of a signature . . .

He is still cycling effortlessly on, cool and relaxed in mind and limb. Every action is automatic and he feels at one with the white road, the hedges and the fields as they slip past. He has found his tempo now and will stick to it. The word *swimmingly* comes to him in a way that it has never before. Or since, he thinks, because this, all of this, is unique, quite unique . . .

At one time he would try to put such a feeling down in his notebooks, shorthand phrases on the paper that would pin the moment for a later time. But either it lost all of its power when he returned to it – a pot-pourri without fragrance – or he never did, he never did. Lately his entries on the blue-lined paper have been flat objective pieces. More of a commonplace book than anything else is how he sees the old journal these days. He has been dipping into the church records again, the parish histories and sundry leather-bound works published at their authors' own expense almost a hundred or two hundred years earlier. These are now his feeding-ground. Copying out passages from them late at night he has found to be a calming exercise, the brain stilled. The pen moves across the paper in its pool of lamplight, transcribing unhurriedly, and all existence outside as well as inside the room shrivels to the page and the words coming forth. Even the expression of his thoughts now seems coloured by that antique but resonant prose. *Coming forth.* Like water from rock. His mind is off again, oh yes, off again, while the rest of him just lazily bicycles on to whatever awaits . . .

That old religion with its imagery burning in the hearts of the faithful. Every bush, every stone, every barren corner of this Valley, for them, the barest remove from that other Eastern landscape. All those dead generations putting their trust in an old and jealous God. Murrain and massacre when they displeased Him, full corn-cribs when His face did shine upon them. Dark times surely with all minds shrivelled to the kernel by superstition and backwoods hysteria. Not all minds though. Not all. One alone standing apart, one man, and that man after

161

his own heart. His very own divine whom he has been back-tracking through all these musty pages so patiently night after night, beneath the green-shaded lamp. The good Doctor hasn't yet surrendered himself completely but he will, he will . . . Only a matter of time before all his pieces fit, and if the written record cannot suffice, then imagination must flesh him, flush him out. But there is enough in print in the old books to be going on with . . .

Now as he works the bicycle along effortlessly all in his own good time, oh, yes, in his own good time, whole passages he has laboured over flow into his head and, so familiar are they, because of the act of slow penning, that they seem almost like his very own thoughts . . .

And from Scotland came not a few ministers, for this land mourneth and the people perish for want of knowledge. And many of these religious professors had been profane, and for debt, and want, and worse causes had left Scotland, yet the Lord was pleased by His word to work such a change in them that they brought to the land a bright and hot sun-blink of the gospel. And verily some of these same men had attained to such a dexterity of speaking of religious purposes by resemblances to worldly things that they would among themselves entertain a spiritual discourse for a long time; and the others present, though these men spoke good English, could not understand what they said.

The chief and foremost brand in this burning assembly was one Doctor Colville, formerly of Kirk O'Shotts, a little active, sharp-eyed man exceedingly quick in all his motions, and noted for his quaint, remarkable and forceful sayings. His gift of preaching was of such an order that many flocked to hear him, coming thirty or forty miles, and there continued from the time they came until they returned without wearying or making use of sleep; yea, but little either meat or drink. And Colville's words fell upon them like gracious rain upon the pastures of the wilderness, and the thirsty land became springs of water.

But presently a darkening of the spirit overtook this gifted emissary of the Lord, making him forsake his former zeal. And there was great dismay among his fellow ministers at the changes wrought in their brother and they taxed him with his new-found habits, for it was murmured now that he did not always go sober to his bed. Further tales had gone abroad too that he had held lewd conversation with a young woman on one of his many journeys, for if he had been a brisk and tireless horse rider in the service of his Lord previously, now he seemed spurred on by a harder taskmaster, so restless was he become in his peering and prying and questioning of the country people in the remote places of the parish.

And so this Doctor Colville continued in his scandalous ways until a deputation of the ministers came to his own house to confront him. But he merely answered them in this manner strangely: 'In my former ministry there hath not one day passed me without thoughts of death, and renewed submission to it; yea, this made me neglect my body and the things of the body, which should have served the Lord, as if it had been the mire of the street. Which now troubleth me.'

New Day

1

Enter the conspirators three, disgruntled and ready now for serious mischief. There have been no pears, not even a pear-tree, as far as they can judge, in that dark, overgrown place they have been fumbling about in for the past half-hour or so. Have you ever searched for fruit at night in an orchard? Touch seems the slowest of the senses and against any faint light there may be still in the sky, the look of the leaves merely confuse the issue. Time after time the hand goes up, only to grab nothing, or nothing but a clutch of stripped foliage, when what the touch has anticipated is something firm, full, rewarding.

At first they slipped from tree to tree silently, moving out from one another, each to find his own bounty. Like children they were in their haste to strike rich first, but then they slowed down as it came home to them. What sort of trees were they trying to plunder? Or were they in a bloody orchard at all? There was noise now, vengeful thrashings, sudden grabs made and branches bent, then broken. And much swearing. They emerged itching as well – and found their way on to the flat paved area, a terrace of some sort, at the back of the house, so enter three conspirators . . .

It's almost a tableau now, each in his own square, positioned. Over there, sitting on an ornamental urn, and with an idea at the back of his head that with just enough pressure it might be made to topple, is Harvey. And over there is Mack. His mind runs to hopscotch. Just give him a little time and he'll invent some chilling variation. Finally, just standing – himself. Stale-mate, is how he sees it. The night, he tells himself bitterly, has been a series of humiliations. All of this blind-man's-buff, too ludicrous for words, yet he puts up with it. And even manages to smile throughout, that hateful, crooked eager-to-please smile he keeps having glimpses of in pub mirrors and the like, just to remind him. He resolves to harden himself from now onwards.

No more grinning. And no more being the conscience of the party either, that's for sure. He'll go his own way, lead the way, in fact, in any future destruction, for it's certainly going to be one wrecking and rending do from now on, and that's also for sure.

In his palm he rubs a leaf while he ponders. It slowly grinds to dead fibre. They should have beaten the trees with sticks. That's always satisfying. Coming home from school, they used to slash a way through the wild rhubarb and the nettles along the river bank for the gunbearers. *Machete* was a word he knew but couldn't pronounce. He knew more about the Amazon than Mack ever would, but Mack was always John Payne in the search for the Lost Civilization. Nothing had really changed.

—Okay. So where's all this action then?

His voice very low, for there's still that lighted window up there among the creepers. But the gibe is unmistakable. They both look at him now. Harvey begins to rock the heavy urn, but that's futile, and he stops when now they look at him.

If he himself doesn't do something at this point it will be too late, his chance lost. He knows it. *Go in there, son, and let him have it. You can do it. The Eddie Cantor Story,* or *Body and Soul,* or was it that time his father handed him a stick and sent him out to fight his own battles with crop-headed Joey Craig? *Yes, silly bugger, why don't you stand there and act it out in your head first? Then Jungle Jim over there will have taken the initiative as usual, and be off again.*

So he starts across the flat stone expanse towards the house with this exaggerated stage prowl, head turning slowly from side to side, finger pressed to the lips. It's an excellent performance, he knows it, and he expects a laugh, a quiet appreciative chuckle, at least, for they mustn't be too contemptuous of that little dormer light up there, but nothing from this dead audience, nothing. He'll need a banana-skin, at least.

These are french windows ahead, he realizes, the real thing, as he gives up on the other two, made to open out when the days are long and halcyon. Closed now of course, but not curtained, because he can see inside.

Hands cupped to his eyes, he can make out . . . books behind glass, a brass clock with a slowly whirring propeller-like pendulum, a lot of pictures, bowls and vases on twin tables, a sofa with a curved back, and all on a carpet that looks Eastern.

He has never seen a room like this one, pictures in magazines and books, yes, and that stage-set for *She Stoops to Conquer,* but never a real room where people can walk about or sit or stand carelessly with a glass in their hand at the mantlepiece.

He thinks, *What am I doing here, staring into this rich room where the rich live?*

It's a panicky moment all right, and he looks over his shoulder at the other two for reassurance. *They aren't there.* The terrace is bare and they're not to be seen. He feels as if he's been set up for target practice. Any second something will come whistling at him out of the dark beyond the footlights, because these stone squares seem lit like a stage. They hold the light, throw it outwards. He's noticing that for the first time, now, when it's too late.

So he's just standing there awaiting the inevitable, when there's a sound, a movement out there in the wilderness that rings the old house. Whoever it is, it isn't the other two certainly for they would be much quieter, but trust them anyway to skulk off and leave him to his fate, his two *buddies,* without a warning. He is more bitter now than ever before, but the emotion is misplaced, inappropriate, as this newcomer heads closer. It may be a policeman, several, deployed cleverly to surround the house after a call for assistance from the old woman upstairs. Are there telephone wires? He looks up, but all is blackness, dense weight of the walls, and beyond that, barely a break into the night sky.

Instinctively he moves now up to and against the chill glass, then on sideways along the brickwork, seeking escape, because not for the world would his feet carry him back across that terrace. How did he ever let himself get into such a position anyway? Like some donkey happily backing into the nearest pair of shafts, and it was no good either saying 'never again' and all that sort of shit, because he was in it, he certainly was and well up to his collar in the brown stuff.

And still making with the wisecracks too, he noticed. Did a condemned man's brain keep on churning out irrelevancies right up to the last? He suspected it did, like the headless chicken.

His hands find a shrub, explore its prickling quills for a moment, then he pulls himself in behind it. It grows close to the wall. There are bare inches in which to manoeuvre, but he manages it, dropping to his knees on the soil at its roots. His face is brushed and tickled, and the smell of earth fills his nostrils. It reminds him of last year, that air-raid shelter, the skinny bit of stuff. Never mind her name, that's best forgotten, everything else about her too, but still he flinches nevertheless, recalling the way she kept on chewing her Spearmint while he fumbled. *Hurry up*, she kept saying, *hurry up*, and once – *Don't be all night.* That did it. As limp as lettuce and he hadn't even her drawers down. Such crudity, oh such crudity . . .

There is someone out there on the far edge, sure enough, just at the edge of the paving, standing. He can hear heavy breathing.

I must look a fright. Through a hedge backwards. She would just sit down for a minute, so she would, on this big plant-pot object. Get her wind back.

Her stockings are ruined, so should they come off? But when she's had a closer look at them by the light of the moon, they aren't half as bad as she'd imagined. She can always twist the ladder around to the back, but anyway it is the middle of the night, for the lord's sake. Enough on her plate without that particular morsel of vanity, and that's no word of a lie. But the light is still on up there, just a wee square in the darkness, and oh, it means everything to her. Salvation isn't too strong a word, for it comes to her what those other words of the hymn must really mean. *Rock of Ages, cleft for me, Let me hide myself in thee . . .*

She still keeps her eyes fixed on that light in the window though, but it won't go out. No. Minnie sleeps badly. *Oh, the long night watches, the long night watches, child. Count your blessings.* She's tired out just thinking it, and dying to slip between the sheets of a certain bed she has in her mind, bars at its wooden head, and at its foot, and the eiderdown is duck-egg blue with a flowery pattern. And the sheets and pillow-cases smell of lavender, and on the round table just within reach is a night-light in case you can't sleep in the dark. People like Minnie think of everything. Rich people.

She sits there on the edge of the empty stone urn, not minding its lip biting into her, it feels like pleasure itself after what she's been through. So good to rest, knowing that in your own good time you can just rise, stroll across to that house and go in. Then to think of the rest of the night in such a bed. A sin really to go to sleep in such a bed, she decides, better to lie awake and feel the cool sheets and smell lavender deeply until morning.

It must be awful to be on the run like a convict, and never know the luxury of a good night's rest. Poor Henry Fonda and his suffering face, afraid to return to his sweetheart. Sitting in the dark stalls it seemed all true, but everything on the screen always did to her. If she ever had money she'd go a dozen times a day, might even have her food brought in to her. On one of those trays with the light shining down. God, the things you could only do if you had money. She often wondered would Minnie leave her any of hers. She rambled on about nest-eggs and windfalls, strange words, but she understood what they meant all right, so she did. She pretended to take no notice naturally but she knew that Minnie hoped she would, for it was her way of trying to keep hold of her. Dear love her, if she only but knew it, she could buy and sell her twice over.

So she laughs to herself, sitting there on Minnie's old urn with the dead plants in it, in Minnie's very own back garden, taking her ease and her none the wiser up in her bed there. She can hardly wait to see her face. What a picture that will be, and no mistake. She means to call up to her. She'll do it softly, so that the old thing won't get too big a shock. That's important, she tells herself, as gentle and soft as one of those wood-pigeons that nest in the top of the trees.

She listens but they must be all asleep by now. There's nothing to be heard but a steady faint sound like a drum somewhere in the fields. She knows what it is. It's a ram pumping water – that's what they call it – and it never stops day or night, although there are times when you can't hear it if there's a strong wind. She has never seen it herself, but she knows it's there all right, down in that low-lying place, where the stream is. That's where it gets the water from. *Bump . . . Bump . . . Bump . . .* She keeps time with the rhythm, a little hiccuping sound after each beat. It's odd really, never resting night and day, just pumping away by itself out in that lonely part of the fields, with nobody near it, like a heart.

Quite suddenly she sees, lying there close to her feet the cigarette butt and she knows just as suddenly that it's not old. She doesn't have to touch it, she just knows, couldn't put fingers to it if she tried, but it looks warm, probably wet a little at one end, a horrible, sticky dampness where someone's lips have been. She makes a rush, keeping wide of it lying there, across the stone slabs over to the window.

—*Minnie! Minnie!* she calls up. – *It's me! Let me in! It's me!*

172

No soft pigeon-cooing, oh no, she's yelling her head off, because even if it doesn't make sense, an ordinary cigarette butt has just frightened her out of her wits. And of course it may be ancient, blown by the wind, swept out even by her own hand to lie there, but her nerves tell her different. Someone has only just thrown it away, she knows, *she knows,* and must be near at hand and even if they do hear her, she can't control herself any more, she's as close to hysterics as she's ever been.

—Oh, Minnie, Minnie, for God's sake, come down and open the door! It's me, I tell you!

And then the next but most terrible thing, for the light goes out, just like that, and she can't believe it at first, how such a thing can be. All around her in an instant things get so much darker and closer, just because one small light is blown out.

She hunts around in a panic now for a stone to throw up at the glass. A handful of dry soil from the base of a bush is all she can muster in the blackness, and up it goes out of her fist to rattle on the pane. She fires another, then another, grains dropping back on top of her head and shoulders, nearly blinding herself with the dust she's bringing down around her, but no light goes on, not even a match flaring. Never has she felt so forsaken as now.

She becomes angry, forgetting the present danger. She'll smash an entrance, so she will, for hasn't she the right? And how can anyone turn out to be so heartless, for she knows she's up there pretending not to hear, like that bloody brass monkey of hers on the mantelpiece. The old bitch with her head under the bedclothes. After all these years to abandon her like this. But it's no use, stones are of no avail, even if she does break a pane.

Now she rushes to the french window to shake the knob in a fury. The door shivers, she can see the room within, so calm, so safe. It seems to dance, moving through the dark glass, pictures and furniture and bits of brass winking back at her. Only this afternoon she had been in there moving about, dusting, and once, when Minnie was upstairs, stretched on the sofa surveying it all, deciding which pieces should go and which should stay when she was mistress. The nonsense of only a matter of hours earlier, the nonsense of a child – but no more. She would never be like that again. The clock could never be put back now.

But she must gather her wits together. There has to be a way in, only a piece of glass between her and safety. Perhaps an open window somewhere? But it's no good searching for that, she knows Minnie and her habit of going over the whole house at dusk. She looks around even more desperately. People have been known to sometimes put keys under a doormat in case they lock themselves out, and Minnie would be terrified of anything like that ever happening to her. But she knows there's nothing under this rough brown square because she shook it only today. There's another of those stone urns though, twin of the one over there she has just been sitting on, but they both must weigh a ton, that other one did anyway. Nevertheless she grips it by its rim, rough and cold, and begins to rock it. The solid thing moves and each time, further off the ground, but now she's in a quandary. How can she get at the key even if it is in there under the heavy base? Her fingers will be crushed, her foot as well, if she dares to wedge that in. She hears a noise near her in the darkness behind a bush – at least she thinks she does – and without hesitation pushes the urn over. It cracks to a hundred pieces, and the sound seems to freeze her blood, no sound like that sound, before or after. She's done a terrible thing, but was driven to it. Such thoughts are hammering in her head, while she's on her knees scraping about among the bits of cement. The thing wasn't stone after all.

But there is a key. It feels old and rusty, and God alone knows what door it's meant for, but still she flies with it in her hand over to the french window and jiggles it into the lock. It turns, *oh, it turns,* she pushes the casement and she's inside Minnie's parlour with its smell of furniture wax and the big green aspidistra, strong and rich.

It's the smell of sanctuary.

—Taken short? Eh, son?

Mack and Harvey bending over to study him, still crouched behind his shrub. He tries to rise swiftly but the cramps in both legs have him tied. The two of them are holding their laughter in.

—We might have to leave him like that, Harvey. You never can tell.

And it is ridiculous to be hobbled this way, he knows, but he's numb from the waist down, he truly is. So as he rubs away at himself, a weak smile on his dial, he's sitting target for the next whispered witticism.

And Mack is in top form again. He can tell. As if he's been saving up malice out there in the dark. And how he must have relished everything he saw and heard. That still reverberates within him. Two faces hanging over him, grinning, and he feels threatened by all this sudden, sick joviality. So he massages his thighs more forcefully, concentrating on a knot of growing warmth in each. Boy Scout blowing on a fire. Once upon a time they were all in the Eagle Patrol and innocent. Remember? Jesus, it seems centuries ago.

—Harvey, wouldn't you say now that Miss Maitland would be only too happy to oblige the boy here? If she knew his position. A spot of light relief. In the right place. Eh?

An unexpected tack this. Distasteful. At least he'll show distaste.

—You've a mind like a shit-house, Mack.

—Well now you know what they say, don't you? The older the fiddle the sweeter the tune.

Harvey bares teeth silently.

No one has raised his voice above a whisper, for they're still prowlers, still up to no good. The old darkened house has cast them in the rôle. He knows he is still overawed anyway. The

175

sheer bulk and spread of it, together with all that unthinking abundance he associates with the wealthy, has turned him in on himself. He resents the feeling, but still he knows that Mack resents it even more in himself. It's one of his own tiny sly observations and he cherishes it. Mack may be cleverer than he is – as at this very moment – but his inferiority complex is much deeper.

And I suppose, he thinks to himself, *the deeper it is the harder one has to work to keep it covered.* Some sort of revenge will be what he has in mind about now though, something damaging. He remembers the post-office bicycle and the way he looked after it slid under, to crash, submerged, against the flood-gates. What old score did that even up? But is he really evil, can he be really as wicked as he seems? To him. *Wicked. Evil.* Sunday-school words. *Mack, you are a sinner, but there must be a speck of decency in you somewhere, a grain, a mustard seed.*

He feels he can rise now, his legs have started to tingle, but Mack is calling up suddenly to the darkened window, his hands cupped like a megaphone, yet whispering still. Minn-ee, let me in. Minn-ee, it's only me, Minn-ee.

Christ, but you are evil, Mack, you really are and there's no redemption for you. – Hasta la vista, he says softly, firmly. – Fellas, it's been a long night.

I mean just how far can this travesty be played out. Until you, Mack, grow sick of it and call a halt?

His legs feel a bit rubbery. He hopes he'll be able to ride home, all right. And what about the old lady waiting up, he hasn't let thought of her intrude up to now? *Better not,* thinks he, *better not.*

The two of them are looking at him. He can see their faces in the moonlight turned in his direction. He has moved away to stretch his legs, make ready. They're smiling again. He has no desire to be their clown any more though, will not allow himself to be re-conscripted. Mack comes closer on his toes, putting a warning finger up. Harvey edges forward too. Once more he's realizing he doesn't know these two, considered as friends, as well as he's imagined, for this is another of those moments of menace.

—You're not going now, are you? Just when the fun's starting.

And it's straight out of the next movie. (Everything is, when you come to think of it.) Widmark up to his sinister tricks with Mike Mazurki in tow. Putting the squeeze on the young crusading D.A., or better still, every jaded private eye rolled into one, but instead of it being midnight in the downtown office with the water-cooler in the corner, big rising bubbles, the dixie-cups – it's Tardree in the small hours. Nothing romantic in such a name alongside Manhattan or Riverside Drive. No skyscrapers, no Yellow Cabs, no Stork Club – just a black hole in the middle of Ireland. It is at times like these that imagination has to finally give up. He tells himself that, shivering a little.

The night air is getting colder, the way he's heard it does before dawn. There's not a sound, just something far off, some machinery or other turning away, a steady thudding.

—You're surely not running out on us now?

Mack makes it sound as if it's the depths of treachery, him merely wanting to get to his bed. And Harvey stirs angrily.

—Now look here—

—No, you look here, you look here. Finger jabbing, show of righteous indignation achieved at last on that pale and puffy face as he closes. If he didn't feel so hemmed in, he'd be laughing right out at this moment. How does one reach such proficiency?

—We're all in this together (*in what, for God's sake, in what?*) but okay, okay, if you're windy and want home to your mammy—

He might well have to fight Mack after all, make the first strike even, at that sneer, he's thinking rapidly, for this is a little too much. More important, and it's an hypocrisy in himself which he recognizes bitterly, he can't afford to let him say more. For even if he does bow the head and walk away, who cares about fighting another day? Too much blood drawn even before he gets out of ear-shot, and that's no lie. So of course he takes the easy and cowardly way out.

—Who's windy? he whispers back fiercely and again – Who are you calling windy?

Mack's mask is now one of outraged innocence.

—I didn't say you were. I said 'if'.

—That's what you said. I heard you.

Mack beseeches Harvey with a look now of martyrdom, but *he* turns away. He knows there will be no fisticuffs after all. Poor Harvey.

—Now look here, don't take the hump. We started off together and we'll stay together.

He can smell his breath, still sweet with beer, as he leans closer. The windsor knot in his tie has worked loose and the jacket with its patch pockets swings open. Disarrayed is the word. He has a moment of cheap triumph. Mack always looks more than a bit common when he starts to sweat. He feels better right away. Even conciliatory.

Then this wizard with the spiky hair – and the grin – the grin of a huckster – what does he do but quickly dip a hand inside his jacket, and as quickly palm a bottle of whisky for them both to see. Not a full one, of course, even he couldn't have managed such deception, but one of those flat and handy five-glass affairs. He has a glimpse of Jaunty Johnnie with hat and cane on the label before it's thrust out to him. A peace offering, and he takes it in the correct spirit, gravely swallowing a roughly estimated third, before rubbing the neck with his sleeve and passing it on. The whisky bites, then spreads. Mack drinks last, then looks at them, the bottle-neck nipped between finger and thumb, moonlight catching the dark glass.

—We can still have a bit of sport, he says.—It's not too late.

Somehow each of them has found his own square to stand in again, to be ready for he knows not what. The light casts their shadows before them on the grained stone to further complicate any pattern of moves they may eventually make. It may only be the whisky, he tells himself, but he finds something marvellous in all this intricacy laid out as though on a board. Yet he feels raised and looking down on it in anticipation, his mind sharp, never so sharp as now, and that which holds its focus is the bottle. It swings gently in Mack's grip. He retains it delicately with what seems the most negligent of holds. But it must not drop. For that emptied bottle to break and shatter just now would be a terrible thing. He watches it intensely. Harvey seems to do so too, he notices. Mack holds them on wires, just moving the bottle gently up and down, causing little flashes.

Then he calls out, and the bottle is travelling towards Harvey for a catch. Harvey holds, then it's on its way to him. The glass

178

feels cold and sticky to the touch. Mack waits now, but he's moved further away, out almost to the edge, almost into darkness.

—Come on, come on, he cries softly, cupping his hands. First variation of the game has now taken place, but there are more to follow.

Mack catches, a cricket toss high in the night air, then straight back to him underhand like a bullet. It slaps into his hands barely a foot above the stone court. Up and over his own lob next to Harvey. Leisurely. Cautious play from him. Then Harvey to Mack, Mack to Harvey, Harvey to Mack. They are grinning. He does too, bearing it. Then out of the air the bottle comes to him, this time whirling. Not flat and weighted as before, and he knows there's spin on it. He sweats, watching it, it's hanging in the air, a glint in it, on it. In his grip the thing wriggles.

He wants to annihilate Mack next time, throws his loaded hand up high instinctively, then lets it fall. They're grinning at him again. So it's back once more to Mack with just that little evil screw of the wrist at the last moment, for he's feeling vicious now, will match anything that's offered. Crouched like a tennis player on the stone, he's in all this body and soul, snaps his finger, narrows his eyes, *come on, come on, let it fly hard and fast.* No quarter given. And it does fly and it soars and darts too, sometimes innocent as a toy, next time a grenade.

All the while the moon rides above, lighting their silent antics, for it might be the oldest of movies they're acting out in energetic mime, Keaton and Co. The scatter of debris over there around that urn's broken stump belongs to some other people. So does the darkened window up there too. And the glass door.

Mack makes a long underhand bowl to Harvey – he's glad it's Harvey – for then the bottle hangs miraculously on an outstretched finger, fixed, and Harvey looks foolish as he reacts to thin air, hands smacking impotently. The wizard has capped it all with a crooked little finger inside the neck. Johnnie Walker mocks them as he wobbles up and down obscenely, black glass winking. Who can follow that – or what?

So the spent missile is drawn back to the arm's full stretch and Mack hurls it far out into the night up and over the trees.

They wait for it to fall. The detonation will surely be something quite colossal, but there is no sound. The bottle rests out there – so that's it – in some soft secret bed to fill slowly with rain. The hedges and ditches are thick with such things, but none will have such a history. To think that he can wax thus over an old bottle.

But Mack is squaring his jacket and tie and putting a hitch to his trousers. They watch this new development, and they're both wondering, for it's not a gesture that signifies finality. And he seems to read their minds for he whispers—Surely you didn't think that was what I meant by *sport*, did you?

They wait, and they're in his hands, blood stirred now to anything he'll put them at, two mounts eager and whetted.

He says slyly—She didn't lock the french windows behind her. You noticed that, didn't you.

And all their eyes, thoughts too, travel over to the shadowy glass, such a thin skin to keep the outside world at bay.

A wedge of Minnie's mousetrap cheese from the covered dish in the pantry. Her heart set on it, or rather her stomach, and she glides through the darkened kitchen towards that desire. It's like swimming in the dark. She knows this old room like the back of her hand, with her eyes shut. There's the table she's scrubbed a thousand times, the Aga's over there, cold of course; there, two rocking chairs, one for her, the other for Minnie, she always likes to think, and to her right the Welsh dresser (always referred to as the Welsh dresser as if that meant something). The delph is about the only thing that gives itself away. *Like a kitling's eye* she thinks for no good reason, but she floats past on a straight course, right to the pantry door, not one bump, and enters the coolest part of the whole house. A tunnel or a tomb. She thinks that just to test her nerves, but they're all right, she's all right now, with the house around her like an old friend.

The cheese is lovely. She sniffs it, can hardly wait to carry it back to the table to begin nibbling. There she breaks it into ladylike morsels, setting them out before her on the bare wood to be enjoyed slowly. Minnie always gets a nice tasty piece of cheddar, she'll say that for her. Not a crumb will remain to ever give her away. She'll be just like a mouse or a ghost passing through. Her nerves are surely marvellous, no mistake about it, to be casually thinking about such things here in this old mansion at this hour. And not a sound, she thinks, as she chews away. Not a sound. Funny too, but she doesn't feel sleepy any more. There's an urge on her to go prowling in and out of rooms, along passages, to open doors and closets, and all in the dark too.

She takes off her shoes in preparation, thinking it a fine piece of cheek to put them on the table instead of under, the act just to prove that the house is really hers to do with as she pleases. And she knows somehow deep inside, that this will be the last time she'll ever be here. It seems strange taking leave of it in the dark this way, but she'll have no regrets.

Sitting there at the table, with her stockinged feet on the rung of the chair, she drowses a moment, not sleepily, just letting thoughts bob through her head like corks on a stream. It's the nearest to contentment she's felt all day, alone like this with her fancies in the darkest, deepest part of the old house. For so long, it seemed, she had been battling against things. It was like carrying a stone on your back. But now it felt as if the weight had been lifted, and soon she wouldn't be able to remember what it had ever felt like.

Her spirits are high all of a sudden, rising inside, a mood on her once more to explore, a restless mood hard to satisfy. She leaves the kitchen and the shoes stay behind on the top of the table, sitting boldly there in the dark, for her to retrieve, just whenever she takes the notion.

Her feet don't make a sound, travelling from the cold kitchen tiles out on to waxed wood in the hallway, where the grandfather clock ticks a deep low beat like another heart, and she puts arms around it in a hug as if it is human and a friend, ear pressed to its case. In the dark she can hear like an animal; smell too. Lavender furniture polish, geraniums, a whiff of Minnie's eau-de-cologne, her rubber galoshes where she keeps them just inside the hall door. But it's not really dark here after all, for moonlight is falling down through the fanlight and through the stained glass on either side of the door. The floor gleams, a great long stretch without a rug to break its flow.

She fancies a slide quite suddenly, something she's always longed to do, especially after a hard stint of polishing down on hands and knees. The wood then always did seem as smooth and as shiny as a rink, but now it really has the look of ice. She can't resist. Anyway, she tells herself, why should she? *Whoosh*, she goes like Sonja Henie, and again, and a further time, hand outstretched to meet the back of the hall-door. She'll try it now with one leg, and does so with barely a wobble. Bravo.

The blood has rushed to her head. It seems to bring madness along with it, for she tears off one of her stockings with its garter, in a fresh impulse, and flings it clear. The soft falling silk lands like a scarf around the carved old wooden darkey at the foot of the stairs. Big white eyes, red lips and monkey-jacket. A regular grinning effigy, there he stands with a lamp in his hands, with what used to be one of her prized stockings draped now around his neck. Then off comes the other one, and number two this time sails up and over a set of antlers that hangs on the wall. Old Hutton Maitland was supposed to have shot the beast in the Highlands of Scotland, silly old bugger that he was.

She feels like having one last look at his sourpuss, because he's around the corner in a big gilt frame, is Minnie's dear dadda. And that one's an equally silly old relic, locked away in her room up at the top of the house and never guessing in a million years what sort of a carry-on is taking place down here among her precious treasures and knick-knacks. To think of the hours she's spent dusting and rubbing Brasso and beeswax into such horrors. Knick-knacks. What a word. It always reminds her of . . . Giggling at her own shamelessness, she quickly stoops and off *they* come. In the next instant she's up on a chair below the row of family portraits and looking for that antique kisser. Then – *ah*, she sighs, stepping down after a moment to admire her handiwork. *Ah*. Quite a picture.

Standing there barefoot she gives the vee sign to old Hutton with his goatee beard and his cross, crabbed stare, but especially to the pair of drawers now hanging down over one hard eye. And still warm – she giggles to herself – still warm, as she feels so free under her frock. She feels so free with her toes spread deliciously in this soft rug. It's like being down at the river bank and running once more on the grass, so safe, so warm and so clean. Once she took off every stitch while Teresa Mullan kept dick, and splashed in a pool. Only for a moment, because she felt scared for most of the time. But the sensation was worth it. She had wanted to be like Hedy Lamarr, and for about a couple of minutes she was. So, now remembering, she unhooks the back of her blue dress and draws it over her head, then carelessly flings it into a corner. She's acting the spoilt society lady. The French maid will follow the trail she's left and pick up every single garment. That's what French maids are for, and so as not to confuse Fifi in her morning search, off comes that very last article. The pink brassiere, only one she's ever had, well-washed and darned, she dangles from the big dinner-gong. That came all the way from Bombay, carried on an elephant's back, so Minnie said. *Oh, Minnie Maitland, to think of you hiding up there under the bedclothes, and missing all this, all of this. Why, it's your very own Hetty's farewell performance, so it is.*

She's dancing before thousands of her admirers, don't you know, and never has The Dying Swan been so wonderfully performed. *More like the dying duck,* she thinks, as her feet get mixed up in one of the rugs, and she nearly collapses with holding the laughter in, but oh, it's so carefree gliding like this, with the air on your bare skin.

Up, down and around the big hall she dances in the dark, just the gentlest of humming coming from her lips. Her arms twine in the air as soft as serpents, and she feels drunk as though on champagne. Then she catches sight of herself in a mirror, the old tall one. For a moment it had held her framed, all of her, and it seemed as if it was a stranger, as though her body belonged to somebody else. She stops. Oh, so much does she want to return to that split second, to be taken unawares, to see herself as others see, but then nobody never has, not even herself, because she has never once seen all of herself like this in a mirror. Like this.

She stands there looking into the dark glass, touching herself very slowly, place by place. How strange she feels, how strange she looks. Not even to know yourself all over, just pieces cut out of you by the mirror at home, the one they all use and never even to think it strange. She's touching herself and watching herself do it.

Presently she comes away from the mirror moving in a kind of daze into the parlour. There she finds a knitted rug belonging to Minnie and she puts it around herself. It smells of eau-de-cologne and face powder. She thinks fondly of the old woman upstairs. *She* will have answers for her.

Up the staircase she mounts, holding her wrap close and sniffing its ladylike smell. One landing, then two, and she's outside the white-painted door. It always reminds her of a nursery door for some reason. She expects to hear baby sounds coming from inside. She listens for a moment, then she whispers – Miss Maitland, it's me. Hetty. Oh, please open the door and let me in.

She waits with her ear pressed to the cool painted wood, and this voice comes at her from within like a cat's screaming.

—Go away. It's too late. I'm not well. Go away! Go away!

2

Once they had travelled to Dublin in the train together, facing across the compartment, unable to look directly at one another because of their excitement. He kept his own eyes fixed on a brownish photographic view of the Rock of Cashel for most of the journey. That barren heap with the Cathedral rising from it like a back-drop and the scattering of obligatory staring peasants with donkey-carts, he could still recall in detail. Yet he couldn't remember what she was wearing. Something over-fussy almost certainly, like her state of mind, because she was still trembling at their daring when they reached Amiens Street Station.

Their destination was a small hotel near the Ballsbridge Show Grounds and they signed the register as cousins. Her nerves could never have withstood the additional strain of posing as anything or anyone else. He was distinctly pent-up himself, he recollected. Wresting his beloved away from the ogre in Holly-bush House for an illicit week-end in the South had left him with a mood of deepest depression and, to shake Minnie out of hers, he felt he had to adopt an air of almost raffish bonhomie. He remembered how he kept excusing himself to go to the bathroom, where he buried his head in his hands, despising himself. Then he began to hate her too and her tremulous ways. The more she fumbled with her cutlery and changed colour for the waitresses to see the more his rage grew, and the coarser his smoking-room manners became.

She retired to her room in tears after dinner, while he plunged into the streets like some ravening commercial traveller. And the mood of the capital was reeking hot. The War had just started and enlistment and final flings were in the air.

A month later he was to learn that two of his best friends had been burned to death in their bell-tent on their first night in

Belgium when a paraffin stove was overturned. Teddy Topping and Harold Duff, the first of that lost generation.

But Dublin's public houses beckoned that night, their music-halls too, for at one stage he was certain he was in the gallery of The Gaiety, squeezing some woman's thigh in the crush. The air was thick with flying orange peel. That stayed with him. Some unfortunate English comedian on stage. The rest of the night became hazy, reeling past in a blur of noise and red faces in bar interiors.

Then in the small hours he was wandering along the quays by himself, no longer drunk. What happened next was something he would gladly have forgotten, but it had stayed with him almost perversely in the finest detail over the years. He could still hear that voice, see that face in the shadows, and the boa which the woman had somehow invested with an almost living suggestiveness, for it drew him towards her, flickering at him like a pale tongue in the darkness. Then it was her scent which next took him, then her little gloved finger brazenly touching, and finally her voice. Now he had been with a whore once before in his life and had seen them parade that very evening around Merrion Square, great ponderous women, for the most part, who offered themselves as naturally as though they were sides of beef, or else the under-nourished and pale slum variant, but this one was like neither.

She whispered softly—I can offer you a moment only, and not only the expression but the voice thrilled him.

Later of course he was to invest the encounter with all sorts of romantic possibilities, but that was months later.

Returned to his hotel room, he scrubbed himself obsessively, then lay sleepless until morning, imagining already the first unclean symptoms. He thought of those gloved hands, the veil – a bizarre touch – then, *what in God's name had it concealed?*

At breakfast he could scarcely raise his eyes. The noise of eating in the crowded little dining-room seemed like thunder, and Minnie's attempts at conversation only turned the blade in him deeper.

When they were due to leave – that was a Sunday morning, and the streets outside were full of people, hurrying to Mass, something which merely served to strengthen his feeling of being alien – he went to her room. He prayed she would have

186

already packed. Let them leave swiftly, and put this place and its events behind them. He knocked, and entered at her command. She was lying on the bed in her underclothing, her eyes fixed on his with a soft dog-like expression. He saw her bosom and her bare feet and arms, but especially those pleading eyes, that look of the sacrificial victim. Two women within hours of each other offering themselves to his lust, but with what difference. They looked at one another, then he backed from the bedroom closing the door behind him with great care. And as the trite phrase has it, the matter was never referred to again.

But the episode had seared something. Such scars rarely heal completely. And now pain of a sort had started up in him again or, rather, guilt, he supposed. But that woman on the quays . . . Had her accent been as well-bred as he'd imagined, or her scent so subtly expensive? Perhaps to his untutored senses then, essence of violets had simply seemed as rare as *Worth*. All so long ago.

He tried to visualize himself as he must have been on that night. So many considerations to obscure the image, the truth though. History for instance, for wasn't the feel of the period so much different? Edwardian sensibilities were surely coarser. He felt certain of that. Memory couldn't have played tricks with the more mundane recollections he had of enormous meals and the quantities of drink they all then consumed – generally strong sensual pursuit of all the appetites. But the past held its aroma jealously. Any occasional whiff released by accident was always much too brief. At such times he ached for the definitive, but of course never got it. It was spread he desired, total compass. He wanted all the past within his grasp, all of it. His mind leaped with the concept. He felt it, and unwisely took both hands away from the handlebars of his bicycle to raise his arms wide. At that particular instant he was travelling downhill quite leisurely but with sufficient momentum to make his tumble bad enough, for the moment he removed his steering grip, the bicycle headed for a low wall, a devil in it.

He fell on the right side of the wall, thank God, for beyond and below slid a tiny stream in the darkness. Its sound sprang up in silence, now that the machine lay still a yard away, one wheel turning. The moonlight caught the spokes. *Silly old coot,* he told himself, *you might have been killed. The end could have come*

here, this way, on this lonely back road, and not one of your famous con-
jectures would have been within a mile of it.

But he had survived, indeed he had, so now what to do but lie here, back against the parapet, and make inventory without panic. And he was as right as rain, he discovered, bar a few bruises. Aches would come later, of course, but liniment would allay those. His luck held. Nothing could interfere with that on this night of nights.

And what a night, he told himself, as he looked up at the great moon throbbing above. He felt at one with every other nocturnal creature, a rare affinity which seemed to rise out of the very roots his two palms pressed. When he was younger, he often would lie spreadeagled in some hidden place to feel that pulse. He was more romantic then of course, and could convince himself readily that there was such a current, a tremor that entered. Stretched out over a bank or a swell of turf, he really felt his body cupped a force. Now he knew it was a delusion. Age had taught him that. But something still remained.

His friends had left to fight, while he stayed behind, and his imagination had been given to it, this place. It must have been about the time that the bond was formed. Never before or since had he been so lonely or embittered, keeping his own counsel in the most secluded walks he could find. He would move along river banks, in woods and quarries, avoiding anything human. He knew his reputation as the eccentric had really stemmed from that time. But why should one more nickname have bothered him? In that flag-waving, red-hot atmosphere, he was already labelled 'shirker'. He used to wish his disability had been something for them all to see, those patriots on the Home Front, a crippled leg, arm, or a blind eye, and not the dicky heart he carried within. That cleared up of course, if a faulty valve can be said to clear up. He tapped his chest now, a quick acknowledgment. *Sound as a bell*, Doctor McCandless had told him, *sound as Big Ben himself*. But he had borne all their sneers then, their spites and long looks after him, as he ducked into some covert to be with his own thoughts. He despised them of course and their posturings.

Beside his shaving mirror he pasted up a verse of doggerel cut from the local paper. It had come from the pen of 'one of our brave boys' who had prefaced his efforts with—*Excuse the writing as I am now one-handed. I have lost my left hand, and am going on 'game-ball'.*

The poem was addressed 'To the Slacker', and he liked to declaim it on his walks, startling the wild life. It went:

> Come, rally up you slackers,
> Take the cotton from your ears;
> Get the blinkers from your optics.
> Face the music, chuck your fears.
> How dare you play the shirker
> And your country's call construe
> As only meant for other chaps
> And not at all for you?

The last line he would always roar out with passion at the top of his lungs.

Yes, he thought, *no wonder these people consigned you long since to the ranks of the local mad ones.* A shake of the head, one finger to the brow, whenever Barbour Brown's name came up, or they caught a glimpse of him between the trees or on the far horizon. The well-dressed one with the binoculars. Him all right. To a tee.

He remounted his trusty metal steed. Like himself, it also bore a charmed life, for the wheels turned as true as ever. Off he sailed none the worse for his spill, and now he beat one-handed time on the handlebars to another ditty he recalled from that far-off period.

> Some say he's in the Navy,
> Some say he fights on land.
> Oh everything that happens now
> Is done by 'Aggie's Man.'

Yes, that ubiquitous folk-hero as well.

How he could remember things, nuggets caught in the sieve of memory. Perhaps they had only swollen with time, though. But it was remarkable, was it not, how they all came from that early time? Little or nothing after the Great War really, when he came to think about it. He could recall the sinking of the *Titanic*, as if it had been last week, the Gun-Running and the Easter Rising too, and that great to-do over signing Carson's

Covenant in people's own blood. Were there any answers to such a conundrum? Others in the same aged ark as himself might well have been able to offer their own solutions, that is if he had not been such a recluse and had troubled to seek them out. But who was there to talk to in this backwater anyway? And he did see the Valley more and more like that, land-locked, and as remote as any Tibetan fastness. Was he really then some kind of tied human insect tirelessly quartering its floor? It seemed at times a penance. Self-inflicted he told himself, as the wheels spun, merely self-inflicted, for it would never do to get maudlin. A tear was always easy to squeeze out. Too easy.

He pedalled on, thinking his thoughts, that inner ebb and flow. A lifetime spent answering himself back, or with such as could not. He should have persevered with Minnie, really he should. He had given up too easily. Even her genteel snobberies should not have been so hard to bear beside what passed for society hereabouts. *More charity, Barbour Brown, that's what is lacking, a little more of that wouldn't do you a pick of harm, indeed no.*

He pressed on and the darkened hedgerows glided past, sleeping. His own bed was the last place he had in mind though, for his eyes felt wide and clear, and each thrust of the pedals he tackled with greater zest. *By heavens, Barbour, you might well out-live the lot of them yet, dicky heart or no. Your tramping has stuck to you, lad, so it has.* The tyres crackled through a drift of fine stones, glittering gem-like across the roadway. The sound struck him as more than pleasing.

Another verse came to mind for no reason, and he spouted melodramatically, remembering a tableau at a village concert, with a local girl dressed as Britannia and someone else in khaki – a man – who declaimed:

> *Throw aside the name of slacker,*
> *Pluck up courage, say 'I will'.*
> *You will win the love of someone*
> *If that vacant place you'll fill.*

Tumultuous applause. Was that red-faced oaf in puttees looking straight at him? It certainly seemed so . . .

But let them stare and nudge one another and whisper their fill. Let them all. He was untouchable. The one who walked alone. He was – but no, that he was not, certainly not that one whose name and exploits appeared everywhere scrawled on walls, cut even into the living bark. There was a beech despoiled, by the church, wasn't there? At least it made the congregation laugh as they entered and as they left. Yes, he enjoyed that aspect – some of the jokes too – but there was a little too much of the seaside postcard world about *Big Aggie's Man* for his real love. No, the hero for him was a cut above such grotesqueries. More subtlety there, infinitely.

And on one occasion the Doctor was seen to be busily carrying large stones into his church and when a collection of people became curious and followed him therein, he promptly fastened the doors on the inside and preached a sermon to them. A further noteworthy diversion of Doctor Colville's on various occasions was the skimming of flat stones and slates along the surface of a lint-dam, an art in which it was remarked he became exceedingly proficient. Oh yes, his very own divine with those private, passionate ways, the man for him all right, leading them all by the nose, every man-jack.

But his journey was coming to its end – he jerked himself back to the present. The house loomed up. Old Hutton Maitland had built it in an early flush of pride. It was to be peopled by straight-backed sons who would shoot, swear and terrorize the country. Stables were laid out before greenhouses, while that old rip waited and waited. But instead he got two daughters who shook at the sight and sound of a gun or a horse, two pale, headachey girls mooning around the place with books of poetry in their hands. Great ones for Elizabeth Barrett and Mrs Hemans. Those ladylike volumes with their limp bookmarks hanging down. And flowers pressed inside. Like two delicate plants themselves, imprisoned and losing sap.

—*Come on*, he used to exhort, in his more breezy moments.—*You must get a bloom into those cheeks. You must exercise. Regular hikes for you, my girl. Shake a leg.*

She would blush at that, Minnie would. He let the sister go her own way. It was obvious she was the doomed one, withering away. That was plain.

He had entered the driveway now, swinging between the pillars, erect, assured, and noting the change in tone his tyres made on the sparse gravel. Conifers now on either side, not the Christmas trees he had remembered. They stretched straight to the moon, full-grown, not a sound or sigh from their branches.

Memories. Afternoons on the drifts of pine-needles. She lay in his arms, not letting him. It was before their Dublin excursion. *My God, he had treated the woman monstrously.* No other way to describe it.

The last fifty yards of avenue he walked, holding the bicycle. When he reached the semi-circular sweep in front of the house – now sadly rutted, and bare in places like an old carpet – he looked around for a place to leave the machine. He would hide it, for there was still a feeling of stealth about this undertaking, there was no disguising that. A heavy rhododendron suited his purpose perfectly, and down went the bicycle in its shadow into deep, damp grass. Straightening up – a touch of stiffness, but nothing great – he dried his hands on his handkerchief, then began to head around the side of the house.

He moved cautiously, there was still enough gravel underfoot to give him away, and surprise was, after all, the essence. *Thank God, she keeps no dogs now,* he was thinking. Not after old Gyp had to be put down.

At the end of the gable, he halted, and carefully fastened his jacket, all of the buttons except the lowest – imagine him remembering that – then the necktie, then a brushing down of the fine trousers – the bicycle clips were in his pocket – and finally he shot his cuffs. Beaux who came calling always did that as their finishing touch. He chuckled. He really did feel ridiculously juvenile, blood coursing, palms moist. A deep breath; then he stepped around to the back of the house.

A heavy garden urn lay shattered near the french windows. It had been perfectly sound earlier. What had happened to it? He thought of Minnie and the dropping level in the sherry bottle. But that was ridiculous, her feeble powers against this heavy rooted thing. No, it had broken of its own natural accord. Age had done for it. Fatal hair-line stretching, inch by inch, over the years until finally –. Dead things always give up their ghost while people sleep. He thought of his Doctor. Sermons in stones.

In front of him the rear face of the old house stretched up high and quite immense to the sky, a growth of creeper softening, blurring its edges. By moonlight now, it reminded him of a story-book illustration. Dark mysterious casements.

And it is now that the shock strikes as his eyes rove from one window to the next, because there is no light up there any more, that topmost one is as blind and as black as any of the rest. The house is totally dead to him in an instant. He shivers, an old fool out of place suddenly, a joke in an antiquated suit.

Still, he hesitates, staring up at that window. Yearning. He knows there is nothing more to be said or done, yet he lingers. *How, why*, he asks himself. How had he not noticed it earlier, why had the lamp been quenched? Ridiculous and quite mad of course, to believe, as he must have done, that an effort of will could somehow control a distant hand reaching out. But on such a night, he was convinced of it, sure of anything he once fixed his mind to, and he had held that bedroom and that lamp so firmly, oh with such ferocity as he pedalled towards it.

So he stands now in the middle of the flagged expanse, looking up – already his eyes are watering – but he is fixed. Like a toy soldier, he thinks, to that General in the sky, looking down and having his laugh. Constant tin soldier with heart of gold – but realities are all about him. It's cold for a start, he may well get his death out of this night's work, and as for time he doesn't dare make an estimate.

He listens. Not a breath, just that faint pounding that never falters, distant, illusory. It echoes his own respiration. He wonders what it can be, where it comes from, this mimicry.

He has his hand in his pocket feeling for his clips, enough is enough after all, when he sees a movement near the glass of the french windows, the merest flicker caught out of the corner of the eye. Instantly he feels alarm, and that is curious, for why, the adventure is resuming after all, and so much better too than he anticipated, for she is in there moving about, amenable. He won't have to pitch gravel up to that high window after all, none of those novelettish tricks.

But still he's disturbed, in spite of such thoughts. He hesitates, looks around for some other way to approach the windows, obliquely. The idea has also hit him that he's vulnerable suddenly – the light suit, the moon, this cleared stage. He half expects a loud threatening voice to ring out.

As casually as he can manage it, he moves backwards, keeping his eyes fixed all the time on the dark glass until he reaches the shadows. Then quickly he glides across the length of the ruined terrace right to its end. A low wall there, steps down into more gardens, but he keeps on, brushing the skirting line of rose-bushes, almost as wild, he notices, as any in the hedgerows. He smells their heavy scent. A looping vine touches his cheek, scratches. *My God*, he thinks, *what sort of a shape will I present when I manage to get out of this*, but he presses on, that window draws him, his old obsession. He sidles along the house wall, his coat rubbing dry brick and Virginia creeper, sinister as any cinema villain, until at last he is at the window's frame. There he holds himself, breathing deeply. It's so hard now to take that final step, screw up his courage, but he must look, he *must*. He trembles. Like a swimmer dreading the first cold plunge, he looks into the darkened room.

The moon lays down a broad, motionless swath of light across its centre. Beyond, swim shadowy humps of furniture, with occasional gleams from picture glass and metal. He longs to hold a hand between his face and the glass to pierce that gloom but he remains cautious. He imagines he would still be undetected if anyone happened to look out, and old habits die hard, to see yet be unseen for too long a compulsion to be easily forgotten now. There's the beginning of an ache across his brow, yet he can't resist. He feels he's waiting for something, something to happen.

When it does it's not at all as he's imagined it, at least not on this night, in this place, for it's the product of an earlier fantasy, of several. Indeed he feels something close to fright, for it's as though he's conjured her up, a living essence of so many lustful images, for there she stands, unaware, young, beautiful and altogether naked except for the knitted Afghan lying lightly across her shoulders and breasts. She has her back turned to him – my God, her flanks make him weak; she looks pensive like someone who has stepped out of a frame. He thinks, *First Flush*, and dares a quick rub at his eyes, for what if this vision should dissolve? Perhaps he is beginning at last to reap what he has sown, first crop of tormenting visions. But she's real, she must be. He can touch the glass, cold reality. Her skin would be so warm and young. Just to lay one finger-tip . . .

She's looking at herself in the mirror over the mantlepiece. He draws back. Then she turns around. She's been crying. *But good God, the rest of her, the rest of her.* He wants to lay himself at two bare feet, pay homage to those vulnerable secret places. It's an onrush of love, for not all his fantasies are the sweepings

194

of some whore-house, no matter how select, not all of them. She stands there and she's his, waiting, only a darkened sheet of window-glass between them. He loosens his collar, a new tremble in his hands.

And as he devours her with his gaze, because he'll never be able to move closer, other faces now begin to swim up behind her. They rise slowly from the shadows, like those when a dream changes almost imperceptibly to nightmare. He's seeing them, yet can't bring himself to accept their three grinning ovals. They hover just at the back of the settee – a touch of reality somehow in that fact – but they must be his demons alone, for she does not turn round.

His heart pounds. Something terrible is about to happen in the room, in his head? He knows it, and it begins, and not in his head, for this naked girl turns, sees the three and opens her mouth to scream. No sound reaches him and that is even stranger. He watches everything that happens.

3

Mack got to her first, then Harvey, and him last of all, coming round the back of the sofa where they had lain hidden. One minute she had been standing there, the next Mack had grabbed, and she didn't yell the house down at all. Her mouth went snap as fast as it had opened at first sight of them lined up, waiting to pounce. A sound did come from between clenched teeth, and he thought, *Christ, lockjaw* – or maybe a fit. That's what he was thinking as Mack, then big Harvey, laid first hold, and that sound in its way seemed much worse than any actual shriek which would certainly have nailed them to the floor.

They were down on the rug rolling about in a bright patch of moonlight. He remembered thinking, *Jesus, Hetty Quinn, you look so different without any clothes on. The real thing*, that kept running through his head, *the real thing*. They were pawing and worrying – three dogs with a bone – as through his head also ran, *store it all up*. Especially those things that serious reading could never prepare you for. And the odd thing was that nothing beyond fondling and *steeping* himself roughly but still almost innocently in this way had entered his head.

Harvey got his hand bitten when he tried to gag her. It seemed unnecessary because of that set jaw, the fierce and stubborn glare. They felt the same urge to break her will, he could tell that, all the more angered by the sound of their own exertion, the absence of hers. She was a big girl, a strong girl. At one time or another, they had felt the weight of her rage. That may or may not have been the reason why they were bent on this, but nevertheless her time had finally come. No quarter given, not now, not like before.

This strange room and its contents contained them. It was all like a dream, happening twice, as if destined to repeat itself.

196

Out of the tangle something was resolving itself. Mack was holding her arms. He and Harvey weighted the rest of her. She was so warm, her skin so soft, slightly damp. And she was giving in. All he wanted to do now was lay his cheek to that softness. Mack however was motioning to Harvey, a blaze of the eye, making them both feel stupid, lacking in some fashion. He was hunkered on the rug where she couldn't see. He had a grip on her white arms that seemed more than just firm. He was sweating, his face pale, and of course his eyes were that way they had of looking both hot and cold at the same time. Again he motioned and Harvey started undoing his trouser buttons. Perhaps something would happen about now so that they wouldn't have to go through with it. *Why didn't she call out?*

Murders run in her mind, crimes committed by men the worse for drink, or maddened by the moon. She's thinking such things but still she can't believe they might be happening to her, for she grits her teeth and fights back, and on no account will she yell. She tells herself that. No shouting, *help, help.* She just will not petition any more. But even to entertain such a notion while you're being man-handled like this. Nothing makes sense any more. They're hurting her arms, pressing down on her chest and stomach as well, three brutes who don't know their own strength. But she won't give in to them. She knows she's only making them worse, but nothing will make her cry out. The old woman upstairs is forgotten, it's these three and them alone, she won't now give the satisfaction to. It must be that stubborn streak in her nature people are always on about, how it affronts them.

Into her head comes two gipsy women she saw fighting tooth and nail once in the middle of the street. She kicks and scratches just like the two red-heads now, not caring about anything. She gets a good bite at somebody's hand, she doesn't know whose. There's richness in that, feeling him pull back. What she fears most is them putting something over her face.

Shame at how they surprised her has all gone. At first she struggled only to keep hold of her covering for what it was worth, but when that was quickly thrown aside and her blood began to heat, modesty went with it. It didn't seem to matter. All that was important and told her that they had clothes on

197

and she hadn't, were their buttons and belts and the roughness of cloth rubbing.

They're getting the better of her, she can't hold out an awful lot longer, she knows that – and then what? That girl that time with those coloured soldiers after the dance in Antrim. She had to emigrate. They said she would never be the same again.

But these three specimens aren't half a dozen big darkies with what they've got, not by a long chalk. She makes a last great effort – if she could only get her knee up into where it hurts – for she despises them, she truly does. *Apologies for men,* she's heard it somewhere, *apologies for men,* she wants to shriek it at them and why not? She knows they'd run like rabbits for sure. She'd have the last laugh then all right, for bloody well sure, but she'd be the one left to explain and take the blame as usual. She even hears voices saying, *she must have encouraged them.* They said that about that other girl and the six G.I.'s.

Her strength is slipping away. One of them has her arms bent back behind her head. She can't move her legs either for Harvey Gault is lying on top of her. She can see his face, smell his hair-cream. He's doing something with himself down there with one hand.

And then the wildest thing comes into her head. For no reason she thinks of Joe Peden the fattest man in Tardree. How does his wife Ruby manage to bear his weight, she wonders. It's only the start of a series of such notions trooping through her head, as she's stretched out there on Minnie Maitland's best Indian rug, while the moonlight pours in and down. It's just like an operation she's having without going under. They're doing these things below to her, which she can't see, only feel, mostly one thing, a monotonous prodding. They don't seem to know anything else. She wonders how long they're going to take. How do women manage to put up with this all the time on the top of them?

It's a penance, he tells himself, shivering. It must be, it has to be. Something purgatorial devised specifically for him and him alone. Like a glutton forced to eat sweetmeat after sweetmeat he feels gorged already, yet cannot draw himself away. He watches, he consumes. Every bedroom tableau he has ever spied upon, country wives of every shape and size, dressing, undress-

198

ing, posing, exposing, flesh by the acre, pink silk, but mainly flannelette, alas, that too, all nothing beside this. And as each second passes, new variations, new tempos. The light falls down for his convenience, like something out of the roof of a theatre. He can't help such lyricisms, at least not in the beginnings anyhow. Only the show possesses him and his own vantage, from where he crouches on the flags, his palms pressed to their cold surface. He finds himself shaking with the strain of such a posture, but no other will do him. Unconsciously he has taken on the set and attitude of the pointer. Shall he bay the moon too? He consumes it all, all the sweet secret flexions of soft inner parts he alone can see. He has no desire to be involved, none. It's everything to be outside.

Only much later when he was stumbling off through the drenched fields did it occur to him that he'd questioned nothing, none of the strangeness, not even thought of it as strange: reason suspended, no whys or hows or where was that other woman even, in whose house all this was happening at the time.

But now was now, a present so brutal and so demanding that he pants and feels sweat breaking out. Men of his age have been known to expire at such moments. On the crest of desire. Old husbands with young wives, in bed or out of it, snapping like dry sticks, flopping, then stiffening. The widows never talk of it afterwards, so there's no way of ever knowing exactly what it must be like. Bunty Pottinger's hair went grey inside a year when old Sharman snuffed it on their wedding night.

Beyond the glass the love struggle continues – a composition of moving limbs, sometimes a starfish, sometimes a heaving knot or mound, but ever-changing, always throwing out and back at him ingenuities. Faces, hands, a bare curve of thigh, arm or loin emerge, then quickly withdraw into shadow beneath clothing. Pale flesh threads in and out of the darkened tangle. He waits for each quicksilver glimpse, tantalized. The gun-dog must look a slavering old wretch by now. Pluto eyeing his bone.

Then came the change. No longer could he be fooled or fool himself. Beyond the window-glass the contest was being quickly and brutally decided. He saw the boys' faces and their expression as if for the first time, and he was appalled, not at what he read there, but at his own realization that he could suddenly *identify*. The word shocked. He was witnessing a *crime*. And that word shocked even more, just like everything else inside the moonlit room now. He hadn't allowed himself to recognize the cruelty in that tableau before, but it cried out to him now all right.

And now he was paying his penance, and his exclusive purgatory was to have to crouch there and watch all of it out to its bitter end.

—Will you have a fag, Hetty?

It was Harvey who said it, and not Mack, who was sitting apart, his face turned away. She accepted and took the light from him as well, very calmly, hardly bothering to raise herself. That shawl affair covered her again, but carelessly. She blew out smoke, and he and Harvey watched her with admiration. He wished he could think of something he could do for her, but Harvey had just done it. It was a very odd moment, a gap in time. He could hear a clock ticking in the next room, not another sound. Hetty Quinn looked really terrific, just stretched there with the moonlight falling on her like that. Just like someone in the movies. It was a trite way of putting it, but that was how she looked, she really did, like a million dollars. They were all dangling, even Mack, he could tell, hanging on what she might do, might say, and strangest of all, half in love with her already.

Listening to the sounds of the old house and trying to place each one. Easiest was the grandfather in the hall, painted suns and moons on his ancient dial, faces in them and the big pendulum moved so slowly. And then there were the other clocks that she wouldn't have even heard, except she knew where they were, a china one with shepherdesses in the morning-room, others upstairs, muffled behind bedroom doors. Minnie's was a little brass five-day effort that made no sound because of her light sleeping. And in this room was one spinning away, which never needed winding. She could just see it. There were odd creaking noises too she'd never heard before. Maybe it was because she was always too busy to notice them during the daytime.

. . . . .

200

What's she thinking about, he asks himself, they all ask themselves nervously as her cigarette smoke curls up into the moonlight slanting down. It reminds him of the beam out of the back of the cinema, that way the patterns in the smoke show up swirling. He supposes not many people have noticed that, being more intent on the picture. It would be nice occasionally to let fall to somebody such items. Her for instance. It would be nice to offer for instance quite casually, *what you really need now of course is a long elegant holder to complete the effect – femme fatale, I mean,* but not so long-winded or apologizing. Christ, why did he have to whisper, *I'm sorry,* in her ear like that! And try to kiss her cheek. Why always to be so bloody ingratiating?

So that's what it's all about, that's what all men are after, all they're after, that. Her legs really do look nice and slender against the cream rug with the shawl coming down just the right length. That bumping and boring thing, like a stupid game children would play, not even knowing what it means, just doing it because everybody else does. She played games herself like that once upon a time. A big rough girl who could give as good as she got. She didn't think she was pregnant, common savvy told her nothing could possibly come out of that daft performance. All that pushing to no avail. Just because they had what they had they couldn't rest until they put it to use, but for all it meant to her it might as well be something the cat brought home.

The Mona Lisa smile, he thought, quickening. It was there quite distinctly, he had seen it flicker just for that bare second or two. He looked at Harvey but he was involved for the moment with matches and the next cigarette. As for Mack, he still offered nothing but the back of his head. He couldn't figure him out. But it was she who drew him, stretched languidly in the spread beam of moonlight, while they waited and watched in the shadows, roughly encircling. They were trapped in this room, in this stranger's house by what they had done, and they wouldn't be able to leave until she gave them a sign, a word; impossible to get up and go, feeling that if they did, something terrible might break out at their back. By staying, in a far-fetched way, they might be able to deflect the inevitable. But the smile

201

couldn't be bad, or could it? Maybe she knows something they don't.

Just how would they take it, she wondered lazily, *if she burst out laughing, for if they only realized how ridiculous they look, sitting around like that on Minnie's parlour floor, a right trio of boy scouts and no mistake, with their, oh what have we done expressions.* But they weren't worth much speculation, she didn't even despise them any more, it was too strong a word for what she felt, or rather, what she didn't feel. Nothing, blissful nothing, as she puffed on her second cigarette. She decided she would develop a taste for a lot of things, from now on. She had begun an odd and private score in her head just lying there, adding up, ticking off, altogether quite calmly, how she had come out of it all. Some tears shed – in spite of herself – various bruises in various parts, one or two scratches, but of course worst of all the feel still with her, a damp sticky kind of feeling. She'd love a bath, and a mirror to examine herself all over. Nothing else. Just that.

Anxiety, steadily growing in tune almost with that damned clock in the next room. *How could the others sit there this way?* It was as if he was the only thinking survivor of some disaster, for he was considering police charges now for the first time, headlines, the girl's father, his own, when it came to that. There was no time to be lost, alibis were needed, a good watertight conspiracy the first essential. *For Christ's sake, look at Mack, when he's really needed. But that's what you get,* he was also thinking bitterly, *when you go out on the rampage, with two half-lunatics. You'll never learn, will you. Why, oh why, couldn't you have stuck with your books?*

As long as she stayed put like this she knew she could do any solitary thing she wished with them. *What's on her mind,* they were asking themselves, *what will she do next?* She didn't need to be a thought-reader to recognize that. The answer of course was sweet damn all. Only they weren't to know. She felt sorry for them now more than anything. For the first time in her entire life she felt she really knew these three inside out, body and soul. They had given themselves to her, not the other way round, as they imagined, for she knew things about them now they kept from one another. A piece of information about one gent in particular. That poor soft little thing of his, like a wet snail rubbing against her. *How the mighty are fallen,* she thought. *No lead in your pencil at all, Mack McFarlane.*

He will make his move now, he instructs himself, right now. And let her yell, for he'll be out in the open by the time she gets going. The other two can wait for the full concert, that's up to them, but he'll be out there, heading for his bicycle and the open road and home – that word suddenly very attractive – deep in bed then, as if none of this had ever happened. Could it all be erased perhaps by simply pulling an eiderdown over his head? He had nothing else to pin any hopes to. So he's standing up to face the dark glass, his reflection is there, pale blob of face, so that's what this nightmare has done to him, and then she starts to yell, but not the scream they'd all been dreading, but words, not sense at first, for it sounds like – *It's him! It's him!*

And then his own reflected face seems to break up before his very eyes in the pane, and he sees the others too because they're all staring out now at that other face looking in. She calls out —It's him! The Well-Dressed Man. Don't let him get away. Don't let him get away!

They're still dazed, in between states. Hetty cries—He's been out there all along. (Mack and Harvey both give a bellow) – —*Watching!* she cries, the last word he hears for he's swept out of the room in a current of rage.

Noises off now are subdued, no hallooing, although it is obvious that something, someone, is being hunted. But it's a discreet pack – at the start anyhow – nervous of that window up there. It's cold out here as well. Dawn is not too far off, grey. So the three of them are in league again. Things always come back again to that, no matter what. No matter what happens.

4

He had somehow managed to get himself into a sunken garden that should not have been there. His brain hammered, as he tried to remember, but everything, as he'd once known it, was different. He stumbled over matted grass, clutched at espaliers that billowed out in places from this wall. He started to climb the lattice-work but it crumbled under his touch and soles. It was a desperate act, for how could he know an easier way out if he couldn't even recall the very existence of the place itself? To be trapped at this point by ignorance, an obscenity, but then everything was, he in his stained dandy's clothes, his trembling and panic, his fleeing into this overgrown afterthought of a place. There *had* been a tennis-court here, he had played on it, he *had*.

He sank down behind a shrub, willing himself to be rational. So far they hadn't discovered his whereabouts, but it would be only a matter of time, he told himself, for wouldn't they be drawn down here too, the way he had, this perfect venue for hide-and-seek? He shivered, felt faint, as he heard them calling to one another in low voices somewhere up there at the back of the house. Those careful tones made him fear them much more, fear their intention towards him. When it came, it would be something more than merely violence. He decided that he could bear that, the fists falling, but that other, the unspeakable . . .

He trembled on two wet knees, parted branches to peer out of his hiding-place. The light was coming, birds too beginning to warm up to that heartless dawn chorus. All over the land sleepers close to death, closer than at any other hour of the daily cycle. A morbid connection. *Morbid.* The mind still made jokes. His eyes strained towards the steps at the far end of this low place. He felt he was in a drained tank, steep-sided, and the growing things around were really aquatic. Everything he touched was brimming with water, or already sodden. His clothes affected too by the slow-spreading damp.

At the top of the steps he made out a movement, someone had appeared, standing there, reconnoitring. It had begun. One figure, one of them in his modern garb. He saw him look back as if considering whether to call the others, then start to descend alone. Barbour shrank closer to the earth. The youth came nearer, moving cautiously. He avoided bushes, and their shadows, as if he were nervous of what he might find there. Barbour's heart beat in a new and tearing way, a terrifying turn. How much more could he withstand?

He could see him clearly now, this teenager. Horrid word. Something of the young blood about him, however, the loose, pale jacket, loud shirt and the tie, hair brutally barbered in that current American film-star mode. He had an intelligent look, an air of diffidence lacking in his friends. They were still seeking him in that other part. Their voices seemed to be carrying much more than previously. The boy was almost upon him. Barbour crouched lower. His clothes must betray him, as obvious as those his hunter wore, a queer connection surely. He must see him, he *must*. Throw himself on his mercy? Not a brutal face. Could he possibly hope? The boy was now stock-still directly opposite where he shook and palpitated. His heart? The old trouble? To finish up in this place, a mystery for the County Coroner. He prayed for more time, just a little extension only. *Please God, not in this sink of a place. Not here.*

Then the boy turned his head, and they were looking at one another, face to face. The boy drew back and Barbour scrambled feebly on to one knee. They held silence there in that drenched moonlit jungle, their confrontation reminding Barbour of that island encounter of Defoe's. A shaking old Crusoe drew himself up. Desperately he sought a little dignity, where it would come from he had no idea, but he managed, was managing somehow, to move his lower limbs, was walking past and away, he was, towards the distant stone steps. He reached them, and when he had climbed half-way the first shout came at his back.

He fell with the shock, expected as it was, then he was struggling up and running aimlessly as the first chorus now from the full pack broke in the still air. Half-crouched, Barbour

Brown, that erudite and private figure in the twilight of his years, scurried from one shadow to the next, a little like some crippled game-bird. He was well and truly scented now, and the yells came unabated. He heard the crash of breaking glass. They were even stoning the old greenhouse. The destruction angered him, that and the thought that he might have taken refuge in among those dusty rows of dead and dying plants.

Half hysterically he shouted out, the most pathetic things coming to his tongue.

—I am old enough to be your grandfather, he called.—I saw Gladstone once!

It stopped their cries only for a moment, then they had swung around baying, hallooing again in the direction of his voice. He ran dodging across the bright square of terrace. He saw the french windows. Perhaps he could find refuge there, inside the house which had once sheltered him. Time spent, times remembered, in civilized company, talk, pale sherry glinting in the decanter, firelight and the perfume of women's hair and their bodies as they moved. How had he managed to fall into such straits to be out here, abandoned this way to wild animals. They wanted his hide, his blood. Nothing less would do them. He knew that now.

He looked through the glass, mere seconds, no more, thoughts come so fast, so fast, and there was the girl standing there looking back at him. She was fully clothed, had a glass in her hand. Had it all been a bad dream then? He took a step, he must be smiling, he felt, *a little spot of difficulty, m'dear, amnesia or an hallucination, more likely, hazards of anno domini, you know. I wonder if you might possibly* . . . Those eyes held nothing for him, cold, so cold.

Barbour Brown, tattered old tramp, he knew what it felt like, turned to stumble away back to the shadows once more. Somewhere over there lay the open fields. . . .

Here's looking at you, she toasted herself. Out there that lot were still busy running around at her bidding, would you believe it, while in here she was enjoying a nice drop of the best. She looked at her reflection in the mirror, for surely the change in her must show. Inside as well as out, she told herself. She touched herself, spread her two hands over her breasts, held them there a moment. They felt heavier, firmer. She'd never thought of them in such a way before, any way really – down below there too. She couldn't really describe what she felt. All she knew was that many things seemed clear to her now that had always been mysteries before. Things the older women talked and laughed about among themselves, things she would sometimes pretend she knew about too, but never did. And they were not the sort of things you could put into words either, one or all of them. It was a general feeling of knowing, of understanding everything, all rolled up, that she had. *Here's to you,* she whispered to the glass, *here's to the new you.* She took another swallow of Minnie's best sherry. She couldn't wait to put her new-found knowledge to use. But she had already started, hadn't she? She listened to the sounds coming from outside. The fools were beginning to make too much of a racket. She supposed it would be up to her now to get them out of this mess in some way.

And various people testified that they had heard the Doctor conversing in strange tongues on his night-time ramblings as well as moanings and groanings and other loud cries. Oh certainly, oh most certainly . . .

> *Can't you hear the sounding bugle?*
> *Earl Kitchener calls to you*
> *Will you fill a place that's vacant*
> *Like a British man so true.*

He was in a trench which circled round to the front – of the house. They were still making their heathen din. But:

> *Come on, dear Irishmen!*
> *Come on.*
> *There's no time to wait.*
> *The whole world's looking at you now*
> *Come – ere it be too late.*

Across that stretch of gravelled no-man's-land he ran, crouching, brightly illuminated by the moon. He reached the shelter of a hedge and flung himself into its dry bed of leaves. Haven here for a little while at least. The enemy out there were still at their filthy tricks, hoping to flush him out into the open. But they had mistaken their man this time, for:

Here lie the Central Antrim boys
Who will lead the Huns a dance . . .

He began crawling along the dry sheugh (he had a pang of homesickness at the word) keeping head well down and body close to the earth. He had aches in every part, but there was no turning back, he must at all costs hold firm, for:

The wave of Northern valour
Is like the advancing tide,
And nought can cure or curb it,
And nought can change its stride.

On, on, until what's this up ahead, metal gleaming? An obstruction? He approaches it cautiously. No knowing what fiendish design is behind this tangle. But ah, he recognizes it for what it is – two bicycles stowed away cunningly like his own. *Their* bicycles. In a trice both are successfully immobilized, front and rear tyres flat as pancakes, valves flung far into the deep grass. It is a moment of triumph, brain over brawn. Is that cheering ringing in his ears?

There was another hearty outburst from the Welcome-Home committee when Mr Houston Lancashire presented our first V.C. with a large box of choice cigarettes . . .

Stiffly, proudly, Barbour Brown – a name fit for any hero – starts on his long way across open country. The sun is rising. The new day ahead has all the appearance of being yet another scorcher. The only sound is that deep throbbing pulse he has noticed before, drifting over fields from its hidden course among the meadow bottoms. *The heart-beat of the townland,* he observes, yes, that's what it is, the heart-beat. His feet move softly through the dewy grass. He leaves long, gleaming tracks behind him, but that's of no consequence, not at this time, for in his head he is once more dipping into his dear Doctor's history . . .

And some spoke of their children's terrors in the dark hours while others testified that their animals had been bewitched. Yet many more blamed entire domestic calamities on the solitary night-walker, their droughts, fires and floodings, as well as all manner of sickness in the family. But the elders weighing such tales could not point the finger at any single truth coming out of the whole business.

At last a young girl was brought to them to be examined, weeping sorely. The Devil himself had entered her while she was undressed, she told them. She had suffered his lewd gaze upon her while her limbs had turned to water. The elders pressed her saying, What manner of human form did he appear in, because it was well-known that such a disguise was customary. The maid replied: 'It was the night-walker. It was he who entered me . . .'